Holding Off
for a Hero

by

Gail MacMillan

This is a work of fiction. Names, characters, places, and incidents are either the product of the author's imagination or are used fictitiously, and any resemblance to actual persons living or dead, business establishments, events, or locales, is entirely coincidental.

Holding Off for a Hero

Cover Art by *Tina Lynn Stout*

The Wild Rose Press, Inc.
PO Box 708
Adams Basin, NY 14410-0708
Visit us at www.thewildrosepress.com

Publishing History
First Champagne Rose Edition, 2012
Print ISBN 978-1-61217-439-6
Digital ISBN 978-1-61217-440-2

Published in the United States of America

She floored the gas, and they took off with a squealing of tires.

"Hey, hey!" he yelled. "Slow down! The speed limit is 100 km. You're heading to 130!"

"Look, I told you, I'm in a hurry!" she exploded. "I've got a ton of things to do back at the cabin. You see," she continued, quieting and sounding sly, "I'm having a party tonight. I have to get ready."

"A party? You're having a party? At the lake?" *Ah, man, that just about tears it.*

"Actually, a bachelorette bash. One of my teacher friends is getting married next week, and a bunch of us decided we'd give her a real whing-ding of a sendoff...up at my cabin where there'll be no witnesses. Teachers and the likes of myself have reputations to think of, you realize." She cast him a wicked glance.

"So there'll be music and a lot of noise and..." The Professor's blood pressure would skyrocket when he gave him this information.

"Oh, y-e-a-h." She dragged out the last word.

"Couldn't you have it somewhere else? Like a male strip joint in town?"

"Didn't you hear what I just said about teachers and others of that ilk? We can't be seen parading into one of those places. Our superintendent would suspend every last one of us. Anyway..." She looked over at him. "I don't see why it should be such a big deal for you. You don't have to keep banker's hours. If the noise bothers you, stay up, watch a video, and sleep in on Sunday morning."

"Okay, okay, but will you please keep your eyes on the road? And slow down! There's a speed trap somewhere along..."

Behind them a siren wailed.

"Quick!" she ordered, pulling over as the police cruiser rolled alongside. "Hunch over and clutch your chest!"

Dedication

To the real life Emma
and her own special hero

Chapter One

"Help! He's drowning! Help!"

Frasier MacKenzie leaped out of his white Ford Bronco, his German Shepherd dog at his heels, and sprinted toward the dock, where a woman in a striped bathrobe, a white towel turbaned around her head, stood shrieking and pointing out over the fog-draped water. Tearing off his jacket and shirt, he ran to the end of the pier.

"Where is he?" He paused beside her, hopping on one foot and then the other as he tugged off his running shoes.

"Out there, over to the left! Hurry, hurry, he can't swim! He's only three years old!"

Frasier dove into the cold September waters of Loon Lake and struck out with long, powerful crawl strokes. From somewhere in the blanket of mist ahead of him came frantic splashing sounds and muted whimpering.

"Take it easy, son. I'm coming."

A small round head, a black mask and ears, and a pair of thrashing paws emerged from the water. He missed a stroke. *What is it, the Loon Lake version of the Loch Ness Monster? No, damn it, she's sent me to rescue a Pug!*

Eyes huge with fear, front paws thrashing, the little dog emitted frantic whimpering sounds as he battled to keep his wide mouth above water. The next instant he submerged.

"Hang on, fella." Frasier grabbed him by his collar before he could sink out of reach and pulled the sputtering Pug to the surface. "Take it easy,

1

fella. You're safe now." He swung about and headed for the dock.

"Oh, Bruiser, oh, my precious sweetie! I was so scared!" The woman dropped onto her stomach and reached for the Pug.

Frasier hoisted himself out of the frigid water and squinted up at her through the lake water running down his face as she got to her feet. Above that ugly housecoat, large green eyes and a peaches-and-cream complexion enhanced one of the prettiest faces he'd seen outside of a movie theatre.

"Thank you, thank you, thank you!" she breathed, sincerity glowing out of those fantastic emerald eyes. "I don't know what I'd have done if I'd lost Bruiser. I couldn't help him. I can't swim either."

"Bruiser?" Frasier rose to his feet and pushed back his dripping hair. About his own age, he guessed, she stood a good ten inches shorter as they stood facing each other barefoot.

"Yes, like the dog in *Legally Blonde*."

Who names their dog after something in a chick flick?

"I'd advise you to keep him away from docks...at least until he learns to swim," he said. "Why can't he swim? I thought all dogs could."

"He was thrown from a jet ski as a pup...before I adopted him. He's been terrified of water ever since. Up here he's started chasing frogs." She cuddled the Pug and kissed him. "He must have chased one out onto the dock and right off the end. The fog probably confused him. Instead of paddling toward the dock, he was heading away from it."

The little dog began to choke.

"Oh, Bruise! What's wrong?" Her face crinkling, she looked down at him.

"He's swallowed a lot of water. Give him a bit of the Heimlich maneuver."

"What?" She swung the Pug to face Frasier.

"Squeeze his belly just below the ribs. Here, let me..."

As he stepped forward, the little dog issued a belch. A stream of lake water laced with kibble fountained over Frasier's chest.

"Bruiser, good boy!" She kissed the top of his head.

Just what I needed. Dog barf on top of ice water.

"Oh, I *am* sorry." She looked up at Frasier as he snatched one of his discarded socks and scrubbed at his chest. "We haven't even thanked you yet. Please...come up to the cabin. You can dry off while I make breakfast. By the way, I'm Emma Prescott." She clutched the Pug in her left arm and extended her right hand.

"Frasier MacKenzie." He dropped the soiled sock, wiped his hand on the seat of his wet jeans, and acccpted hers in it. "And Scout." He indicated the German Shepherd. "You're staying here?" He pointed to the two log cabins barely visible through the fog. "I thought I was the only one living at Loon Lake."

"You're my neighbor?" Emma Prescott perused him, head to toe.

"Apparently. My job keeps me in this area. What about you? This is a long way from civilization for a woman alone."

"My apartment in town suffered smoke and water damage in a recent fire. It's not easy to find a place that accepts dogs...as you probably know." She indicated Scout, who looked up at Bruiser and slowly began to wag his tail. Bruiser wiggled his in return.

"Agreed. But way up here? This area is pure wilderness. I assume you work in town?"

"I'm a guidance counselor at Carleton High School," she said. "A forty-five-minute drive to work doesn't bother me if I have this lovely place to come home to each night."

"Yeah, it is nice," he agreed glancing back toward the pair of log cabins on the lake shore behind them.

Backed by mountains with hardwoods beginning to develop their autumn hues of gold, orange, and red, and fronted by wide, wilderness-surrounded Loon Lake, the two little chalets nestled near its shore would make a great photo cover for an outdoor magazine.

"It is isolated, though, for a..." His voice trailed off as he realized he was about to repeat himself.

"For a woman alone? I feel a lot safer here than in an inner-city apartment. But enough chitchat. You must be freezing. Come up to my cabin. I'll whip up some bacon and eggs."

She started to turn away, but he stopped her.

"Okay. I'll run over to my place and shower. I don't think you want someone in my condition at your table."

She gave him a head-to-toe appraisal. A mischievous twinkle lighted up her eyes. He got a flash of how a woman feels when a man ogles her.

Damn, I'm not going to blush, am I?

"O...kay." Holding the Pug in her arms, she headed toward the shore.

Through lifting layers of fog, Frasier watched her go up the steps and into the first cabin, the one previously unoccupied. What was he going to do about her? Emma Prescott had just become an unexpected crimp in his plans. He'd have to tell the Professor and get his take on the situation. One thing he knew for certain. He had to get rid of the woman and her disruptive little dog. His project was too important to allow anyone or anything to foul it.

As he started toward his own cabin, he saw a dusty black Sundance parked beside her cabin. The rust patches along its lower sides declared it a senior citizen, and its near-bald tires screamed for replacement. *Damn it, the woman must have more guts than brains to trust an old wreck like that to get her over miles of wilderness roads. Guts or the wisdom of a dodo bird.*

****

The tantalizing aroma of toast, bacon, and coffee greeted him when he strode up her verandah steps twenty minutes later. Man, he was hungry! He'd been driving since 5:00 a.m., and he'd thought all he wanted to do was crawl into bed for a couple of hours. That dive into the September chill of the lake had driven away sleepiness. Hunger and a desire to learn more about Emma Prescott had replaced all other feelings.

Better the devil you know...

"Come in." She put a plate of toast on a table set for two. "You're just in time. Hi, Scout," she greeted the dog at his heels. "I've got scrambled eggs for you and Bruiser."

Her cabin, similar to his, consisted of a common room that served as living room, dining area, and kitchen, with two bedrooms at the rear adjoined by a bath. Log walled with a big fieldstone fireplace along the right side, both cabins had all the modern amenities without losing any of their rustic charm.

Her home got only a miniscule bit of his attention. Emma Prescott in jeans and an orange T-shirt that fitted her just right in all the proper places held ninety-nine percent of his interest. Her hair hung loose, a shoulder-length tangle of chestnut curls. He caught himself staring. Man, he'd been up here in the bush way too long to be suddenly faced with this kind of temptation—temptation he knew he had to ignore.

"Scrambled eggs?" He snapped himself out of it.

"Great for their coats." She placed two bowls, one large, one small, on the floor, then watched, a smile tipping her lips, as the dogs dug into their respective containers. "Now, come, sit." She swept out a hand to indicate a chair at the table, where two steaming cups of coffee waited.

As he sat down, she took two plates of bacon and eggs from the oven.

"Dig in," she invited, placing them on the table. "Orange juice?"

"Please." When she came to his shoulder to pour juice into his glass, he caught a whiff of something that reminded him of a morning after a spring shower.

Ignore it, just ignore it.

"You haven't told me what your job is." She sat down opposite him and flashed a smile that seemed brighter than the sunlight beginning to glide in through the cabin windows.

"I'm an associate professor of biology, working on a research project for the University of New Brunswick," he said. "I'm searching for evidence of the Eastern Panther."

"Really?" Her forehead furrowed.

"You have a problem with that?" He picked up a piece of crisp bacon.

"No." She focused on her food for a moment, then dropped her fork with a clatter and met his gaze. "Actually, that's not true. I *do* have a problem with it. A very big problem, as a matter of fact."

"And that would be?"

"I believe the money spent on these so-called research projects would be better used on improving the lives of human beings. For example, stopping the flow of illegal drugs, alcohol, and tobacco flooding over the US/Canadian border in this area and infecting our kids like a lethal virus."

"How could this be accomplished?" He spread plum jam on a piece of toast.

"By using the money from unnecessary research

6

projects such as yours to employ more officers to patrol the area. There are acres and acres of unmanned border in these woods, and they're infested with criminals who couldn't care less about the young lives they're ruining."

Her voice rose, concern in every heated word.

"Hey, just a minute." He held up a hand. "I have to object. Finding actual scientific proof that the Eastern Panther still exists in these woods would provide important new biological information about a species long believed to be extinct."

"Look, there's about as much hard evidence to support the existence of an Eastern Panther in this province as there is to prove the actualization of a sasquatch in British Columbia." She leaned across the table toward him, eyes narrowing.

"I beg to differ." He picked up his cup. "There have been sightings, researchers have found scratches on tree trunks..."

"And people have seen hairy monsters, too."

"Hairy monsters?" He felt a grin twitching at his mouth.

"Okay, laugh. But if you dealt with kids every day who are having their lives destroyed by illegal substances, you might not find it so amusing."

"I'm sorry." He looked over at her, impressed by her vehemence. "I guess we'll have to agree to disagree."

"Most definitely." Her eyes flashed emerald fire.

They finished their meal in silence.

"Thanks for breakfast." He stood. "Come on, Scout. I think it's time we left."

"Now, there I can agree with you. I have to get myself ready for school and Bruiser for Doggie Day Care."

She snatched up their plates. At the dishwasher she clattered them inside with more force than necessary.

7

****

Back at his cabin, Frasier paused on his verandah to gaze out over Loon Lake. The sun was burning off the mist, turning it to gossamer gold. One of the loons for which the lake was famous hooted its haunting call. Another chuckled a reply.

Frasier drew a deep breath of the cool, clear air and wished he could live and work here forever. He didn't mind the locals monikering him the Hermit of Loon Lake. Maybe that's exactly what he was, what he wanted to be after the past turbulent years.

He twisted his mouth in a grimace. *Fat chance of that now.* Suddenly there was Emma Prescott and her annoying little dog. They had to be gotten rid of.

"Come on, Scout. Let's go inside. We need to do some serious thinking."

****

"There's a woman living in the cabin next door." Frasier let the words gush over his cell phone an hour later. "Her name is Emma Prescott."

The line fell silent. Then: "When did she arrive?"

"Within the last couple of days, while I was meeting with you in Fredericton. She said there'd been a fire at her apartment building in town and she couldn't find another place to live with her dog. She has a Pug."

"Strange she couldn't get anything closer to Carleton. I presume she has a job there?"

"She says she's a guidance counselor at the high school."

"Attractive?"

"Yes, sir."

"Very?"

"Yes, sir."

"I'll have her checked out. But you'll have to get rid of her, regardless of what I discover. She'll put our entire project in jeopardy."

"Understood. How do you suggest I go about it?"

8

"You've always been creative. You'll come up with something. I'll expect to hear all about it at our meeting in Carleton tomorrow. And Frasier, one more thing."

"Yes, sir?"

"I know you've been living up there for four months with very little...ah, shall we say, social life? I can appreciate how you must be feeling, but don't get involved."

"Yes, sir."

"I'll get back to you shortly. In the meantime, remember this project won't last forever. Once it's done, you'll be free to romance any young woman you fancy...provided she's respectable."

"Yes, sir."

The line went dead. Frasier held the deserted phone out from his ear and stared at it. What a pickle! Under favorable conditions, having a beautiful woman like Emma Prescott as a neighbor could have been a dream come true. Under the current circumstances, it could only spell one huge black mark on his career, not to mention the end of his involvement in a project in which he had invested every ounce of physical and emotional energy.

Scout leaned his chin on Frasier's knee. He patted the dog absently, his gaze roving around the cabin, hoping for an inspiration.

Ah-ha! His guitar leaning against the wall beside the fireplace brought the flash of an idea. It had been a while, but maybe, just maybe...

****

That evening Frasier was sitting on his front verandah steps when Emma arrived. The warm, balmy fall twilight couldn't have been better for his plan. When she braked to a stop, he drew a deep breath, strummed the guitar resting across his knee, and began to sing.

9

She got out, opened the back door for Bruiser, paused, and swung to look over at him. Instantly he felt stupid, sitting there bare-chested, hoping to scare the daylights out of an innocent woman. Unfortunately, it had been the only plan he'd been able to come up with. As she continued to gaze over at him, he stopped, took a swig from the long-necked bottle that had been sitting on the step beside him, looked back her with narrowed eyes, then slid into Bruce Springsteen's classic "I'm on Fire" lyrics.

A slow smile broke over Emma's face. She threw her purse onto her verandah and trotted across the lawn, Bruiser at her heels. She wore those same form-fitting jeans that had devoured his attention that morning, along with a yellow sweatshirt with Carleton High School emblazoned across the front of it. A lot of schools and businesses allowed casual dress on Fridays. *But did she have to look so good in it?*

"Not bad." She paused at the bottom of the steps and grinned up at him, hands on her hips. "You wouldn't have another one of those in that cooler?" She indicated the bottle on the top step. "I've had a heck of a day."

"Yeah, okay, I guess." *Man, this couldn't be going more wrong.* He laid his guitar aside and opened another beer.

While she waited, Emma gyrated and sang the next verse so completely off-key he winced.

She paused when he handed her the bottle. Taking a pull on it, she sat down beside him. "Come on, play for me, my man. It's Friday night, and we…at least I…deserve to kick back." She grinned over at him. "You've got an okay sound."

****

When she and Bruiser left, two beers and an hour later, Frasier pulled on his shirt. Ominous black clouds had gathered over the far end of the

10

lake and were moving steadily in his direction. *A bellwether of what lay head for Frasier MacKenzie and his new neighbor?* His best bad-boy performance hadn't done a thing to unnerve Emma Prescott. If anything, it had only served to form a bond between them since, as Emma had said, they were both fans of Budweiser and classic Boss.

Dragging his cooler, his guitar in his other hand, he went back inside his cabin. Tomorrow was another day. He'd think of something tomorrow.

****

Hammering woke him four hours later. Rain and wind buffeted the cabin. In the living room Scout cavorted, whining.

"What the—?" He stumbled out of bed, pulled on his flannel pajama pants, and headed for the door.

Halfway there, he stubbed his toe and cursed. Muttering expletives, he yanked open a drawer by the sink and grabbed the .38 lying inside.

The hammering grew louder, more persistent.

"Quiet!" he hissed to Scout as he eased the door open a crack.

In the illumination of her verandah light, Emma Prescott bent over the top of her car, pounding on the sunroof gaping open into the storm. He dropped the gun on a table by the door and, bare-footed and bare-chested, headed down his front steps, flinching as cold September rain and wind buffeted his bed-warm body.

"What *are* you doing?" He had to yell to make himself heard above the storm.

"My sunroof is stuck open! Give me a hand! Hurry, before my car gets flooded!"

"Why didn't you close it before you went to bed?" He trotted across the yard, annoyance negating the discomfort of pebbles and pine cones pricking his feet. "Don't you realize you're inviting car thieves?"

"Who's going to steal a car up here?" Water

dripping from the end of her nose, she turned on him, drenched hair plastered about her face, a transparent raincoat covering pink flannelette pajamas. "Are you going to help me or not?"

"Okay, okay. Move back. Let me see what I can do." He leaned across the car's roof and threw his weight against it. Nothing. "Have you got a tarp?"

"A tarp?"

"Yeah, a big plastic sheet."

"I know what a tarp is, but I don't have one."

"Plastic garbage bags?" *Geez!* Icy water trickled down his back and into his pajama pants.

"Yes, right, yes, I do." She turned and ran into her cabin.

Damn it, damn it, damn it. He gave the offending opening a whack. This woman would drive him crazy.

"Here we go." She ran back toward him, sounding cheerfully exuberant. "I've cut one open so it'll fit across the entire top."

"Give me one end of it, you take the other, go around to the driver's side, and open the door. I'll open the passenger one, then we slam them simultaneously, okay?"

"Great. Got it? Good. One, two, three...doors open."

Together they opened the doors and stuffed the ends inside.

"One, two, three, doors closed!"

"There!" He gave the black plastic covering a pat. "That'll do the trick until morning." He backed away from the car to check their handiwork, trod on something sharp, and yelped.

"What?" She pushed wet, straggling hair from her face.

"Rock. I'm barefoot."

"Oh, right. I should have guessed."

"Guessed?"

"Bare chest, jammie bottoms. Doesn't follow you'd be wearing your bunny slippers."

"Look, you brought me out of a nice warm bed with that hammering." *Could she possibly get more annoying?*

"I sort of figured that out, too." The chuckle in her words sent a flush of warmth over him. "Those pj pants have to be the male equivalent of a wet T-shirt."

Damn and blast! The thin flannel clung to him like a second skin, the porch light providing enough illumination to highlight the fact. He uttered a guttural sound and suppressed the urge to shield his male dignity with his hands.

"I'm going back to bed." He turned and headed toward his cabin. "Ouch!" A pine cone found his instep.

"Lookin' good." Her words echoed after him. He muttered an expletive that would have made most women blush...but probably not Emma Prescott.

****

He was waiting for coffee to perk, twenty minutes later, when Scout uttered his sharp bark.

"Frasier, it's Emma." A knock on the door followed her announcement. "I've brought something to chase the chill." A short pause, then, meekly, "And say thanks."

She's never going to leave me in peace, never!

Wearing jeans and moccasins, the plaid flannel shirt he'd pulled on after his hot shower hanging loose and unbuttoned over his chest, Frasier opened the door and scowled out at her.

"Wow! What a night!" Swathed in a yellow oilskin and matching sou'wester, she scuttled in out of the wind and rain, a large thermos in her hands, the Pug at her heels. "This will warm us up." She placed the jug on the table.

"That isn't necessary." He closed the door as

Scout and Bruiser greeted each other with wagging tails. *Ah, man, her dog is turning a perfectly trained guard animal into a tail-wagging pet.*

"Oh, but it is." She removed her dripping hat and coat, gave them a shake, and hung them on a peg beside the door. Beneath, she was wearing a gray jogging suit. "Where do you keep your mugs?"

She glanced speculatively around the room. He gave up.

"Third cupboard to the right of the stove, second shelf."

She peered into the shelf and took out a pair. "You know, you really should tidy up in there." She poured golden brown liquid into two mugs. "Just to make sure you don't have mice. This is the time of year they try to get inside for the winter. Even leaving the door open for a minute to let your dog inside can give a pair time to scamper into the place. And you know what that means."

"Okay, okay, I'll try to find time to clean my cupboards."

"I'm sure you could take a few minutes out of your busy schedule."

Sarcasm, and after he'd just helped her prevent her car from flooding.

"Here. Git this down ya, and I reckon ya'll live ta fight another day." Before he could retort, she handed him a mug and grinned. "Heard that bit in a movie, liked it, and was always hoping for a chance to use it." She sat down on the couch, indicating the chair across from her. "Come on, matey. Take a load off and give it a go."

"Yes, well, I think once is enough." He sat down. *Damn, it was hard to stay annoyed with those drop-dead green eyes twinkling over at him.* He raised the drink to his mouth.

"Ahhh!" His head flew back. "*What* is this?"

"Hot buttered rum. The very best thing to drive

out a chill." She took a sip, grimaced, then smiled brightly. "I might have gone just a tad heavy on the rum."

"I'll second that." He put the mug on the coffee table and shoved it away. "Since I don't drink…"

"You can't term this drinking." She pushed the mug back at him. "It's medicinal. Anyway, when did you become a teetotaler? I remember you savoring a few Buds earlier this evening."

He glanced over at her, then down at the liquid in the mug. That first mouthful was already easing its way through him, chasing out the cold. Maybe he could file it under the heading of medicinal. Maybe it would help ward off a cold or flu. He couldn't risk getting sick at this point in his project. He took a cautious sip.

"Not bad," he admitted.

"There ya go, me lad." She grinned broadly. "If ya git a mite tipsy, I promise not to go takin' advantage of ya."

"Another movie?" He leaned back in his chair and felt his lips curling up at the corners. Whatever else she might or might not be, Emma Prescott definitely wasn't dull.

"Same one, actually. Wish I could remember the title. Have you got any favorites?"

"Anything with a good story line and great characterization."

"Ah, so you would enjoy a good seafaring adventure." She urged the Pug onto the couch beside her. "Books?"

"Again, anything with a good story line and great characterization."

"You're a bit of a generalizer. That covers a good section of the library."

"Yeah, well, my taste is pretty eclectic. Makes life interesting."

"I just bet it does." She slanted him a sly glance.

"What is that supposed to mean?"

"Well, in women, for example. You probably like blondes and redheads and brunettes equally... whichever takes your fancy at any given moment. Not very romantic."

"Oh, and you are? Do you have someone special in mind...tall, dark, handsome, clever as Einstein, sensitive as a sunburn, and as devoted as a St. Bernard?"

"And that would be a bad thing? Much easier to deal with than your eclectic outlook."

"Point conceded." He stifled a yawn. "This conversation is beginning to sound like an ad in a hook-up column. It's time we abandoned it and went to bed...separately, that is."

"Don't flatter yourself with any really premature thoughts." She got to her feet and headed to retrieve her hat and coat. "Good night, Professor MacKenzie. Sweet dreams...about an Eastern Panther."

"Associate Professor," he called after her.

She slammed the door on the words.

He looked down into the liquid left in his cup. *Might as well finish it. Does seem to be warming me up.*

Ten minutes later he stood. And staggered. He caught the edge of the table and waited for his equilibrium to return. *That stuff packed a wallop.* Of course, he hadn't had more than the occasional beer in a very long time. Those two Buds on the steps tonight had been his first multiples in weeks. He drew a deep breath, made certain his feet were under his command, and headed for the bedroom.

Inside he stripped off his clothes and fell naked back into bed. A chuckle echoed from his throat. He brought himself up short. What would the Professor say if he discovered the events of this past night? *Damn!* He clutched a handful of pillow. *Emma Prescott, you're trouble, big trouble. You have to leave*

Loon Lake soon, very soon.

He snored.

****

Frasier awoke to the rattling of his phone and the sensation of having eaten a huge chunk of cotton wool. He dragged himself up onto an elbow and slapped a hand over the cell on his nightstand.

"Hello." The word was a croak.

"Frasier, is that you? What's wrong?"

"Nothing." He pulled himself sharply to a sitting position and grimaced as a streak of headache slashed across his forehead. "Must have overslept a tad."

"A tad? Do you know what time it is?"

"I believe it's..." He paused as he tried to focus on the clock radio by his bed. "Just going on 9:00 a.m., Professor."

"You should have been out on surveillance two hours ago. Do you think those big cats sleep in? What's happened to you?"

Emma Prescott happened, that's what.

"My neighbor had some difficulties with her car. I...we were up late trying to repair it."

"That woman again! Frasier, you've got to get rid of her. We can't have her living in our project area."

"Yes, Professor. Understood, sir."

"Then do it...now! I've checked her out, and she appears to be exactly who she's said she is. Still, we can't have her mucking around in our operational area. I'll meet you at the Department of Natural Resources in Carleton at 11:00 a.m. for further briefing. Don't be late."

"Yes, sir."

He replaced the phone on the nightstand and heaved a sigh. Tracking down his elusive quarry would be easy compared to getting rid of Emma Prescott.

17

He pulled himself out of bed and headed into the bathroom. A roiling stomach and the pounding ache above his eyes were fair punishment for letting Emma ply him with liquor. He should have been smarter. He shouldn't have accepted her invitation to breakfast. He shouldn't have tried to frighten her off with that ridiculous bad-boy performance. He shouldn't have tried to fix her car. He shouldn't...

He stopped. The woman had only stepped into his life yesterday morning, and already he had a laundry list of involvement with her.

****

Frasier showered, shaved, and dressed with more than usual care. He figured he had to at least look efficient for his supervisor.

When he stepped out onto his verandah wearing tan Dockers, green silk shirt, and brown suede jacket, he felt ready to face the Professor, a man who tolerated no sloppiness either in mind or body. Putting on a pair of Foster Grants, he hoped the bloodshot would have left his eyes by the time he got to town.

"You stay here and watch the place," he called back inside to Scout on his way to his SUV.

Glancing at his watch, he slid into the driver's seat. He barely had time to get to his meeting. That run up the mountain to check for tracks hadn't allowed him time to spare, but he had to have his latest findings ready to report.

He turned the key in the ignition. Click. Again. Click. Click, click, click.

Ah, not now. Son of a...

He cracked the hood, got out, and shoved it up. He hadn't a clue where to look for the trouble. A couple of wires appeared unattached, but where to reconnect them...

"Car trouble?" Her voice made him lurch upright and bang his head.

18

"It would seem that way." He rubbed the sore spot and struggled to keep his cool.

"If you need a lift to town, I'm heading in to do a little shopping. You're welcome to ride along."

He hesitated. *Spend more time with Emma Prescott? Ah, man!* But he did have to get to town.

"Okay. Thanks." He slammed the hood, locked the vehicle, and shoved the keys into his pocket. "I have a meeting with Professor Taylor to discuss the project at 11:00 a.m., and he doesn't take tardiness well."

"Where's Scout?" she asked as he joined her in the walk to her car. "He's welcome to come, too. Bruiser's in the back seat. He'd enjoy company." In jeans, a yellow turtleneck, and a denim barn coat, her hair pulled back into a ponytail that stuck out of the back of a baseball cap, she looked way too attractive. Not someone any man with a drop of testosterone would want to get rid of.

"Thanks, but I'm leaving him here...to look after things."

"To protect your place from what...rogue rabbits, bandit bears, dastardly deer?"

"We're not that far from civilization that some of your disgruntled students can't find this place."

She whirled on him, hands on her hips, green eyes flashing. "Are you implying my kids might...?"

"Are we going to town or what?" He cut off what could escalate into an all-out argument.

"Okay, sure, get in." She jerked open the driver's door, then jumped back as a gush or rain water flooded off the garbage bag roof cover. "Open your door so I can pull this off."

Grinning as he watched her brush droplets from her jacket, he opened the opposite door. While she shook water from the sheet of plastic and began to fold it away, he slid into the passenger seat. And yelped.

"What the hell...?" Jumping out, he scrubbed at the seat of his pants.

"What now?" Emma paused to look over at him, the question coming out in an exasperated sigh.

"Bloody seat's soaked!"

"Oh, stop whining!" She bent into the back, brushed aside Bruiser's overtures, and pulled out a snowshoe. "Here, sit on this."

"You carry snowshoes in September?"

"Never got around to putting them away. Anyhow, it'll soon be winter. So are you going to sit on it, or what?" She shoved it across the roof toward him.

He hesitated, picturing himself meeting the Professor in wet pants. A guttural sound issuing from his throat, he grabbed the snowshoe and adjusted it over the drenched seat. As he tried to settle on the leather-thonged contraption, he vowed he'd find some way to get rid of Emma Prescott, even if it cost him the last shred of his dignity.

Chapter Two

"You *do* know this vehicle needs new shocks? Damn!" Frasier bounced high and ducked as the car struck another exposed root. He'd lost count of how many times he'd had to dodge as she jounced the car along the woods road. The pummeling his backside was taking from the snowshoe had to be making bruises.

"No, and I don't see how you would, either." She navigated a sharp turn that would have sent him slamming against the door if he hadn't been wearing a seatbelt. "You didn't seem all that mechanically talented when I found you staring into the innards of that fancy four-by-four as if it were some kind of Chinese puzzle."

"Yeah, well, a person doesn't have to be a genius to feel this car hitting the road like a sledgehammer. Ouch!"

She'd bounced them over another rock. He flew as high as the seatbelt would allow. This time his head smacked against the roof before he boomeranged back onto the snowshoe.

"Bet you didn't realize snowshoes were so rigid." She cast him a quick glance from behind emotion-concealing Ray-Bans. Twitching at the corners of her mouth rankled him to the core.

"No, I didn't. But then I never thought I'd be riding one over a potholed woods road with the female equivalent of Mario Andretti trying to break a record for recklessness. Slow down!"

"Look, I want to get my shopping done and return to the cabin asap. I have a ton of work ahead of me. You must have things to do, as well. I don't want to waste any more of the taxpayers' money than necessary by helping you slack off." Acidity colored her tone.

"Okay, okay. Just pay attention to the road. I see a deer up ahead, so unless you've got some twisted desire to murder Bambi…"

****

Ten minutes later she swung the car out onto the chip-sealed secondary road that led to the highway. Frasier was about to heave a sigh of relief when she floored the gas. They took off with a squealing of tires.

"Hey, hey!" he yelled. "Slow down! The speed limit is 100 km. You're heading to 130!"

"Look, I told you, I'm in a hurry!" she exploded. "I've got a ton of things to do back at the cabin. You see," she continued, quieting and sounding sly, "I'm having a party tonight. I have to get ready."

"A party? You're having a party? At the lake?" *Ah, man, that just about tears it.*

"Actually, a bachelorette bash. One of my teacher friends is getting married next week, and a bunch of us decided we'd give her a real whing-ding of a sendoff…up at my cabin where there'll be no witnesses. Teachers and the likes of myself have reputations to think of, you realize." She cast him a wicked glance.

"So there'll be music and a lot of noise and…" The Professor's blood pressure would skyrocket when he gave him this information.

"Oh, y-e-a-h." She dragged out the last word.

"Couldn't you have it somewhere else? Like a male strip joint in town?"

"Didn't you hear what I just said about teachers and others of that ilk? We can't be seen parading into one of those places. Our superintendent would suspend every last one of us. Anyway…" She looked

22

over at him. "I don't see why it should be such a big deal for you. You don't have to keep banker's hours. If the noise bothers you, stay up, watch a video, and sleep in on Sunday morning."

"Okay, okay, but will you please keep your eyes on the road? And slow down! There's a speed trap somewhere along..."

Behind them a siren wailed.

"Quick!" she ordered, pulling over as the police cruiser rolled alongside. "Hunch over and clutch your chest!"

****

"That went well." Ten minutes later she waved a cheerful goodbye to the officer and headed back out onto the road. Within seconds she'd accelerated to the top of the speed limit. "Better watch it from here on in, though. I don't think the fact that you two happened to be buddies in university will save us twice in one day."

"*Us?*" He felt another flame of exasperation shoot through him. "*You're* driving! *You're* the one who got *u*s stopped for speeding. Consider yourself fortunate that Constable Roy and I shared a dorm in university. Otherwise, that tall tale you started to tell him about me, a.k.a. your boyfriend, developing chest pains while we were making love would have landed us both in deep trouble."

"I could hardly stuff a pillow under your shirt and say you're in labor, could I?" Emma's equally exasperated tone lashed back at him.

"Oh, and I suppose you've pulled that scam and gotten away with it?"

"Nearly." She shrugged as she swung the car into a merge section of the four-lane that led to Carleton. Frasier ducked when an eighteen-wheeler flashed past with inches to spare. "Unfortunately, the officer insisted on escorting my friend Mandy and me to the hospital. He even rushed in and

23

brought out a wheelchair for her." She chuckled. "You should have seen his face when Mandy pulled that rolled-up sweater from under her T-shirt.

"I assume you were fittingly fined?"

"Oh, yeah. He even managed to get a couple of points shaved off my license."

"Good. Smart fella."

"He is, actually." Tires squealed again as she changed lanes. "I really enjoyed dating him. But it soon became obvious he and Mandy were way more compatible. I was happy when they got together. It's her bachelorette party I'm hosting tonight. She's marrying Constable Jeff Cooper."

Frasier felt a sudden urge to pound his head against the dashboard, but he was afraid to take his eyes off the road as they careened in and out of lanes.

****

When she double-parked in front of the Department of Natural Resources offices in Carleton, he climbed out, pulled free the snowshoe stuck to his bottom, and heaved it into the back seat. His "thank you" was a wheeze of relief.

"Don't forget," she called as he started to close the door. "I'll meet you in the SuperValu parking lot in an hour and a half. Let's synchronize our watches. It's 11:00 a.m., so…"

Damn! He'd forgotten the drive back to the cabin.

"Okay," he muttered. "I'll see you then."

****

At 12:15 p.m. Frasier headed for the supermarket. He'd met with the Professor, given an account of his progress, received a reprimand regarding the level of his success and of his failure to get rid of Emma, and dispatched a mechanic to Loon Lake to check out his vehicle problems.

Finding Emma's Sundance in the parking lot, he

24

leaned against the passenger door to wait. At 12:30 p.m. she emerged from the supermarket, pushing a full cart.

"Looks like it's going to be quite a party." He frowned at the noisemakers sticking out of one of the canvas sacks. Grinning, she slipped into the driver's seat to crack the trunk.

"Yeah, well, a girl only gets married once...hopefully." She joined him at the back of the car, raised the lid, and lifted a large pink shopping bag from its perch on top of several bottles of wine, three quarts of liquor, and two cases of beer. "Hold this while I put the heavy stuff on the bottom."

While Frasier stood holding the bag and watching her pile the trunk full of party favors, the police cruiser that had pulled them over on the highway eased to a stop beside them.

"Glad to see you made it safe and sound, Frasier." Constable Vince Roy rolled down his window and grinned. "But maybe you should be careful with the contents of that bag, or next time she *will* be rushing you to the hospital with chest pains." He drove away, chuckling.

Frasier looked down at the cherry pink bag. On its side, silhouetted in gold, was a curvaceous female image in a minimalist's idea of a bikini. Beneath it glistened the words "Nice n' Naughty."

"Argh!" Frasier shoved the bag in on top of the groceries and headed for the passenger door.

"Hey, hey, careful, mister! You'll crumple everything!"

"Crumple? Crumple?" He swung on her. "Right now *I'm* feeling pretty crumpled. Can we just head back to the lake...within the speed limit, if that's at all possible? I want to get home without any further life-threatening or humiliating moments."

"Okay, fine." She slammed the trunk, then watched as he pulled open the passenger door. "Oh, by the way, there are marks that look like some kind of grid on the back of your pants. Must have gotten there when you sat on the snowshoe. Guess it was a bit dirty. I'm surprised someone at your meeting didn't mention it to you."

****

At Loon Lake the mechanic's bottom stuck out from under the hood of the white SUV. He straightened when Frasier approached.

"Nothing serious," he said, wiping his hands on a rag. "Just a couple of wires disconnected."

"Disconnected? How? Could they have jarred loose coming up the trail?"

"Hardly. Pulled clear off." The mechanic stuffed the rag into the back pocket of his coveralls. "Someone did it on purpose. You know of anyone who wants to give you a hard time?"

Frasier shrugged. "I'm here on a university research project. I don't know anyone in the area except..."

He turned to look at Emma busily unloading her car while the dogs danced around her.

"Been foolin' around on the little woman?" the mechanic followed his gaze and grinned. "Better be careful, buddy. I remember one gal who put sugar in her boyfriend's gas tank after she caught him cheatin'."

"She's not my little woman," Frasier snapped. "How much do I owe you?"

"Hundred fifty."

"What? To connect a couple of wires?"

"Travel costs and know-how. You couldn't get it going on your own, now, could you?"

"No." Frasier pulled out his wallet.

Had Emma been responsible for the vandalism on his vehicle? The idea didn't make sense. She'd offered to drive him to town. Still she had been in their dooryard in the night. Had she pulled those

26

wires off on her way back to her cabin after she'd left him mellowed out on buttered rum? Had it just been buttered rum, or had she perhaps added something more potent? If she had, where had she gotten it? *You're getting crazy, MacKenzie. The Professor said she was okay. Leave it there.*

****

Frasier came out of his cabin in jogging clothes, Scout at his heels. He hadn't gone for a run in a couple of days. Now, with Emma in the neighboring cabin, he could take the German Shepherd with him. No one would invade the area with someone in evidence in broad daylight. At least there was one perk to the lady's invasion of his space. He began stretching exercises on the verandah.

Scout gave a delighted bark, then rushed down the steps. Turning, Frasier saw Emma, also in running gear, on her front porch, the Pug beside her as she limbered up. His dog rushed up their steps to join them, then both dogs raced off to roughhouse in the yard.

"Hi, neighbor!" she called. "Heading out for a run? Great! I love company."

No avoiding it. He locked his door and went to join her. Adjusting to each other's pace, they started down the trail. *Getting to know her better could be a good thing. An opportunity to find out her weaknesses.*

"This is great!" she enthused as they jogged down the trail, sunlight dappling their way, the two dogs at their heels. "Bruiser is a good companion, but he's not much of a talker."

She flashed him a grin. Reflexively he grinned back. *The lady had charm. Charm and great looks. And she was funny and bright and— Stop it.*

"Do you run a lot?" she asked.

"I try to make it most days."

"I'm afraid I only manage weekends, and then

27

not always. With a job that has regular hours and a fair commute, I don't have the time."

"Was that another dig about my work? Because, if it was, I can assure you I work much better than a forty-hour week. Furthermore…"

"Gee, you're quick to take offense! That wasn't what I meant at all!"

"Sorry. I guess I am a bit prickly…ever since you made that crack about my project being a waste of taxpayers' money."

"I'm sorry, too. Without research, how would we ever increase our knowledge? As an educator, I should have been more appreciative of your work."

They jogged in silence until she stopped.

"Tired?" He hoped. He had to best her at something.

"No, just time to turn back. I have a lot to do. Hey, how about a race? See you at the lake."

Leaving him in a metaphorical cloud of dust, she dashed back up the trail. *So this is how Wiley Coyote feels behind the Road Runner.*

"Argh!" He took off after her. He had to let her win. His father had taught him to be a gentleman even when he felt least inclined. Nevertheless, the thought of her coming out on top again irked him.

Running behind her, close enough to give her competition, he couldn't help enjoying the way the curls of her ponytail bounced, the rhythmic movement of her shapely hips. The view made coming in second almost worth it.

"Argh!"

He went sprawling into the mud of a trail not yet dry from the previous night's rain. Lost in his perusal of Emma's derriere, he hadn't noticed the Pug darting in front of him.

The Pug's yelp drew her attention. Emma swung back.

"Bruiser, what happened?" She knelt beside the

dog struggling to right himself. "Frasier, are you okay?" She swung toward him as he scrambled to his feet.

"I'm just fine, but maybe in future you could keep your dog in heel position so I know where he is." He brushed grime from his hands and knees.

"Sorry. Forget the race. We'll walk back...in case you did hurt yourself. Are you sure you didn't skin your knees?"

"Yeah, yeah, I'm sure." He had a flashed vision of Emma offering to kiss them better. "Let's just get going, okay? I've got things to do, too."

He'd skinned his hands and felt pretty sure his knees had suffered the same fate. *Damn this lady and her annoying dog!*

"Frasier?" She moved close in front of him. "You've got mud on your face. Here, let me."

She pulled up the bottom of her sweater and used it to wipe his cheek, treating him to a view of a taut, bare midriff and a bit of sports bra. He sucked in his breath.

"There." She pulled her sweatshirt into place and stood back. "Much better. Can't have an associate professor of biology running around with mud on his cheeks."

He caught her taunt and started off at a pace that made his knees smart but his pride feel at least a bit better.

Back at his cabin, Frasier washed his hands and knees, applied antiseptic, and changed into his bush clothes. In jeans, sweatshirt, boots, and jacket, he strode to the storage shed at the rear of the property and backed out his ATV. With more vehemence than necessary, he revved the engine, ignored Emma who stood on her verandah waving, and, with Scout galloping behind him, tore off, up into the mountains. Not only did he need to do some serious searching to satisfy the Professor, but he had to get away from *her*. He hadn't had skinned hands or knees since he was seven years old. In less than a single day in her proximity he had both, and had been made to feel like a clumsy kid.

And she'd foiled him again. In any of the chick flicks he'd endured with last year's romantic interest, even accidentally kicking the heroine's beloved pet would have been grounds for a verbal battle. Inevitably it would have ended with the heroine clutching her critter and striding away. Words like "I never want to see you again!" were generally thrown back over a retreating shoulder.

But not his nemesis. No, sir. She'd expressed concern for both of them, leaving no room for a fight that would make her pack up and leave Loon Lake. *Damn!*

By the time he'd reached the summit of the mountain that rose up directly behind their cabins, he'd cooled down. He remembered how great she looked in jeans that clutched her body in all the right spots, and how her hair shone in the sunlight, and how her jade eyes lighted up when she was happy or angry or excited. And the way she smelled when she brushed up against him. And what that brushing up did to him.

Forget it, man. Just forget it.

He braked to a stop, removed his crash helmet, and pulled binoculars from his saddlebags. Miles and miles of forest and streams spread out below him. Not for the first time, the enormity of the task the Professor had assigned to him threatened to overwhelm him. It was like looking for a particular grain of sand on a beach. Nevertheless he knew he had to make good on it. The importance of this project overrode every other consideration...even Emma Prescott and her killer body and teasing emerald eyes.

"Eastern Panther, where are you?" he asked.

Scout looked up at him and whined.

"Yeah, you're probably right, boy." He lowered the field glasses and bent to pat the dog. "I may be going a little nuts. Being the hermit at Loon Lake isn't as easy as it sounded when I took on this assignment." He stashed the binoculars, replaced his helmet, and started the bike. "We'll just take a quick look down the other side of the mountain before we head home. It'll be getting dark soon, and Ms. Prescott's guests will be arriving. I suppose I should take at least a cursory look at them."

****

Frasier shut the door of the storage shed, flipped the lock, and headed for his cabin. He paused to look out over the calm surface of the lake and listen to the calls of the loons. The evening promised to be perfect, clear, and with the first hints of frost. He sucked in a deep breath and enjoyed...for a moment. Destroying the twilight hush, a car revved into earshot. The first of Emma's party guests. He grimaced.

He got to his verandah just in time to see a Cavalier brake at her front step. Five women piled out, laughing uproariously, shrieking as they pulled packages from the trunk.

Oh, yeah. Frasier shook his head, turned, and went into his cabin. *The games are about to begin.*

Within the next hour four more cars, each containing their full complement of women, pulled into the cabin area. He sat behind a half-drawn mini-blind and watched.

In the late evening dusk, Emma's cabin seemed to rock with music and laughter. At 10:00 p.m. a black SUV drove into the yard and a man swung out. Tall, broad-shouldered and, from what Frasier could see in the illumination of his vehicle's interior light, good-looking, the newcomer pulled a black box from the seat beside him, then went up to the door and knocked.

The minute Emma answered, he pushed a button and raucous music blasted. Frasier heard the female cacophony escalate at the speed of light when Emma drew the man, gyrating, inside. Hoots and catcalls echoed out into the wilderness night.

Damn! She's hired a stripper!

****

"You've got a stripper in there, haven't you?" Frasier faced Emma in the shadows on her verandah and yelled at her above the beat of bump-and-grind music and the hoots and cries of enthusiastic female encouragement. It was 2:00 a.m. He'd given up trying to ignore the din.

"What if we have!" she shouted back at him. "We're all over twenty-one, and so is he!"

"And everyone is drinking and planning to drive home after this fiasco! Don't you realize how dangerous that is?"

"It's a sleepover. The only one who'll be leaving tonight is our exotic dancer, and he's stone-cold sober."

"Okay, okay, just keep it down. I've got to get some rest." He turned and strode back toward his cabin.

"Lookin' good," echoed in his ears. Glancing back he saw her raise her wine glass in a salute. "If you ever need extra cash, you can entertain a bunch of us ladies anytime."

"Argh!"

At 3:00 a.m. he pulled a pillow over his head and tried to blot out the raucous drinking song that rattled his windowpanes.

At 6:00 a.m. he struggled out of bed. Silence had fallen over the wilderness a couple of hours earlier. Blurry-eyed from lack of sleep, he showered, shaved, dressed, and pulled the power mower from the storage shed. It eased his frustration to give the start cord several mighty yanks before the machine roared into life. While he pushed it up and down the lawn surrounding both their cabins, he felt a smug if (he realized) childish satisfaction. *Try sleeping it off now, ladies.*

When he finished, he got out a hammer and nails and repaired a few loose planks on his front porch. Even more childish? Maybe, but he couldn't resist. Revenge and an opportunity to make life unpleasant for Emma Prescott had been just too tempting. A half hour later he watched as her guests trickled out of her cabin, climbed into their cars, and drove away.

Maybe this afternoon she'll pack up and leave, he fantasized.

****

"Frasier." As the last of her visitors' cars disappeared down the trail, he looked over to see her standing alone on her verandah. She waved to him, skipped down the steps, and jogged over to join him. How, he wondered, could she possibly appear so chipper after partying most of the night?

"Any more of that coffee?" She gestured to the mug in his hands.

"Yeah, I suppose." With a sigh he pushed out of his lawn chair and headed inside.

"Thanks," she smiled as he handed her a cup. "That crowd was more than a little thirsty this morning. They drank up every drop I had. But we sure had a good time."

"I heard." The words reflected his grumpiness.

"Oh, sorry. Well, don't worry. I don't have any more friends in immediate danger of getting married, so that will be the end of it...for a while. What about you? Planning any bachelor bashes in the near future?"

"No." He took a sip and stared out over the lake, determined not to let her exuberant good humor finesse him out of his belligerent mood.

"Maybe you should have a bunch of guys up for a night of male carousing." She finished her coffee and handed him the cup. "It might iron out those cranky kinks in your disposition."

She jogged back to her cabin, the Pug prancing at her heels.

"Argh!" Frasier threw the remains of his coffee out over the grass, got up stiffly, and headed back into the house. He had work to do and, by damn, he'd do it in spite of Emma Prescott, her annoying friends, and her ridiculous little dog.

****

The rest of the day stayed blissfully quiet. Colorful autumn leaves drifted lazily down in the warm sunshine. No sign of life issued from the neighboring cabin. Emma Prescott and the Pug must be sleeping off the results of that wild bash, he decided as he set out with Scout for a hike up into the mountains. Ostensibly he would be in pursuit of his quarry, but actually he was simply out to enjoy the peace of the beautiful autumn day. It would have been better if he weren't feeling punch-drunk from lack of sleep.

They traveled around the base of Mount Carleton, then up Mount Head until the trail dissolved into a mass of boulders he'd already scaled one day a week previous, looking for the Eastern Panther with no results. As he stopped to stretch cramped muscles, he looked up into the clear, blue autumn sky and wished he was simply in the area for recreational purposes, just out to enjoy this magnificent wilderness.

An image of himself enjoying a picnic in a mountain meadow replete with daisies, warm September sunshine, and Emma flashed across his mind. He banged his hand onto his forehead. *That woman again!* She'd burrowed into his brain and

34

lodged there, determined to drive him nuts.
****

At 8:00 p.m. Frasier was scanning maps of the area, laid out on his kitchen table, when he heard her yelling and the Pug barking furiously.

"What now!" He looked down at Scout in exasperation. An autumn dusk had descended, and he snatched up a flashlight on his way to the door. "Stay!" he ordered his dog, and the Shepherd sat down beside the fireplace.

When Frasier stepped out onto his verandah, he saw Emma, with Bruiser beside her, shooing two black bear cubs away from a pair of coolers on her lighted porch.

"Don't!" he yelled starting to run toward her. "Get back inside! Their mother could be…"

As if on cue, something big and black lumbered muttering and snarling out of the shadows. Frasier sprinted up her steps, snatched the yapping Pug, grabbed Emma by an arm, and propelled all three of them inside as Mama Bruin charged. He tossed Bruiser onto the couch and slammed the door, bolting it, all in one swift sequence of motions.

"Are you crazy?" The words were a ragged rush of expelled air as he swung to face her. "Didn't anyone ever tell you never, *never* to mess with a black bear's cubs?"

"No." She stood staring at him. For once she had the decency to look shaken. "Black bears aren't exactly grizzlies. Usually they run away when you shoo them."

"Unless the 'them' happens to be a sow with babies she thinks are being threatened. Then she becomes a grizzly at heart, willing to attack and kill anything that dares molest her kids."

"Well, how do you expect me to know all that, Mr. Associate Professor of Biology or whatever you are!" Her color was returning, and with it her spirit.

"I'm a guidance counselor, not an animal behaviorist. What was that?"

A loud crash issued from just outside the door. Frasier strode to a window to see the sow batter open one of the coolers. When the contents scattered across the lawn, the cubs scrambled to retrieve the treats.

"That does it!" Emma reached for her cell. "I'm calling the rangers and telling them to come and get their bears!"

"Hold it!" Frasier caught her hand. "This isn't Jellystone Park. If you call those guys, they'll tranquilize the mother, and transport her a hundred miles away. Her cubs could die without her to care for them. Do you want that to happen? Is a cooler and a bit of food worth the lives of two innocent little bears who were only looking for a lunch?"

He was lying. He knew rangers would never transport a sow without making certain she had no dependent cubs. But he also knew he couldn't have those guys scouring the surrounding bush and scaring off his quarry.

"They'd do that?" Her hand released its hold on the phone. It dropped back onto the table.

"Seen it happen."

Man, I hate lying.

"Okay, okay." She stood beside him at the window and watched the trio gobbling up gourmet cheese, the remains of two fruit and vegetable trays, and a bag of crusty Italian rolls. "Luckily I kept the leftover booze inside. The only thing worse than a hungry bear would be an inebriated one, right?"

He turned to look down at her. In the light glowing in from the porch, he saw a grin spreading across her face. Suddenly they were both laughing, laughing so hard that Bruiser braced himself on four sturdy little legs and let out a full-bodied Pug howl in an attempt to join in.

"Damn it, Emma Prescott, you'll turn my hair gray yet," he chuckled finally.

Her laughter quieting, she looked up at him.

"I'd never want to do that," she said softly. "You have terrific hair."

She touched him lightly just above the temple.

For a moment he stood gazing into those amazing jade eyes. She was beautiful and bright and funny, and he wasn't made of stone. *Damn, damn, damn!* Battling his instincts, he forced himself to step away and turn back to the window.

"They're leaving." He looked out at the bears ambling into the forest. "But we'll have to be careful around sunrise and sunset...that's when they could come back looking for more easy pickin's."

"Okay." She turned away, too, clasped her hands behind her back, and looked demurely down at the floor.

He felt his body react. Above bare feet, in a faded plaid shirt and frayed jeans, she exuded the most potent, natural, innocuous appeal he'd ever encountered. He had to get out of there. Fast.

He'd made two strides toward the door when she stopped him.

"Frasier?"

Her voice caressed his name. He half-turned toward her, his hand on the knob. "Yeah?"

"Thanks. I'm sorry if Bruiser and I have made things difficult for you. We'll try to keep out of your way in the future."

"Great, terrific," he heard himself croak as he yanked open the door.

He vaulted over the verandah railing, ran to his cabin, and took the steps two at a time. It didn't help. As he paused and turned to look out across the dark lake to the black silhouette of the mountains beyond it, he chafed with pent-up frustration.

He struck the post beside him an open-handed

37

smack. There'd been women enough in his past, more than he'd wanted at times, but none had gotten under his skin like Emma Prescott. He had to get himself under control...fast.

From inside the cabin Scout whined.

"Coming, boy." He drew a lungful of frosty air. Opening the door, he was met with the Shepherd's cavorting welcome.

"Ah, come on." He tried to brush the dog's greeting aside. "You're a highly trained, no-nonsense guard dog. Don't start imitating that foolish Pug."

The Shepherd paused, then turned and walked slowly back to the hearth, tail drooping.

"Okay, okay! Geez, come here, you big baby." He hunkered down. The dog turned, stared at him for a moment, then bounded back to knock him onto his behind.

"Just one indignity after another since that lady arrived at Loon Lake," he muttered, struggling to right himself as Scout proceeded to wash his face with a long, wet tongue.

****

He decided to go to bed early. Emma's party and getting up at 6:00 a.m. had taken its toll. He opened the window on the side of his room next to Emma's cabin. He enjoyed falling asleep listening to the hooting of an owl and the gentle rustle of a soft breeze in the pines. He even liked the yelping and howls of coyotes.

The open window would also allow him to monitor any unusual comings or goings around her place during the night.

****

"What the...?!"

He bolted upright as heavy metal music burst into the room like a blast of cannon fire. He blinked and stared at the luminous dial on his bedside clock glowing in the darkness.

6:00 a.m. Who could possibly be blasting music at 6:00 a.m.?

As his senses cleared, the only possible answer came to him. She must be up and getting ready for school. So much for the soothing wilderness sounds of hooting owls and breezes soughing softly through the pines. He fell back into the bed and covered his head with a pillow.

****

Putting his ATV in the storage shed behind the cabins late that afternoon, he remembered he hadn't checked the fuel for the generator that provided electricity for both cabins. With Emma's cabin also consuming energy, he'd have to replenish it more often.

He stopped short. Why hadn't he thought of it before? All he had to do was shut off her power supply, feign ignorance about getting it started again, and she'd have to leave. He headed for the generator shed, whistling.

****

"Frasier."

He was taking a pan of barbecued chicken from the oven when he heard her calling him. A crafty smile kinking his lips, he placed it on a cooling rack. He'd heard her arrive a few minutes earlier. By now she'd have discovered her power outage. Of course he'd offer to help, give her supper, and a place to sleep for the night, but he'd tell her he couldn't correct the problem. He'd advise she move out the following day.

"Frasier!" She was coming up his steps. "My power was off when I came home." She walked past him as he opened the door. "Mmmm...something smells incredibly good."

"Barbecued chicken." He watched her cross the room to sniff the dish. "No power?"

"No. Breaker must have kicked out. Dad showed

me how to remedy the problem when we came up here years ago. Our family used to spend vacations up here when I was a child. That's why I was able to turn it on when I arrived last week. Simple, really. It couldn't have happened long ago. Nothing in my refrigerator or freezer spoiled."

Stupid, stupid, stupid. Of course she knew how to operate the generator.

She paused and favored him with a glittering smile.

"Frasier, this chicken looks absolutely amazing. Do you mind if Bruiser and I stay for supper?"

He felt like banging his head on a hard surface...again.

"Frasier?" She was looking up at him, emerald eyes questioning. "Supper? Do you have enough for two?"

"Oh, yeah...sure."

"Great. I'll go over to my cabin and make a salad. Brusier, you stay here and play with Scout."

Foiled again! He took a pair of plates from the cupboard and began to set the table for two. May as well make the best of it. Maybe he could make her talk, find her Achilles heel, something that would drive her away from the lake for good.

It didn't happen. Emma proved the perfect dinner guest, bright and cheerful, with an extensive knowledge of current events, books, movies, and music, and a sense of humor that had him chuckling more than once. He became so enthralled he forgot his plan to pump her for personal information. Only when he watched as she waved back at him when she and the Pug headed for their cabin did he realize she'd once again upended his plan.

He piled dishes into the dishwasher and headed off to bed, feeling a complete idiot.

He awoke shortly after 7:00 a.m., stretched, and got to his feet. Scout bounded off the end of the bed

40

and headed for the door.

"Okay, okay." He walked groggily across the cabin to open it for him. "So you need a bathroom break." Coffee, that was what he needed. At the counter he filled the machine, set it to brew, and headed into the shower.

Back in the kitchen area fifteen minutes later, he filled a cup and headed out onto the verandah. From the sunlight beginning to stream in his windows, he gathered that another beautiful autumn day was already on deck. Drinking his coffee outdoors in the peace of a wilderness morning provided one of the perks of his job, and this morning there was no rock music blaring. He didn't want to waste a minute.

He pulled in a deep breath of clear mountain air. Something caught his peripheral vision. He swung to the right, toward his neighbor's cabin.

Scout lay on Emma's verandah watching while the lady herself sat on the bottom step with the Pug. An assortment of birds, rabbits, and squirrels formed a semi-circle around her as she fed them from her hand.

A Disney heroine and her little forest creatures. All I need is for an Eastern Panther to stroll out of the trees and lie down among that menagerie, never mind that my guard dog is watching as meek as a lamb!

"Don't you know some of those creatures are rodents, that you're encouraging squirrels to come around the cabins and, given half a chance, into them?" He strode down his steps and started across the yard. The wildlife scattered.

"Look what you've done!" She stood to glare at him. "It takes time to gain their confidence. Now you've blown it. I'll have to start all over again! Your dog does a better job of dealing with the little forest creatures than you do, Mr. Biologist!"

"Squirrels are rodents. If they get into our cabins, they will make one hell of a mess. Wildlife is supposed to be just that. You're not supposed to go around making pets of them. As for my dog, I'd appreciate it if you'd refrain from modifying the behavior of a well-trained guard dog. Making friends with birds and bunnies does nothing to enhance his abilities."

"Oh, for heaven's sake!" She picked up her basket of seeds and crumbs. "I can't imagine any of these little animals as the kind of threat that requires a one-hundred-pound German Shepherd to thwart. Come on, Bruiser. We have to be on our way to town." She started up the steps, then paused to glance back over her shoulder. "Some of us have jobs that require us to show up at an appointed hour."

Frasier stifled a retort as the screen door banged behind her.

"Come on, Scout. You've had enough mellowing for one day...for a month—hell, for the rest of your life."

The big dog stood, stretched, yawned, and came down the steps to join him. Together they returned to his cabin.

****

"Frasier! Frasier, help!"

He bolted from the chair at the table. It had been three days since the power outage incident, and they'd been relatively Emma-free. After their barbecued chicken supper together and their 7:15 a.m. meeting over the birds and bunnies, the only evidence he'd had of her presence was the occasional blasting music at 6:00 a.m. and the sound of her old car leaving and returning each day.

In long strides he crossed the room and out of the cabin, Scout at his heels.

At the top of the verandah steps the stench enveloped them. The Shepherd muttered a strangled yelp and skidded to a halt.

"Wimp," Frasier labeled his companion, but he put a hand over his own nose as he looked around for Emma.

"Frasier! Over here!" She came around the corner of her cabin waving her hands in front of her face. "Bruiser chased a skunk around back and he...the skunk, that is, peed all over him and the rear wall!"

****

"I thought you were supposed to use tomato juice." Emma watched, ten minutes later, as Frasier, stripped to the waist, sudsed a snuffling, struggling Bruiser in a washtub on his verandah.

"Doesn't work as well as this pet shampoo developed specifically for the situation," he said, trying to speak without letting any of the rising fumes into his mouth. "I discovered it last summer when Scout got sprayed. But *that* was an accident." He slanted a narrowed-eyed glance up at her. "He stumbled across a skunk while we were working in the bush. He's always had enough sense not to chase one."

"Oh, so you're saying my dog isn't as clever as yours!" Emma's hands went to her hips, her chin jutting forward. "Just because Bruiser isn't a one-hundred-pound Einstein doesn't mean..."

"I didn't say that." Involved in his heated conversation with Emma, Frasier let the Pug slip in his hands. The little dog submerged in the soapy water.

"Frasier!" Emma's cry sent him grappling into the tub for the Pug's slippery body.

Snuffling and blinking, Bruiser emerged, drew a deep, shuddering breath, and sneezed. Mucus and soap suds fountained across Frasier's bare chest.

"Argh!" He held the Pug out at arm's length and looked down at the mess. "What does this dog have against my chest?"

"He couldn't help it." Emma gathered the subdued little animal into a big bath towel. "Besides, you almost drowned him."

"Drowned him! I'm trying to save his annoying little hide from burning with the acid in skunk spray!" Frasier scrambled to his feet and began wiping himself clean with another of the towels Emma had supplied.

"Okay, okay, we didn't mean to be ungrateful, did we, Bruise?" She bent to kiss the Pug's furrowed forehead, then grimaced and drew back. "He needs rinsing." She handed the towel-wrapped dog back to Frasier. She pulled the tub across the verandah and upset it down Frasier's steps.

"Hey!" he protested.

"It's only a little soapy water." Emma righted the tub and put it back in place. She grabbed the hose lying on the planking and started to refill. "And, by the way," she slanted a teasing glance at his chest. "You clean up real nice."

He struggled to look exasperated, but Emma's teasing had started that uncontrollable ripple effect down his body.

****

"You can't go back to your place tonight." Frasier stepped into his living room where he'd left Emma and the dogs while he hosed the rear of her cabin. "I threw some of that scent-neutralizing shampoo over your back wall and washed it down with the hose, but it will be a while before things are tolerable over there."

"Okay." She surveyed her surroundings. "I assume this is a two-bedroom?"

"Same layout as yours. I'm using the one on the left." He went into it and brought out a navy terrycloth robe.

"Give me your shirt and jeans," he said handing

44

it to her. "I'm going to throw mine into the washer. I may as well do yours at the same time."

"This has to be the worst ploy ever used to get a woman out of her clothes." She accepted the robe and looked up at him, green eyes twinkling. "Implying that she stinks isn't exactly romantic."

"Well, you do," he snapped. "We both do. Romance isn't what's in the air around here. Go into the bedroom and change."

"Aye, aye, sir." She turned and headed into the bedroom, Bruiser prancing at her heels.

Why had Emma Prescott landed squarely in the centre of his life and plans? Was there some malevolent super power out there using her to destroy his hopes of success? Worst of all, now she would be living with him.

****

Sleep didn't come soon or easy to Frasier MacKenzie. In the next bedroom lay Emma Prescott: gorgeous, frustrating Emma Prescott. As much as he tried to tell himself she was a major detriment to his work, he found his thoughts sliding back to images of teasing green eyes and the feeling of her fingers stroking his hair.

"Good night, Frasier. Good night, Scout."

Her words, sultry with sleep, drifted into his room.

"Good night, Emma...and Pug."

He rolled onto his belly and stifled with his pillow the groan that followed.

****

He awoke the next morning and sniffed. Coffee. Toast. And, unless he was very much mistaken, bacon. He pulled himself up on one elbow and sniffed again. Yeah, that was definitely it.

He scrambled to his feet and headed for the shower in the bathroom connected by doors to each of the two bedrooms. Stepping into the flow, he stifled an inane desire to burst into a rendition of "Figaro." He settled for the old Dwight Yokum tune, "I Ain't That Lonely Yet," being careful to keep the volume below that of the gushing water. He didn't want to experience another humiliation like the one his failed Boss/Bad Boy imitation had produced.

****

"Good morning." *Ah, damn!* The sight of her frying eggs barefoot and clad only (he guessed) in one of his plaid flannel shirts, which hung to just above her knees, had made his voice crack like it hadn't since he was fourteen. He cleared his throat and tried again. "Good morning."

"Good morning yourself." She turned to smile at him, a spatula in one hand. Seated on the floor beside her, both dogs watched her activities with rapt attention. "I thought I'd make us a little breakfast. It's the least I can do after all you've done for my boy. I hope you don't mind that I borrowed this." She pirouetted to display her attire. "I took it out of your closet while you were sleeping."

"Too late to say no." Man, he must have been sleeping way too sound if he hadn't heard her. "I appreciate your making breakfast," he continued, advancing toward the well-filled coffee machine. "But won't it make you late for work?"

"It's only 6:00 a.m. After we eat, I'll run over to my place, dress in something that hopefully doesn't reek of skunk, and be on my way. I'll leave the dishes for you."

"Okay." He poured a cup of coffee and sat down at the table as she placed a plate of eggs, bacon, and toast in front of him. "You must miss your music." He slanted a glance up at her.

"Oh, Frasier, I'm sorry." She paused and looked down at him. "That must be really annoying. I didn't realize you can hear it all the way over here. I crank it up so I can listen while I shower. I'll keep it down from now on, I promise. I should have guessed you're not an early riser. *Your* job doesn't require regulated hours."

He raised a hand to protest the slur on his project, but she'd turned away.

"There's orange juice in the pitcher." She got her own breakfast from the stove and sat down opposite him. "Can you keep Bruiser today? He's still a bit too odorific to attend doggy daycare."

"Sorry, I have plans. Scout and I are cruising a big area..." He was still smarting from her remark about his project.

"Bruiser can keep up. He and I often go for long hikes. Just tie his leash to your belt so he won't get lost. Please?"

Gorgeous green eyes begged.

"Okay, okay, but just this once. Whether you agree with it or not, I have a research project to complete. Babysitting small white balls of trouble isn't part of the plan."

"Thanks." She flashed him a radiant smile as she buttered her toast. "It'll be just this once."

He told himself he didn't hear her add the qualifier, "Probably," under her breath.

****

"Frasier, are you up? It's Emma...and the Bruise."

As if she needed to identify herself. He leaned forward and turned off the burner on his stove, where he'd been about to make French toast.

She'd come back from school the previous evening, picked up her clothes from his dryer, been friendly in a neighborly way, and gone home with her dog to spend an apparently quiet Friday night alone. This morning he'd gotten up early, made coffee, and carried a cup out onto the sunny verandah to enjoy it while he mulled over a couple of maps. Emma's little cabin had remained blissfully quiet. Sleeping in on her day off, he hoped as he went back inside to prepare his breakfast. Maybe he'd be able to get out on patrol before she awoke.

But now here she was, up and hollering at him. What was equally annoying was that, at the sound of her voice, Scout had begun to dance eagerly around him.

"Yeah, yeah, she has that annoying Pug with her," he addressed his dog. "You don't have to act so pleased." With a resigned sigh, he headed for the door, Scout prancing happily beside him.

"What is...?" He stopped in mid-sentence as he pulled it open and was confronted by an astonishing Emma. Dressed in a floor-length gown of brilliant yellow that billowed out into an amazing circumference about her feet and a matching picture hat of astounding proportions, she looked like a giant sunflower. Or, he thought, eyeing the flounces, ribbons, and bows, an escapee from the set of a Civil War movie.

"What...?" He stared.

"I'm maid of honor at Mandy's wedding." She put down the Pug she'd been carrying under her arm, and he dashed off to play in the yard with Scout. "And I don't need any smart remarks. Mandy's mother, who isn't well, has always dreamed of an antebellum wedding. Mandy and Jeff have decided to oblige her."

"I thought for a minute you were an advertisement for sunflower seeds."

"What did I say about smart remarks?"

"Sorry, ma'am. What can I do for you? Grease you so you can stuff yourself into your carriage yonder?"

"Fine! I'll manage without you." She whirled and started back down the steps, but one of her ruffles snagged on a nail on the porch rail.

"Hang on there, ma'am." He stepped out onto

the verandah. "Don't go frettin' yourself, missy. I'll have you all free in two shakes of a lamb's tail."

Carefully he freed the chiffon ruffle, then stood back as she rounded on him, eyes narrowed, forehead puckered.

"Your servant, ma'am." He swept her a deep bow, quirked a crooked, rakish grin, smoothed an invisible moustache, and suddenly she laughed.

"It *is* a ridiculous get-up," she chuckled. "But Mandy has been my best friend for years. I owe her for a whole bunch of favors."

"What boon were you about to request of me?" He peeked at her under the huge brim of her hat.

"Will you keep Bruiser today? I know, I know," she added quickly as he winced. "I said it would only be that once...probably. But this is an emergency. Doggie Day Care just telephoned to say they're closed today because one of the clients has been diagnosed with fleas. They have to fumigate."

"Mandy's the one marrying the Mountie you played fast and loose with last year?"

"Well, I'd hardly call it fast and loose, but yes, that's the one. Now will you help out?"

"I suppose." The acceptance was a sigh of resignation. "But just once more."

"Thank you, Frasier MacKenzie. You're my hero." She leaned forward over the voluminous skirt to give him a peck on the cheek, lost her balance, and tilted. He caught her before she capsized, and righted her on her feet.

"I do declare, that went very wrong," she murmured, straightening her hat. "But never fear." She brightened. "Lean over."

He obliged and she planted a chaste kiss on his cheek.

"That's it?"

"Of course." She fluttered her eyelashes. "It's the most a lady can do within the bounds of propriety.

Now, I'd be ever so grateful if you'd help me to my carriage and stuff me inside." She offered her arm.

"Surely." He took her arm. Together they went down the steps and across the lawn to her car. He opened the driver's door.

"Maybe you should put Bruise in your cabin," she said. "He's never happy being left behind. He's sure to try to stow away while we're getting me inside."

"Okay."

He was back in a moment, the Pug secured inside with Scout.

"Let me take off this hat and put it on the passenger seat," she said removing it from her carefully arranged coiffure of curls.

When she bent into the car, the hoops whirled up. Frasier found himself confronted with Emma's bottom encased in a pair of yellow drawers that stretched to her knees, where they flowered out into a froth of ruffles.

"Where did you get the Little Bo Peep panties?"

"They're part of the outfit." She straightened and turned on him. "They're designed for just such eventualities as this. If my skirts don't behave, at least all that a gentleman will see is a pair of calf-length undies."

"Not exactly the most fetching things I've ever seen." Frasier was all-out grinning now.

"And have you seen a lot of fetchin' things, sir?" She frowned up at him and fluttered her hand in front of her face in feigned distress. "I declare, sir, you are a rogue!"

"Come on," he chuckled. "Let's get you settled inside...somehow. The only way I can see is for you to remove your dress and put it in the backseat until you get to the church. If we bend those hoops, you'll never be able to straighten them properly in time for the wedding."

"You do have some novel ideas for undressing me." Emma stood looking at him, hands on her hips.

"Well, then you tell me how you're going to get into that car without crushing that ridiculous get-up."

She looked down at her skirts, then at the driver's door still hanging open.

"You're right. Here, start unbuttoning." She turned her back to him to display a long line of fabric-covered buttons. "It took me a half hour to do them up, and I haven't got time to unfasten them."

"You're not naked under this thing are you?" he asked apprehensively. "If you are, you'll be putting my ability to behave as a gentleman to an acid test."

"I'm wearing a chemise, of course." She gave her curls a southern-belle toss. "No southern lady would go about neck-ed under her finest gown."

"Good," he breathed. He began to unfasten the dress, the softness that was Emma beneath his fingers.

"What did you say?"

"Nothing, nothing. You'll have to put on a shirt or something to drive to town. That chemise may be all well and good up here at the lake, but if you get caught for speeding again, an officer of the law might misconstrue what you're up to."

"Oh, I hardly think that would a problem." As he finished releasing the last button, she turned back to him and let the dress fall in a soft puddle of yellow about her. "I think he might be quite smitten with what he sees."

Standing in front of him in yellow pantaloons and some kind of corset thing that nipped in her slender waist and all but forced her breasts over its lacy top, she cocked her head to one side and smiled up at him.

"You can't drive to the church dressed like that." His fingers raced to undo the buttons on his chambray shirt. "Wear this." He thrust it at her.

"Why, Frasier MacKenzie, you are the most charming, old-fashioned man I've ever met." She paused, looking up at him. "Given half a chance, a young lady might just become smitten with you." She took the shirt, pulled it on, and buttoned it.

"Better?" She pirouetted, eyes twinkling.

"Much. What time is the wedding?"

"Eleven a.m."

"Then you'd better be on your way."

He gathered up her gown, opened the rear door, and deposited the voluminous folds and springy hoops carefully inside.

She slid into the driver's seat and turned the key. As the motor coughed to life, she squinted out at him in the sunlight.

"You're a gentleman, Frasier MacKenzie. And definitely Bruiser's hero."

He watched as she drove down the trail and into the trees.

"And you're quite a lady, Emma Prescott," he muttered as he headed up the steps and into his cabin.

****

"So how does it feel to be a married woman?" The wedding was winding down as Emma attempted to take a chair beside the bride. Her dress blossomed up on its hoops with a display of yellow knee-length bloomers.

"Damn!" She abandoned the idea, remained standing, and pushed it back into place. "Mandy Cooper, I swear, no one but you could persuade me into a get-up like this! This marriage of yours had better be forever, because I won't do this again!"

"Mandy Cooper." The bride looked up at her best friend. Emma could swear she saw stars in her eyes. "Doesn't that have a lovely ring? Mrs. Cooper. I love it! Emma, you should give serious thought to getting married."

"You think so, do you? Well, first I have to find the perfect man."

"You mean that hero type? The one on the white horse who fights for the right and never, ever fails?"

"Something like that."

"Look, I caught a glimpse of Frasier MacKenzie in Carleton the other day." Mandy's eyes were twinkling. "He may not have a white pony, but he does have a white SUV, and he is one total hunk. So unless he's an absolute dud in the personality department..."

"No, definitely not. It's just that he's already married—to his job—and sees me as nothing more than an imposition. Furthermore, he's a long way from being a storybook hero. He's a dull associate professor of biology." She gave Mandy a playfully disparaging toss of her head. "I bet he wears reading glasses and sleeps in flannelette pajama bottoms!" She fluttered her eyelashes, gave her skirts a flounce, and sashayed away, hips swaying, but not far enough to avoid hearing Mandy's take on the situation.

"What's up with Emma?" Mandy's new husband, resplendent in his Royal Canadian Mounted Police uniform jacket of red serge with black jodhpurs and shining brown riding boots, joined her.

"She's in denial," Mandy chuckled. "She's protesting her lack of interest in the gorgeous hermit of Loon Lake way too much. All I can say is Frasier MacKenzie had better be careful. It's not only the Royal Canadian Police that always get their man, Constable Cooper. Emma Prescott has quite a distinguished record, as well."

Chapter Three

At 10:00 p.m. Emma's car labored up the trail to Loon Lake. Frasier snapped on his outdoor light and stepped out onto the verandah into the warm autumn darkness, the Pug under his arm. He didn't trust the little dog not to run in front of the moving car. After she'd braked to a stop, he placed him on the planks and let him scamper down the steps to meet her.

"Bruise! Hi, my boy! I missed you. Have you been good for Frasier...I hope?" She scooped the little dog up into her arms.

"Didn't expect you home until the wee, small hours," he commented, coming down the steps to join them. She'd swapped her antebellum getup for jeans and his chambray shirt.

"It was a long day, the music matched my outfit, and..." She hesitated, then continued looking up at him when he stopped in front of her. "I had this sudden desire to come home."

"Missed the little guy, did you?" Frasier tried to ignore the gentle innuendo in her final words as he reached out to rub the Pug's head.

"Yes." The word continued the nuance.

"Well, no need to worry. He had a great time roughhousing with Scout."

"Good."

"You changed your clothes."

"I couldn't stand all those buttons and bows. The minute the reception ended, I dug these jeans out of the trunk and put on this shirt you so gallantly loaned to me."

"Glad it came in handy."

They stood staring at each other in the mysterious darkness of the wilderness night. An owl hooted back in the bush, a coyote howled. Bruiser shuddered.

"The little guy isn't comfortable out here," Frasier heard himself saying. "Would you like to come in for a nightcap? I have a bottle of Chianti."

"Sure, why not?" Emma didn't hesitate this time.

Following her up the steps, he told himself he'd invited her in because it was wise to get to know your adversary. It definitely wasn't because she looked and smelled terrific.

****

Ten minutes later they sat in Frasier's cabin, enjoying glasses of red wine in front of a fire crackling on the hearth. The dogs lay curled up asleep on Scout's dog bed at their feet.

"They had a big day of running and jumping," Frasier remarked, looking down at them. "Plum wore themselves out, ma'am."

"All right, that's the last southern joke for today." She grinned over at him. Then she sobered. "Frasier, I heard something strange at the wedding today."

"Not about the happy couple, I hope?"

"No, no. But it was vaguely disturbing. I was talking to Roc Hard..."

"Who?"

"The exotic dancer who performed at Mandy's bachelorette party."

"Oh." He felt a corner of his mouth twitching. "Roc Hard. Right."

"Well." Emma flashed him a disparaging glance. "He told me about an incident that happened when he was leaving here that night."

"He was ambushed by a bunch of overheated

55

women?"

"Frasier, do you want to hear what I have to say, or not?"

"Definitely. Go on."

"When he left my cabin, he said he saw two shadowy figures running into the bush. Frasier, do you think someone was spying on us?"

"Naw." He forced himself to be dismissive. "Mr. Hard Roc must have been imagining it. Too much gyrating probably unhinged his brain. Peeping Toms are rare up here. Unless..." He paused.

"Unless what?"

"You have a jealous ex who's stalking you."

"As if! Come on, Frasier, this could be serious."

"Okay, okay. If you're uneasy, I'll get Scout to sleep over at your place. I guarantee no one will get past him."

"Did I say I'm uneasy?"

"No."

"Okay, so let's just forget it and move on." She took a sip of wine.

"Fine. Aside from the costume and the music, did you enjoy the wedding?"

"It was absolutely beautiful." She leaned back with a sigh. "I don't think there's anything so colorful and romantic as a wedding that includes members of the Royal Canadian Mounted Police. Never mind that Mandy was a dream in a white antebellum lace gown. The wedding album will be amazing."

"I assume you were included in some of these photos?" A thought flashed into his mind. "With your escort?"

"Yes. He looked terrific in his uniform."

"Him being?"

"Your university chum, Vince Roy, the officer who pulled us over on your way to town. Remember him?"

"Yeah." *Ah, man! Vince, lady's man extraordinaire.* He turned back to his wine, a chaffing sensation rubbing at his gut. Vince was not only far from ugly, he was clever, with a sense of humor that never failed to charm the ladies. "How did that come about? He called you for a date...like Jeff Cooper a year ago?"

"Don't be ridiculous. History doesn't necessarily repeat. He's a good friend of Jeff's. Seems there's a brotherly feeling among a lot guys in the RCMP. Plus..." She looked over her wine glass at him, eyes sparkling. "Both Mandy and I agree. He looks like a poster guy for the Force in his red serge. And when he put on that Stetson to drive Jeff and Mandy away from the church in a carriage drawn by two white horses... Well, let me tell you, he had more than a few ladies' full attention." She fanned herself with her fingers.

"What about you? Do you plan to see him again?"

"Maybe. He did mention the possibility of our getting together for lunch or coffee. Why? Do you know some deep, dark reason why I shouldn't date a member of one of the most respected police forces in the world?"

"No, of course not." Green eyes taunted and teased, and he turned away. "It's just that Vince had a reputation in university...like a love-'em-and-leave-'em one."

"Ah, ha! A handsome, charming rake! How intriguing." She chuckled. "Come on, Frasier, lighten up. I'm not a vulnerable seventeen-year-old, ready to fall hopelessly in love with the first Adonis in jodhpurs and shiny knee-high boots who comes along. Vince is a nice guy, but he's not my type."

"And your type would be?"

"Someone a lot more dependable, someone who'd be there when I need him, someone who wants a

57

forever relationship, someone who'll love me and only me as much as I'll love him and only him."

"Big shoes to fill. Kind of like the guy on the white horse thing."

"Perhaps, but I'm not about to give up looking. Now how about some music? Think you can manage something?"

"Manage?" He got up and went to get his guitar from where leaned against the far wall. "Listen up, woman."

****

When he paused for breath twenty minutes later, Emma leaned back on the couch, narrowed her eyes, and looked over at him.

"What?" he asked.

"I'm thinking I've seen or heard you somewhere before. You perform much too well for an amateur. Were you ever in a professional band?"

"Played a few gigs during my university days." He chorded absently and avoided her eyes.

"Really?" Emma used the word that Frasier was coming to learn indicated skepticism.

"Yeah, really."

"No big shows, no best-selling CDs, nothing like that?"

"Do I sound good enough for any of that?"

"Yes, as a matter of fact, you do."

"Well, I'm not. Now pour me some more wine, woman. I'm intolerable dry."

"Frasier?" She paused, the bottle above his glass.

"Hmmm?" He strummed the guitar. *Man, I'm enjoying myself...too much.*

"Did you ever consider marriage?"

"Consider marriage?" His fingers slipped on the strings. "I guess like everyone has...in a general sort of way."

"What does that mean?" She poured, topped off

her own glass, and put the bottle aside.

"I mean I've never gotten up close and personal with the subject."

"Never?"

"Never. What about you?" Ah, ha, an opening. A way to start questioning.

"I've never gotten up close and personal either."

"So what brought the subject to mind tonight?"

"If you think I'm going to say you did, you can put your ego away, Associate Professor MacKenzie." She resumed her seat. "It was Mandy's wedding, of course." She leaned back, pulled her feet up onto the couch, and clasped her arms around her bent knees. "She and Jeff looked so happy. All that red serge and the shining boots and perfectly brushed Stetsons. Sets off the bride's white to perfection..." She sighed.

"So you're looking for a fairy tale on top of all that other stuff you mentioned." He strummed a few soft, romantic bars and quirked an eyebrow, Clark Gable style, in her direction. "Guy on a white horse who never, ever trips over a Pug and falls on his face in the mud."

"Come on, Frasier. You could be romantic if you wanted to be. Lord knows you have the looks."

"No kiddin'?" *Damn it, don't blush, you fool.*

"Yeah. Or..." She stood. "Maybe I've had too much wine and you're looking better than I'd normally judge you to be. I'd better be heading home. Thanks for everything."

"I'll walk you over." He put the guitar aside.

"Oh, for heaven's sake, Frasier." She headed for the door. "It's only a few yards to my place. What can happen?"

"Bears, coyotes, and, with luck, an Eastern Panther." He followed her outside, then grabbed her by an arm, brushed the door shut to keep the dogs inside, and yanked her back into the shadows of the cabin wall.

"What...?" she began, but he held a finger to his lips.

"Over near the road," he hissed. "Moving shadows. Two men. Don't move."

"Frasier, I don't—"

"Emma, quiet."

For what seemed an hour but what Frasier knew could only have been a few minutes, they stayed where they were. Suddenly, down the trail, the wilderness silence was shattered by the roar of an ATV. As the sound indicated its retreat, Frasier stepped out into the middle of the verandah and muttered an expletive. If Emma weren't here, he'd go after them, follow them, find out what they were up to. But he couldn't in good conscience leave her alone, not even with Scout as her guard. Men roaming these mountain trails in the middle of the night were definitely suspect.

"What do you think they were doing, prowling around our yard?" Emma looked up at him. "Poachers?"

"Possibly. Look, Emma, I want you to sleep over here tonight. It appears they've left, but I don't think it's safe for you to be alone."

"Don't be silly." She brushed aside his suggestion. "I'll lock the doors and windows. Both cabins have security systems. If you hear mine go off, you can rush to my rescue. And anyhow..." She opened his cabin door and let out the Pug. "I have a Dutch Mastiff to keep me safe. Good night, Frasier MacKenzie. Sweet dreams."

****

Water and uneasiness cascaded over him as he rubbed soap across his chest. Those guys were pretty damn bold. Or desperate. He wished Emma had agreed to stay with him. He knew he wouldn't get any sleep waiting for her security alarm to go off. What a night! To top it off, she thought she

60

recognized him. *Damn!* He threw back his head and let the flow of misting water rinse his body. He had to get rid of her fast, before those prowlers got any more aggressive—or she had time to do any more remembering.

Ten minutes later he stepped out of the shower, toweled himself dry, and pulled on fresh clothes. Before long he had a pot of strong coffee brewing and the .38 out on the cupboard. It was going to be a long night.

He took out his cell and hit the professor's number.

"Sir? Yes, I know it is late, but there's been a development... No, sir, the lady hasn't left yet, but there's another complication. Two men lurking around the cabins... Yes, I agree, sir, I should be able to handle the situation. Normally. But now I have her and her annoying little dog to look out for, until I can get rid of them, that is... Yes, I will get rid of her. Sorry to have disturbed you, sir."

****

His larder looked as bare as a bone that Scout had had in his clutches for a half hour. "I have to take a run to town," he told the German Shepherd. "I'll leave you outside to guard both cabins. I shouldn't be long."

Scout looked at him with sad eyes.

"I know, I know. You haven't had a break in a very long time. Soon, buddy, soon."

In Carleton, he parked outside the SuperValu store and strode inside, eager to get what he needed and return to the lake.

"Hi, Frasier." A familiar voice hailed him as he threw a pair of T-bones into his cart. "Eating for two now?"

"Vince. Good to see you. How are things with you?" He turned to face the officer, who was in civilian clothes and pushing a shopping cart, as well.

"Could be better. I'm hoping to get posted out of this little town to somewhere a man can at least hope for a promotion. Not enough action here. At least not for me." He grinned at Frasier. "Some of us have all the luck. Panther patrol, Emma told me."

"Yeah, well, as of yet I'm not sure if it's good or bad. Vince, have you got a few minutes?" An idea had flashed.

"Sure, just as soon as I pay for this stuff and pile it into my car. How about a beer at the local watering hole, Joey's Pub?"

"Sounds like a plan. Meet you there in fifteen minutes."

****

"I seem to recall you were a Bud man, so I took the liberty of ordering for you." Vince Roy indicated the sweating longneck on the bar when Frasier seated himself on the stool beside him.

"You've got a good memory." Frasier took a pull on the beer, glanced around the nearly empty bar, and lowered his voice. "Vince, what do you know about Emma Prescott? What's the local buzz about her? This is a small town. There has to be gossip."

"You, Frasier MacKenzie, interested in gossip?" Vince Roy drew back in pretended shock. "I remember you as one of the least inquisitive guys in our dorm...about gossip, that is. You had that philosophy of evaluating people for yourself. Have you become one of those nosey old professors with nothing better to do than live vicariously?"

"I hardly think so. It's just this particular lady. I'm getting conflicting images of who and what she is. I'd like to get the opinion of someone I know is trustworthy and dependable."

"You make me sound like a faithful old hound dog." Vince took a drink, then quirked a smile at his friend. "What is this really all about, Frasier? What are you doing up at Loon Lake?"

"You know about my project, the Eastern Panther."

"Okay, okay, fine. Ghost chasing and pursuing Emma Prescott."

"Get serious, Vince. I really want to know about her."

"Okay." He drew in a deep breath. "Well, there's conflicting views. To ninety-eight percent of the people who know her, Emma Prescott verges on sainthood for her work with kids involved with drugs."

"And the other two percent?"

"Think she may be involved in the business. The fire at her apartment a while back only enhanced their case. She didn't initiate an investigation. In fact, she did all she could to foil our efforts. She said she didn't want any kids hauled in for questioning, that it would only serve to widen the gap between her and them in the trust department."

"Sounds like a logical if unwise reason."

"To you and me, maybe. To those who aren't in her corner, it looked like a cover-up born out of fear of retaliation."

"I can see where it could look like that to people out to make her look bad."

"Especially when we're reasonably certain someone on the staff at Carleton High is involved in the drug business within the school. Well, got to go. I have a hot date tonight, and I have to start cooking that stuff I bought. See you around, buddy."

"Yeah, see you." The words sounded flat and absent-minded. Frasier MacKenzie was lost in pondering.

****

"Good evening." Emma was sitting on her verandah when he came around to the front of his cabin from putting his ATV in the storage shed. "Any luck?"

63

"No." He drew a deep breath and stretched tired muscles. He'd been riding the bike all day after another night of very little sleep. He needed a meal and a hot shower and a soft bed. He definitely didn't need Emma calling out to him like a wilderness siren.

"If you need any help..."

"Thanks, but no thanks."

"Would you like to come for supper? I made this huge turkey dinner, and there's just Bruiser and me." She paused and looked over at him, a little wistfully. "It would be nice to have company for Thanksgiving."

"Thanksgiving. Do you know, I'd forgotten. I work pretty much twenty-four-seven up here, so holidays and such just sort of slide by."

"Well, then, here's one you won't miss. Will you come?" She tilted her head appealingly to one side and smiled at him.

Man, she is beautiful. And I am hungry. And it would be nice to have company on Thanksgiving ...even if I did forget about it until now.

"Thanks. Just give me a couple of minutes to wash up. Is Scout invited, too?"

"Of course. Bruiser needs company, as well."

He turned and headed into his cabin, whistling.

****

"I brought wine." Frasier tapped lightly on her screen door fifteen minutes later. He'd showered, shaved, and pulled on a pair of Dockers and a blue chambray shirt in record time, trying to tell himself it was simply because he wanted to get over to her cabin, have dinner and a quick look around, and return home in time to get to bed in anticipation of an early morning. But he knew this wasn't the case. He wanted to be with the totally gorgeous Emma Prescott.

"Thanks." She turned from draining potatoes at

the sink and smiled. "Put it in the refrigerator, will you? I have a bottle of my father's very best homemade white, chilled and ready. We'll save yours for next time."

Next time. She was making plans. The idea simultaneously pleased and distressed him. *Damn!*

"Fine." He did as she instructed. "That dinner smells incredible. I've been living mostly on stuff from the freezer...nuking it up when I come in at night. This will be a treat. Thanks for inviting me." Struck by a shaft of pride, he smiled. Here was Frasier MacKenzie, detached gentleman, at his best. Now if he could just maintain the ruse for the next couple of hours...

"Well, then, I'm glad you decided to join the Bruise and me." She cast him one of those room-brightening smiles. The detachment in which he'd been confident seconds before melted like ice in a microwave. "I made us a pitcher of martinis. There's time for a drink before all these goodies—" she gestured toward to the laden stovetop— "reach their peak."

"Sounds good." *One drink and only one drink.* He could manage one drink. Her father's homemade wine was probably as lethal as brook water. He had to stay safe from Emma Prescott getting him tipsy this time.

****

"That was delicious." Frasier leaned back on his chair and touched a napkin to his lips. "Best meal I've had in months."

"I'm glad. We'll have to do this more often." She arose and began to clear the table. "I love to cook, but there's not much point, living alone. Maybe we could pool our groceries...each pay half, and I'll cook, you clean up."

"Yeah, well..."

"Oh, okay." She paused at the sink and turned

back to him. "It's still too early for that kind of arrangement. I tend to be impulsive. We'll just leave things as they are…for now." She rinsed a plate and turned back to him. "Why don't you sit by the fire and finish your wine while I make coffee and slice the pumpkin pie."

"What about my cleaning up?" Feeling lazy and lethargic, he got to his feet. *Too much food after a long, hard day in the outdoors. And her father's wine was really good.*

"Didn't we just decide to put that idea on hold?" She threw a smile back over her shoulder as she set up the coffee to brew. "Go, sit by the fire. You've had a full day. I heard you leaving at the crack of dawn. Don't you ever take a day off?"

"I will when the project's completed." He stifled a yawn as he sat down in front of the crackling flames. The evening had grown frosty. He'd lighted the fire while she carved the turkey. The room, with two replete, contented dogs sleeping at his feet, had a comfortable, homey feeling. He missed this kind of life. His eyelids drooped…

****

"Frasier." Her voice drew him out of the depths of sleep. He blinked and looked up at her.

"Sorry." He pulled himself upright as he tried to clear the fuzz from his mind. "Long day, great food…"

"No need to apologize, but it *is* getting late, and you did say you've planned an early start in the morning. I've wrapped up your pie so you can take it with you."

"Thanks." He got to his feet and swayed. How much wine had he had? He remembered three glasses. "Come on, Scout. We've overstayed our welcome."

"Definitely not." She smiled up at him. "But we're both working people, and tomorrow is a work day."

"Yeah, right, a work day." He made his groggy way to the door, then turned back to blink at her. "Thanks, Emma Prescott, for a terrific Thanksgiving."

"Next time, your place," she grinned.

"Yeah, next time, my place," he muttered and floundered rather than walked out the door, Scout at his heels.

Vibrant cold air cleared his head on his way back to his cabin. He fitted the key into the lock and paused to draw in a few deep breaths before stepping inside.

"Man, her dad's wine packs a wallop," he told Scout as he snapped on lights and turned up the thermostat. It felt chilly after the warmth of Emma's hearth and home. "That's the second time she's fouled me up with liquor. It won't happen again."

Fool me once, shame on you. Fool me twice, shame on me. His mother's words suddenly echoed in his head.

While he piled paper, kindling, and wood into his fireplace, another thought struck him. Maybe it hadn't been just the wine. Maybe she'd put something in it...like maybe she had the last time she'd given him a drink. But why? He threw a match into the materials on the hearth and watched while they burst into flame.

Damn it, Frasier MacKenzie, do you seriously think Emma Prescott drugged you, then planned to come over here and rummage through your stuff? Man, you're getting way too paranoid. Anyhow, the door was locked.

"Come on, Scout. Let's hit the hay." He set the firescreen in place and headed for the bedroom. "I'm getting a little crazy."

When he stepped into his bedroom, he stopped. The window was open, curtains fluttering in the breeze. No wonder the cabin was chilly. Annoyed, he strode across the room and shut it with a bang. Fortunately the Professor hadn't been around to witness the botches he'd made that evening. Tomorrow he'd pull up his socks, figuratively speaking. He sat down on the edge of the bed and pulled his literal ones off. No more letting a pretty face, a great body, and a bewitching personality romance him into making a total mess of the job he'd come up here to do.

A few minutes later the soft strains of "Tequila Sunrise" wafted from her open window. Frasier MacKenzie moaned, rolled sideways into his bed, pulled the covers around him, and fell asleep.

****

The next day, after patrolling from dawn until 9:00 a.m., Frasier headed into Carleton. He needed to talk to Roc Hard. He figured morning would be the best time to catch the exotic dancer resting up either at the male strip club or wherever he lived.

The strip club fronted on a side road that was little more than an alley between Main Street and a quiet area of town where schools, churches, and the hospital were located. Frasier knocked on the locked door several times before it was opened by a brassy blonde, her California-girl coloring betrayed by the multiple wrinkles of too many tanning sessions.

"What?" she snapped, clutching an electric blue robe about her thickening body. Her eyes were bloodshot and sported deep purple bags.

"I'm looking for a guy who calls himself Roc Hard."

"What's the problem?" Her eyes scanned him from head to toe. "Your old lady got the hots for him and you've come to scare him off?"

"Nothing like that." Frasier pulled out his wallet and extracted a couple of crisp twenties. "He danced at my girl friend's stagette last week, up at Loon

68

Lake. He told her he saw two guys running away from her cabin as he was leaving. Her ex has been giving us nothing but grief. If it was him and one of his buddies…" Frasier crumpled the bills in his fist and slammed it into the palm of his other hand.

"I get the picture." She eyed the bunched-up money. "Come in. Nigel's apartment is upstairs."

She held the door open, and Frasier followed her into a big room with chairs piled on tables. A catwalk ran from a stage at the far end down its entire length. A bar filled a side wall. The odor of stale booze and heavy perfume made Frasier's nose cringe.

At the top of a flight of stairs carpeted with a dirty runner, the woman paused and pointed. "Number three, love. You may have to knock more than once. He was out on a gig till near dawn. He'll be dead asleep." She snatched the twenties from Frasier, tucked them into the top of her robe, and, with a sly smile, left him alone.

"Nice lady," he muttered, heading for the door marked with a tarnished brass numeral three.

He knocked once, twice, three times before a disgruntled male voice responded.

"Keep your britches on, mate. I'm comin'."

The man Frasier had seen at Emma's cabin on the night of the party opened the door. He looked different this morning from the well-groomed guy in the black, Zorro-type outfit. His long hair was a greasy tangle and he had dark circles under his eyes as he faced Frasier and pulled on a shabby navy robe over his nakedness.

"What is it, chum?" he squinted out at him. "If it's about your old lady gettin' the hots for me, don't worry. I never mess with customers."

"Nothing like that. I'm curious about two guys my girl friend said you saw hanging around her cabin up at Loon Lake."

"Ah, Emma's place." He moved aside. "Come in, mate. Emma's one terrific lady. I don't blame you for being a tad jealous."

Frasier stepped into a shabby apartment where living room, bedroom, and kitchen were one. Beer cans and empty take-out containers littered the table and floor. A bed in one corner held a tangle of sheets and a rumpled duvet. A single bare window looked out on a brick wall.

"Give me a minute to think." He crossed the room to where a coffeepot rested on a warmer. "Need a caffeine jolt to get going after a show like last night's. Some of those ladies, man, you wouldn't believe."

"I'd believe." Frasier pulled a wry face. "Used to be a performer myself."

"Do tell. Never would have pegged you as a dancer. Where'd you perform?"

"All over. I was a rock musician."

"Ah, groupies and the like. Pretty wild stuff."

"Yeah, pretty wild. Now about those guys you saw at Emma's."

"Sure, sure." He poured two cups of black coffee and handed one to Frasier. "Big guys, six feet or better. Broad shoulders, one of 'em sporting a bit of a belly. Aside from that..." He shrugged. "They were dressed all in black and wearing ski masks. Sorry I can't give you more. I like Emma. Only met her a couple of times, mind you, but she impressed me as a very fine lady. You're one lucky bloke." He raised his cup in a salute.

"Yeah." Frasier took a drink of his coffee. His taste buds cringed, and he placed the cup on the cluttered table and headed for the door. "Thanks...Nigel."

"No problem. If you need a hand to keep those bums from bothering Emma, I'm your man."

"Thanks, I'll keep it in mind."

70

Everyone, even male strippers, loved Emma, he thought as he made his way back downstairs and across the shadowy club room. He stepped out into the bright sunshine half blinded after the darkness inside. And bumped squarely into Emma.

"Frasier, what are you doing here?" she gasped. The group of women accompanying her stopped to stare.

"Ah...nothing." He felt heat flooding up his neck. He wasn't prepared to tell the real story in front of a group of females he didn't know, some of whom might well have been at Emma's party and would be horrified to learn about peeping toms.

"You?" He tried to turn the focus on her.

"It's lunch break. We use this shortcut to get to the sandwich shop on Main Street. But you still haven't..."

He caught her by an arm and drew her away from the gawking group. "Can we talk about this tonight?" he hissed.

"I guess." She looked up at him. "Frasier, has this got something to do with those men Nigel saw running away from my cabin?"

"Nigel? Nigel? You know his real name?"

"Yes, of course. You don't think I'd hire someone I didn't know..."

"How did you meet him?"

"At the sandwich shop. He eats there too. Frasier, are you jealous?"

"Yeah, right." He forced a guffaw.

"Emma, are you coming?" one of the women called. "We only have a half hour."

"See you tonight," she said and turned to leave. Green eyes twinkling, she swung back, rose on tiptoes, and planted a kiss squarely on his lips.

"'Bye," she breathed and trotted off to rejoin her friends.

"Wow, Emma, is that the hermit at Loon Lake?

71

He's a hottie!" he heard one of them remark as they started toward Main Street.

"Shhh!" Emma admonished, glancing back at him, a familiar wicked grin curling her lips and brightening her eyes. "He's got an ego the size of an elephant. Don't feed it."

****

"Okay, explain."

Frasier opened his cabin door at 5:30 p.m. that evening to face a disgruntled-looking Emma.

"I don't run around checking up on you, so what gives you the right to pry into my business?"

"You're referring to my visit to the strip club?"

"What else?" She brushed past him, head held high, the Pug at her heels looking equally indignant.

"I thought I should check out exactly what Mr. Shaky Stones saw after your party." He watched as she threw her purse onto the couch and plunked herself down.

This wasn't going to be easy.

"Oh? And just exactly what did you discover? That it was a couple of my jealous ex's stalking me? Or could it have been someone from my nefarious criminal past?"

"Do you have a couple of jealous ex's or a criminal past?"

"Neither is any of your business!" Green eyes flashed emerald sparks up at him. "Since you have no interest in me, you have no right to an explanation, and I'll thank you to exercise your nosiness elsewhere!"

"I was just trying to make sure that you—that we both—are safe." He leaned a shoulder against the doorframe and crossed his arms. "I have equipment that belongs to the university, including that SUV and the ATV. I can't risk having it stolen or vandalized. Sorry if I overstepped any boundaries."

She stared up at him for a few seconds, then

heaved a sigh and stood.

"No, I'm sorry. I see your point. I've had a lousy day, but that's no excuse to take it out on you. A student overdosed on some concoction a drug dealer sold her, and she nearly died in my arms before the paramedics got there. But that's not your fault."

As she moved to pass him on her way out, he caught her gently by an arm.

"No, I'm sorry. I understand how you must be feeling."

She looked up him, her eyes widening.

"Frasier, did you lose someone to drugs?"

"Haven't most people? Drugs are becoming an epidemic in this area."

"Do you want to talk about it?" The compassion in her eyes and expression almost made him crack, almost made him tell her his story. Scout bumped his knee, and he came out of it.

"It was just a general comment. Now you'd better head home. The Pug looks hungry."

****

The following morning Frasier stood on the sidewalk outside the Department of Natural Resources office and heaved a deep sigh. He'd just received the dressing down of his career. Six weeks into the project and, according to the Professor, he hadn't made any significant progress. He hadn't even managed to get rid of that pesky woman. Furthermore, if he didn't soon find some evidence to support continuing his work, he'd be recalled, the job handed over to someone else.

He looked up and down the street, then jogged across to where his SUV stood parked on the opposite side. *What to do, what to do.* He swung into the driver's seat and sat thinking. Up the street, kids spilled out of the high school. Lunch time. Emma would be on a break. Maybe if he talked halfway straight with her, told her the presence of

Gail MacMillan

her and her dog was detrimental to his project... It was worth a try.

He got out of his vehicle and strode down the street and into the high school.

"Will you tell me where I might find Emma Prescott?" he asked the pretty blonde standing behind the counter in the main office. A shorter, stouter, older, darker woman stood beside her. "I'm Frasier MacKenzie, her neighbor up at Loon Lake."

"Oh...Frasier." The blonde blinked at him. "Emma mentioned you. You'll find her in her office. Take the first left on your way up the corridor. Her door is the third on the right."

"Thanks." He flashed her a smile and left. Outside the door he noticed his shoelace was untied and knelt to fix it.

"Wow! Emma knows how to pick her neighbors."

A grin twitched up the corners of his mouth as he overheard the blonde's voice.

"Emma's *picked* more than her fair share of men, if you ask me," another female voice responded sarcastically. The chubby, dark woman, he assumed.

"Come on, Mildred, that's not fair," the blonde said. "Emma's a beautiful woman, with a terrific personality. Guys are attracted to her like lint to a black suit. We should all be so lucky."

"Umph! Well, I hope this one understands that no matter how gorgeous he is, he's only seasonal. By winter she'll have someone else, believe me. Our Emma's got to hold the record when it comes to smashing hearts. It's like all her men come with an expiry date."

Frasier straightened slowly. So Emma had had a lot of guys. He should have suspected. He remembered the words in the background check the Professor had provided: "No serious sexual relationships, no present partner or significant other." Initially that statement had made him feel good for a reason he refused to acknowledge. Now it haunted him as he walked down the hall, took a left, and began counting. He should have known she wasn't the innocently seductive creature she appeared. Absolute unassuming turn-ons like that didn't exist, not these days.

He paused outside the third door on the right. Through the glass upper half he saw Emma, her back to him, handing a roll of money to a stocky young man dressed in jeans and a black sleeveless T-shirt. His muscular arms were tattooed, he sported an earring, and his head was shaved.

Emma's companion spotted Frasier over her shoulder, grabbed the roll of bills, and shoved it into the pocket of his scruffy jeans. With a jerk of his head, he indicated the man stopped outside.

Emma turned, for a moment looked startled, then hurried to open the door for him, delight brightening her face.

"Frasier! What a surprise. Come in. I'd like you meet Jesse Jones."

"Jesse." Frasier stepped into the cramped office with its scarred oak desk, uncurtained windows, and overflowing metal file cabinets and extended his hand.

The younger man hesitated, looking Frasier up and down critically. "You Miss Prescott's old man?" he asked, chewing slowly on a wad of gum.

"Just a friend."

"Yeah, right. Cool." He ignored Frasier's proffered hand, cracked his gum, and with a final, insolent glance at the older man, sauntered out of the room.

"Don't forget, Jesse. Get the very best *legitimate* deal you can on that equipment," Emma went to the door to call after him. "We worked hard to raise that money. Remember I'll need receipts."

She stepped back into the room, closed the door,

and looked up at Frasier. "Not a bad kid, really. But lately he's been keeping company with one student who's been trouble from the get-go. I'm trying to win him back, keep him on my side, but sometimes I think I'm fighting a losing battle." She heaved a sigh.

"Don't give up. It's a fight well worth winning."

"Thanks for the vote of support. Now to what do I owe the honor of this visit?"

"I was in town and thought maybe we could have lunch...if you're free."

"Sounds like a plan." She reached for her purse and jacket hanging on a canted wooden coat rack behind the door. "But what did that last bit mean...'if you're free'? Seemed to hold a hint of sarcasm."

"Sorry. I overheard the school secretary and a friend commenting on the trail of broken hearts you've left behind."

"By Gail's friend, I assume you mean Mildred Carter...stocky, dark, formidable? She doesn't seem to like me for some reason I've never fathomed."

"Maybe jealousy?" He opened the door for her, then followed her outside and waited while she took a collection of keys from her purse and selected one to fit into the lock.

"You think?" She looked up at him, astonishment widening her eyes.

"Yeah, I think. Come on." A grin quirking up a corner of his mouth, he took her arm and headed her down a corridor that smelled of cafeteria lunch and gym sneakers.

****

At the junction where two corridors intersected, they nearly collided with a tall, muscular, blond man striding around the corner. His face looked as if it had been chiseled from granite. There could be no mistaking the anger in his expression.

76

"Emma." He halted, glanced at her, then glared at Frasier. "Mildred said you had a visitor."

"Brock, I'd like you to meet Frasier MacKenzie, my neighbor up at the lake." Emma smiled benignly. "Frasier, this is Brock Kelly, our gym teacher."

"Mr. Kelly." Frasier extended his hand.

"The legendary hermit of Loon Lake?" The man's tone filled with sarcasm. "You must be getting hard up to take on a backwoods recluse, Emma." He ignored Frasier's hand. With a slight shrug, Frasier let it drop to his side.

"Brock, there's no need to be rude." Emma glanced about at the corridor crowded with students on their lunch break and lowered her voice. "And definitely no reason to cause a scene."

"No, I suppose there isn't." He let a sneer distort his features. "You're free to hook up with whoever you choose. But watch it, man." He turned on Frasier, and anger again took over. "She'll dump you like yesterday's garbage the minute she finds something she thinks is better."

Brock Kelly swung about and strode away, narrowly avoiding knocking several students out of his way.

"Former boyfriend?" Frasier took Emma's arm again and began to steer her toward the front entrance.

"We dated for a while, nothing serious...at least on my part." Emma avoided his gaze. "But Brock read a whole lot more into it. Sorry you had to get the brunt of his unwarranted jealousy." When she paused while he shoved open the door for her, she tilted her head and continued, "By the way, I had no idea you were a.k.a. the hermit of Loon Lake."

"Yeah, well, hardly something to brag about." He herded her down the steps and up the street toward his vehicle. "Local joke. Where should we eat? We hermits seldom frequent the restaurant scene. I'm up for anything but the sandwich shop. I prefer not to share a table with Roc Hard a.k.a. Nigel."

"Afraid you might suffer by comparison?" She cast him a teasing glance.

"Yeah, right." He opened the passenger door.

"Well, if it's any consolation, I think you'd make a great stripper. So there." Green eyes twinkled as she took her seat and fluttered her eyelashes.

He guffawed and strode around to the driver's side.

****

On Emma's suggestion, they drove a few miles out of town to a small restaurant overlooking the Northern Passage River that flowed past Carleton. Surrounded by lofty, soughing pines, the rustic eatery had few customers on an off-season weekday noon hour. Frasier was glad. Shown to a table overlooking the river through a stand of lofty pines, they ordered, on Emma's suggestion, clam chowder in a bread bowl.

"You're familiar with the menu," Frasier said, settling back in his chair.

"I've been here a few times." Emma took a sip of the ice water the waitress poured. "Too bad it's midday and we're both going back to work. They have a terrific wine list."

"So you're familiar with that, too. Did you come here with Brock the Rock?" The words erupted harsh and suggestive. *Kick yourself, MacKenzie...hard.*

"Frasier MacKenzie." She pulled herself up straight, crossed her arms, and looked directly into his eyes. "If I didn't know better, I'd think you were jealous."

"Jealous! Don't be ridiculous! We're neighbors... friends, nothing more. I'm just curious."

"Well, let me set you straight." She relaxed in her chair, green eyes narrowing to wickedly twinkling slits. "Sure, I've had a few men in my life—most of them nice guys—but I've never found what I'm looking for...yet."

"And, pray tell, what might that be?"

She paused, looked down at her hands clasped on the table in front of her, then said softly, a tad embarrassedly, he was surprised to observe, "A hero."

"A hero?" Astonishment raised his tone, and he struggled to moderate it as he repeated, "A hero?"

"Yes, a hero." She raised her gaze to meet his defiantly.

"Not many of them around these days." He toyed with the silverware.

"No, not many."

Her tone had suddenly softened, and when he glanced up, she was looking at him with a gaze that rattled the cage around his heart. He remembered she'd called him her hero on the day he'd rescued Bruiser from the lake and again when he'd de-skunked the little pest.

Sunlight filtering through the pines beyond the window cast gently swaying shadows over the snowy tablecloth, and he saw her hand sliding slowly through them to come to rest over his.

He stared down at her fingers covering his in the sensuously changing light, feeling the warm tingle filter up his arm and then race through his entire body. *Emma, Emma.* Her name pounded a tattoo.

"Frasier?" She moved her hand carefully over his, and when he managed to look up, to meet her gaze, he saw the question there. Sweet Jesus! How much was a man supposed to sacrifice for his work?

"This isn't a good idea, Emma." The words came from somewhere deep inside. They ripped and hurt as they came out. "I've got a job to do, and..."

"Oh, for God's sake, Frasier!" She wrenched her

hand back and glowered over at him. He'd never seen her so angry. "Your job! Ghost chasing!"

"Yeah, well, at least it doesn't involve giving wads of cash to tough-looking students!" Frustration made him uncharacteristically cruel.

"That money is to purchase sports equipment!" She was on her feet facing him, outrage spilling over. "Trusting Jesse to buy it is a step on his road back. If you had even a pinch of logic in that suspicious brain of yours, you'd know the only way to gain trust is to give it!"

She grabbed her purse and jacket from the back of her chair and strode out of the restaurant, head held high, back defiantly straight. He scraped back his chair to follow her, then felt the weight of keys in his pocket. A grin began to kink his lips and he slid back into his seat.

When she stepped back into the dining room a couple of minutes later, he saw a lot of her anger had drained away. As she approached their table, he got up and pulled out her chair.

"I forgot," she said sheepishly. "Your vehicle. And I'm not angry enough to walk eight miles back to school. Anyway—" she drew a deep breath as she sat down and folded her hands on the table— "I'm hungry."

Green gaze met blue. Slowly they both began to grin.

"Sorry," she said softly.

"No, I'm sorry. Damn sorry. If you only knew how much I wanted..." He stumbled over the explanation and couldn't finish.

"I think I do." The words, gentle and laced with understanding, nearly blew him away. "But the timing isn't right. Let's just leave it there. Friends?"

She extended her right hand across the table. He hesitated, then folded it into his. "Friends."

The waitress arrived with their lunch. Frasier

could only hope clams didn't have the same effect as oysters. He'd had about all he could handle in the way of sexual frustration for one day.

"Tell me about your work."

"What's this? An effort at polite lunch conversation?"

"Don't be snide. No, I really would like to know more about what you do."

"Okay." Frasier settled back in his chair. "I'll give you a bit of the history of the Eastern Panther. That should prove boring enough to put you to sleep."

"I doubt it, but go ahead."

"Well, perhaps the first sighting of what we've come to call the Eastern Panther was made by Cabeza de Vaca in 1513. He reported seeing some type of lion in the Florida Everglades. Several years later, the English sea captain Sir John Hawkins reported a similar sighting. Over the years these cats were reported farther and farther north. By the mid-1800s, Pennsylvania had become home to a few. Later still, there were reported sightings in Vermont and Maine."

"Were these animals that had migrated north from Florida?" Her eyes were bright with interest. Inspired, he continued.

"That we don't know. If I'm able to get a DNA sample for a cat in these woods, we'll have proof, but until I do, all we have is speculation."

"Tell me more."

"Fear and bounty hunting were largely responsible for destroying whatever specimens might have existed in the Appalachians around that period. Then, of course, there were those we now call consumptive users of wildlife. Collecting species by killing them was an accepted practice by these individuals. They saw themselves as naturalists and conservationists, but they were among the most destructive forces to a species as rare and teetering on the brink of extinction as the Eastern Panther. Fortunately, these days we can use tranquillizers, not bullets, as a means of examining an animal."

"Fascinating and more than a bit sad."

"Unfortunately, during the mid-eighteen hundreds, when the Eastern Panther would have been fighting for its existence, they became trophy animals with a bounty on their heads. Accused of devastating young farm animals for food, the cats were hunted down and slaughtered.

"In actual fact, pigs and calves weren't their natural prey. Their main food source was the white-tailed deer. They only resorted to raiding farms after settlers had killed off a lot of their normal nourishment or driven it out of the area with towns and agriculture. I don't like to think how many kittens must have been left to die motherless in their dens when their foraging mothers were killed by farmers or bounty hunters. There are mounted specimens in several New England museums that bear witness to this slaughter."

"But did they attack people? I've heard horror stories." Emma spooned into the chowder.

"I haven't found any confirmed accounts of cats we can identify as Eastern Panthers attacking human beings, although there are many attributed to similar big felines in the western section of North America," he continued. "They're known as mountain lions, much bigger than the cats I'm out to document. Some of those out there reach two hundred pounds, while the Eastern Panther, to the best of our knowledge, averages around one hundred."

"So what you're saying is that, according to historical data, we have little to fear from an Eastern Panther?"

"No, not at all. These are big, unpredictable cats

with the strength and temperament to attack and kill a human being if they feel threatened. What I am saying is that they're reticent creatures who avoid people. It's only when we press them into untenable situations that we can come into serious danger."

****

Driving back to the lake that afternoon, Frasier mulled over what he'd learned about Emma Prescott that day. First—and what should have been least important—he had learned she'd had men in her past. Probably a goodly number, and probably most were as good-looking and muscle-bound as that gym teacher. Second, he'd seen her giving a large roll of bills to a student who had drug connections written all over him.

He knew it was wrong to judge from appearances, but he'd been around long enough and seen enough to be able to form a pretty accurate conclusion. Sure, she'd said it was for gym equipment, but that was only after she'd seen him, been aware that he'd witnessed the transaction. Afterwards she'd tried to seduce him over lunch. Damn, he hoped he was wrong, but the entire situation had begun to gnaw at his gut.

****

"Emma." Brock Kelly stopped her as she was locking her office door at the end of the school day. "I'd like a word with you."

"I'm not sure I want one with you, Brock." Emma turned to face him and dropped her keys into her purse. "After the way you behaved in front of my friend Frasier today, I think it's best we keep our relationship strictly on a professional level."

"Yeah, well, sorry about that." He looked abashed for a moment before he picked up again and continued. "But I thought you and I had something going, something pretty good. Now Mildred tells me you're living up in the wilds with nature boy as your next door and only neighbor. What's the story, Emma? Are you enjoying more than the lake?"

"Okay, Brock, that's enough!" Emma started down the deserted corridor toward the main entrance, but he caught up to her and seized her by the arm.

"Emma, I'm warning you. People are talking about you and that guy living up at Loon Lake. As a guidance counselor, you've got a reputation to protect. I suggest you move out of that cabin and get yourself back to town tonight!"

"And I suggest you release my arm." She glared up at him, green eyes snapping. "I'm over twenty-one and unattached. If I choose to have a relationship with Frasier MacKenzie, it's my affair and certainly of no concern to you. We dated, you played around, and that was the end of it. I don't want to waste my life on two-faced creatures such as yourself. Now, are you going to let me go, or will I have to yell for the custodian? I warn you, you don't want me to do that. We both know what a gossip Mr. Higgins is. He'll have the story all over school by 9:15 tomorrow morning."

He hesitated a moment longer. Then with a powerful guffaw, he let her go, shoving her aside as he headed for the front door.

"But don't say I didn't warn you, Emma Prescott." He paused when he reached it and turned back. "It's not safe for you to stay up at Loon Lake with that man. I've warned you. That's all I can do."

He went out into the autumn afternoon, the door closing slowly on its air hinge after him.

Emma waited until she felt he'd had time to get to the car park and drive away. Then she adjusted her purse on its shoulder strap, hefted her briefcase more firmly in her hand, and followed him outside.

What could he possibly have meant, she

wondered, as she got into her car and headed off to Doggie Day Care to pick up Bruiser. The very idea that she had something to fear from Frasier MacKenzie was ludicrous. He was just what he appeared to be...an associate professor from the provincial university, with the single-minded purpose of finding the mythical Eastern Panther.

****

Friday night again. Frasier straightened from poring over the maps spread out on the table in front of him and tiredly rubbed the bridge of his nose between his thumb and index finger. Searching for the proverbial needle in a haystack would have been an easier assignment.

He glanced at his watch. 8:00 p.m. Huh. 8:00 p.m. and Emma wasn't home. Jolted back to the moment, he knew he hadn't heard her overworked, under-serviced car. He couldn't have missed its arrival. The vehicle needed a new muffler, along with shocks, springs, tires, and probably a whole bunch of other stuff a professional mechanic would spot in a minute.

He crossed the room to peer out at her cabin. It formed a black silhouette against the backdrop of mountains and forest in the autumn darkness.

"Damn it, where are they?" he asked Scout, including the Pug in his concern. "They're always home no later than 6:30."

He opened the door and crossed the verandah to stand on the top step. Loon Lake and its surrounding mountains lay encased in darkness. Overcast hid the moon and stars. A cold dampness suggested rain wasn't far off.

A coyote yelped and howled, the cry echoing in the frosty silence. Not an environment for a woman alone with a small dog.

And then he heard it. A scream. The unmistakable, hair-raising scream of an Eastern

Panther.

"Sweet Jesus!"

For a moment he stood riveted in place. A second scream sent him bursting back into the cabin and over to the drawer by the sink. He yanked it open and grabbed the .38 inside.

"We're going to look for them," he told the dog as he checked its load.

He shoved the weapon into his belt. Cold sweat began to trickle from his armpits.

Then a car, an old car, came within earshot, bumping and roaring up the trail toward the cabin.

"Thank God!" He thrust the gun back into the drawer, grabbed a flashlight from the counter, and strode outside.

****

"What kept you?" The moment the words were out of his mouth he regretted them. He sounded way too concerned.

He shone the flashlight on her as she emerged from the car.

"Good God, what happened?" All the annoyance left his tone as he breathed the question in a gigantic exhale.

Her jeans were coated with mud, her hands and face smeared with grime, and there was a tear in her faux suede jacket.

"I had a flat tire a couple of miles from here." She stared up at him like a deer caught in headlights. Suddenly she began to sob, great wrenching sobs that shook her slender body and sent fat tears coursing down her dirty cheeks. "I just got it changed when I saw eyes, big glowing yellow eyes staring at me from the trees. And then it screamed. Oh, Frasier, you can't imagine that scream! Far worse than anything in the bloodiest horror movie!"

"Emma, did you see it? Did you actually see an Eastern Panther?"

"Damn it, Frasier MacKenzie! I've just had a horrible experience, and all you can do is ask stupid questions?"

"Ah, Emma, Emma." He gathered her into his arms, the flashlight bobbing shafts of illumination around the clearing as it went behind her back. "You're safe now. Come on, let's get you into your cabin. I'll start a fire while you clean up."

Keeping his arm protectively about her shoulders, he let Bruiser out of the passenger seat, then herded her toward the steps. Once inside, Frasier snapped on a couple of lamps and headed her toward the bathroom.

"Get a hot shower," he said. "I'll start a fire and rustle up some food."

She turned back to him, her tear-streaked face wrenching at his heart.

"You...you don't have to...not the last, I mean. I brought a you-bake pizza, and there's a bottle of Dad's homemade wine in the refrigerator. I was planning on treating you tonight because you were so good to Bruiser and me. Some treat, right?" She tried to grin but her lower lip trembled.

"It's a super treat." He leaned forward and planted a light kiss on a clean spot on her forehead. "I'll put the pizza in the oven. Now, go, get out of those filthy clothes before you get sick."

"Always the romantic, aren't you?" This time she was able to feature a weak grin. "Last time you got me out of my clothes, it was because you said I stank."

"Go." He turned her about and gave her a gentle push toward the bathroom. "And be careful. You're teasing a man who's been celibate a very long time."

"Really?" She glanced back over her shoulder as she reached the bathroom door. "I would have thought..." She gave him a head-to-toe appraisal, winked, then disappeared behind a door.

Recovering fast. He headed out to her car for the pizza. *And ready to torment the daylights out of me again.*

So the Eastern Panther did exist, and nearby. That complicated the situation. He paused, listening to water running in the shower, then made a quick trip over to his cabin for a bottle of Chianti. Although he hated to admit it, he no longer trusted any booze supplied by Emma.

He opened it, placed in on the table, and went to check the pizza in the oven. Browning nicely. Too bad the rest of his life wasn't going so well. The close proximity of the panther made it even more important that he force Emma and her funny-looking little dog away from Loon Lake immediately.

By the time she returned, he had two chilled glasses waiting.

"Better?" She spread her arms wide and smiled. She was wearing a pink jogging suit, her hair, freshly blown dry, looked like curly silk, and her face scrubbed clean of makeup reminded him of Doris Day and the girl-next-door types in all those ancient movies he'd watched on late night TV when he couldn't sleep after shows. His gut wrenched, and he swallowed hard.

"Much." *Ah, damn. If you only knew. Hell, man, get a grip!* "What about emotionally?"

"Much also." She accepted the drink and sank down on the couch in front of the fire with a sigh.

"Want to tell me about it...again?" He sat down in a chair opposite her.

"Yes." She took a sip of wine. "Now that I've gotten over my basic hysteria, I would. But first let me tell you about my day. That will bring me back to earth." She curled her legs up under her and gathered Bruiser into her arms. "I have this student...let's call him Ted...who's been coming to me supposedly for help since school recommenced.

He's got huge problems only a full-fledged psychiatrist could sort out, but he refuses to see one. The only reason he consents to come to me is because he'll be suspended or quite possibly expelled for the rest of the year if he refuses. That would mean losing contact with a lot of his customers and potential customers."

"A drug dealer." Frasier sighed, leaned back in his chair, and remembered the student he'd seen in her office earlier that week.

"Previously, but not any longer...I hope. He knows I know what he's up to, but he's clever. Carleton is a small town with a small police force. They haven't the time or resources to catch Ted, and he's well aware of the fact. I try to explain the damage drugs can do, but he just sneers. Sometimes..." Emma leaned back and wearily closed her eyes. "Sometimes I think that boy has absolutely no conscience and that I'm wasting my breath trying to reason with him. The worst of it is the influence he has over other students...like Jesse Jones, the student you met in my office."

"Come on, now." He hated to see her weary and discouraged. He'd become accustomed to the other Emma, the vivacious one with a wicked twinkle in her green eyes that belied a sincere generosity of spirit...and the power to arouse him to the quick. "No one ever said the battle against drugs was an easy one. I believe it's the most serious one this country is facing. Your job is an essential in the war. You're working at the grassroots level to stop teenage users and pushers from creating a whole new generation of addicts."

Her eyes opened, widening as she looked over at him.

"You sound pretty vehement on the subject for a man who's led the sheltered life of an academic and a backwoods researcher," she said.

89

"Yes, well, I've seen the damage drugs can do on a university campus. Not pretty." He shook his head sadly. "Young people ruining their futures, destroying their families. Believe me, Emma, although you may not respect my work, I most definitely respect yours."

"Frasier, I'm sorry." She sat up straight and leaned toward him, jade eyes warm and sincere. "Proving the existence of a species believed extinct *is* important work. The reason I came on so strong against it when you first told me about your project was because I'd just been burned out of my apartment the day after one of the students agreed to go to the police and testify against Todd—Ted, I mean. It took me a couple of days to recover and relocate, and by then he'd changed his mind. Actually it was Jesse. I've been trying to win him back to my camp ever since."

"Probably he was threatened." He looked over at her. "Has the fire marshal given you his report on the cause of the fire?"

"What are you suggesting? That Todd—Ted set fire to my home to scare Jesse...and me?" Her eyes rounded.

"Didn't it occur to you as being too much of a coincidence?"

"Not until now." She jumped to her feet and began to pace. "Oh, God, Frasier, if Bruiser hadn't wakened me with his barking, we could have been killed!"

She stopped in front of him, and he saw horrified disbelief in her expression.

"I'm probably wrong." He set his glass aside and got up to stand inches in front of her. "Just be careful."

He could smell the shower freshness of her, the tantalizing scent of her clean, damp hair. He wanted to take her into his arms and soothe away her shock and fear, but he didn't trust himself. He opted for a light touch.

"Come over to the table. That pizza must be ready by now." He turned toward the stove. "Git a few slices of that down ya, and I reckon ya'll live to counsel another day."

As he lifted the pan out of the oven, she came to stand beside him.

"Thanks, Frasier." She put her hand on his arm and stretched up to plant a kiss on his cheek as he straightened up. "I've been naive. I didn't want to admit children their ages could be so dangerous. I'll be on my guard from now on."

"Good. That's all that's required." He placed the pizza on a cooling rack and took up a cutter.

Steam rose as he sliced into the hot crust. *Appropriate.*

"Hey." She suddenly looked down at her glass. "This isn't Dad's wine."

"No, it's a bottle from my place. I didn't think anything as powerful as your father's vintage would be appropriate with you under serious stress. It could hit you way too hard." He focused on his cutting.

"Frasier MacKenzie, don't you trust me?" He caught the taunt in her tone. When he looked over at her, those resolve-melting green eyes were sparkling. "I'd never take advantage of a nice old professor like you."

"Yeah, well, just taking precautions."

****

"Feeling better?" Frasier returned from putting their plates and utensils in the dishwasher, a mug of coffee in his hand. He sat down opposite where she was curled up in a corner of the couch.

"Much, thanks. By the way, this coffee is delicious." She cradled a mug in her hands and smiled at him. "You're the first man I've known who can come up with a decent brew."

"Oh, and have there been a lot?" he heard himself asking. *Damn, why couldn't he put Mr. Muscle out of his mind?*

"The usual number," she replied, her eyes teasing him over the rim of the cup. "What about you?"

"The usual number," he taunted back and then they were grinning at each other.

"By the way, it's my turn to entertain." She settled back comfortably, and he felt a rush of apprehension wash over him. *What does she have in mind?* "Since I can't play an instrument or sing all that well, I'll tell a story, a ghost story. But I'm warning you, it will curl your toes."

As if you're not already curling them, Emma Prescott. He leaned back in his chair. "But if you're trying to scare *me* away, forget it. I'm on the trail of a catamount, a puma, the biggest and most dangerous cat in North America. Something as insubstantial as a ghost is no competition."

"Okay, here goes." She gave the little dog cuddled up beside her a kiss, then began. "In the 1920s, loggers came to this area to harvest the vast stands of white pine. The men in charge, timber bosses they were called, were tough guys who worked their crews hard in the bitter cold of winter and during the log drives on the river each spring. The most notorious was a man they called Midnight Jim. He worked his men from dawn to dusk, often in waist-deep snow. If there was enough moonlight, he sent them back out into the bush at night."

"A regular Captain Bligh of the forest," Frasier commented, when she paused to take a sip of coffee.

"Exactly. Finally one of his lumbermen had enough. One night after Midnight Jim had ordered them back into the bush, he lay in wait for him outside the privy. When Jim stepped out, the lumberman threw his razor-sharp ax with all the accuracy that had come from years of experience. It hit Jim in the middle of his chest. He died within minutes."

"Damn painful way to go."

"Definitely. But that's not the end of the story. Legend has it Midnight Jim still roams these mountains and forests at night, the ax embedded in his chest, bent on avenging his murder."

"And just how close are we to the place where this alleged killing took place?"

"I'd estimate a few miles. My father took our family up to see the ruins of Midnight Jim's camp several times while we were staying here at Loon Lake."

"Do you think you could find it again?" An idea was forming in Frasier's mind.

"I didn't pay close attention. Why? Do you want to try to catch a glimpse of Midnight Jim?"

"Well, it might provide comic relief from hunting another phantom."

"You're not getting discouraged, are you?" She placed her cup on the coffee table and leaned toward him, concern furrowing her forehead.

"Would it matter to you if I were?"

"Well, of course it would! It's your job, your work, and, I imagine, a big part of your *raison d'être*, right? It would be like my giving up trying to help kids in trouble."

"Thanks," he said and then smiled. "It's good to know someone besides the Professor is on my team. Now..." He got up. "I'd better be going. Scout must be getting lonely over at our place, guarding my research."

"Wait!" She scrambled to her stockinged feet and padded into the kitchen. She put the last slice of pizza in a plastic container and handed it to him.

"What's this, bait? I think the night's events

93

have established there's an Eastern Panther nearby. He sounded hungry."

"Don't be ridiculous. It's for Scout. Poor guy missed the entire evening."

"Not exactly traditional dog food," he said, looking down at the tomato, cheese, and meat topping the pie.

"So who says we have to stick with tradition? Actually, I don't think there's anything really traditional about any of us, and I'm including our dogs in that statement."

No, he though gazing down at her. *Even if you look like a character out of a movie adaptation of a regency novel with an equally old-fashioned name, there's definitely nothing traditional or old-fashioned about you, Emma Prescott.*

"Just be careful, okay? Don't let the Pug out after dark or let him roam more than a few yards from the cabin. He'd make a nice, light snack for the Panther. The same goes for you."

"Are you implying I'm a tasty treat, as well?" She cocked her head to one side, a sly smile curling her lips.

Hell and damnation!

"For a big cat like an Eastern Panther, definitely." Ignoring her teasing strained his nerves to the limit. The words came out as an exasperated sigh as she handed him the pizza slice.

"Okay, we'll be careful. And, Frasier, thanks for caring."

"No problem." As her fingers brushed his on the container, he flinched. "See you in the morning."

****

Instead of going inside his cabin, Frasier let Scout out for a run. Leaning against a verandah post, he watched the big dog sniffing around in the darkness and tried to organize his thoughts. As if he didn't have enough to be concerned about, now an actual Eastern Panther had been added to the list.

Damn it, why couldn't the woman take a hint! Hadn't someone tried to burn her out in town? Couldn't she see danger when it was looking her right in the face? He drew a deep breath and let his gaze roam over the clearing, the lake, and the surrounding blackness of the night forest. Both of them were vulnerable. As for himself, he figured he could handle anything that came his way. He and Scout. But Emma and that innocuous little dog!

He stretched his shoulders, trying to rid himself of the stiffness lurking between their blades. It had been so much simpler when there'd been just himself to watch out for.

"Scout, come on, boy, time for bed," he called to the dog. Together they went into the cabin. Frasier stirred the embers on the hearth and added a log. Yes, it had been simpler when he'd been living alone at Loon Lake. But not nearly as intriguing. Or arousing.

Rain began to spatter on the steps. *Great!* It would wash out any prints the big cat had left in the vicinity of Emma's flat tire incident. *Proof gone.*

****

"Rise and shine, nature boy. It's 7:30 a.m. We've got a cat to catch."

Frasier awoke to the sound of Emma's voice and an incessant pounding on his cabin door. He blinked at the luminous dial of his bedside clock. A thin shaft of sunlight peeked in through his window.

He stumbled to his feet, pulled on his flannel pants, and, rubbing sleep from his eyes, headed for the door.

He opened it to find Emma dressed in hiking boots, bush pants, camouflage jacket, and khaki baseball cap. On her back was a knapsack, and in her hand was a plastic bag with a loaf of bread sticking out of the top. The Pug beside her wore a camouflage vest and a big grin.

"What—?" He could only stare.

"We're going to help you find that big pussycat." She and her dog pushed past him into the cabin. "We figure it's the least we can do to try to repay you. But first I'm going to make us some stellar oatmeal and whole grain toast while you shower and—" she looked meaningfully at his stubbly chin— "shave."

"No, no, really, this isn't necessary." He tried to protest, but she was shoving him into the bathroom. "And I don't like oatmeal," he howled in final, bleak protest.

"Ya will when I gets through with it, laddie." She jerked open the door just as he was about to step into the shower. "Do you prefer peaches or bananas?"

He scrambled for a towel but only managed to grab a washcloth.

"Oh, my." For a few seemingly interminable seconds she gazed at him before closing the door, a chuckle bubbling in her throat.

Damn, damn, damn. He turned on the shower and yowled again. It was ice cold.

Chapter Four

He had to admit he'd never tasted oatmeal like it. She'd spruced it up with cinnamon, laced it with bananas, and topped it with a drizzle of maple syrup.

"Told you," she said, watching as he scraped his bowl.

"It was good," he admitted looking up at her. "But about today..."

His cell phone broke in on his words.

"Professor. Good morning... No, I'm not out in the field yet. Just finishing breakfast. I'll be leaving momentarily."

He looked up at Emma again, and she took the hint. She gathered up their bowls and cups and tiptoed toward the dishwasher. It wasn't far enough for her not to overhear, but at least he wouldn't have her closeness to distract him.

"No, sir, nothing definite yet."

Emma dropped a saucepan and swung to scowl at him. "What about last night?" she mouthed the words.

"Just dropped a pan, sir." He got to his feet and began to pace. "I'm cleaning up breakfast. Yes, I'm leaving now. Yes, I'll give you a full report tonight. Until then, sir."

Frasier stopped, punched End, and replaced the phone in his pocket.

"Why didn't you tell him about last night?" She threw up her hands, eyes rounding, tone pitched with exasperation. "I can't imagine your not being eager to tell him about your first—It is your first, isn't it?—actual evidence of an Eastern Panther! Isn't such proof crucial to the continued funding of your project?"

"I'll do it later."

"When I'm not around, you mean! When you can use phrases like 'she could have imagined it'? And while we're discussing your precious professor, why didn't you tell him I'm in your cabin? We're not doing anything erotic and, even if we were, we're both adults of consensual age." She stopped abruptly and stared at him. "Frasier MacKenzie, you're not married, are you?"

What an idea!

"Yes." He avoided her eyes. "Does it matter? We're just friends."

"Oh, I beg to differ. We're two people living in isolation. I think our marital status is definitely of concern to each other." Her words heated up with each syllable.

"So you think we shouldn't be living up here alone together when one of us is married?"

"It would appear to be rather an unhealthy situation—for the one of us who is married— wouldn't you say?"

"Agreed. Not good for me at all. Now you know why I had to lie to the Professor. Actually—" he drew a deep breath— "he's my father-in-law."

"Great! And just what is the name of your beloved wife, his daughter?"

"Margaret...Maggie."

"How long have you been married?"

"Two years. We were married on June 30th. Maggie wanted to be a June bride."

"Children?"

"Not yet, but we're hoping."

"A difficult wish to fulfill with you up here and her...?"

"In New York City."

"And what does Maggie MacKenzie do in New York City?"

"She's a book editor."

"What company?"

"Look, I've told you I'm married to Professor Taylor's daughter. That should be enough information to set the parameters of our relationship." He stood and went to get his hiking boots from a tray by the door. "I'm supposed to be devoting all my time and energy to this project, not arguing with you. If the Professor thought I had someone, never mind a lady, distracting me, he wouldn't take it well. He might even cancel the entire undertaking. Actually, it would be a whole lot easier if you were to move back to Carleton. I'll help you look for a place that will allow the Pug."

"Why should I be the one to leave? I have as much right to be here as you do. Why can't you find another ghost-chasing location? I'm sure other delusional people have spotted Eastern Panthers elsewhere in the province."

"My work requires me to be in the area; yours doesn't. Anyway, I was here first." *Damn. I sound like a kid claiming first rights to a swing on the playground.*

Instead of the angry reaction he'd expected, a smug, calculating expression slid across her face.

Oh, oh.

Slowly she began to circle him, her gaze raking him up and down.

"What?" He couldn't stand the suspense.

"Frasier MacKenzie, you've been lying to me. You're no more a married man than Bruiser."

"You can't tell if a man's married just by looking at him!" He tried to scoff, but sweat broke out on his chest.

"I can." She paused in front of him, caught him by the shirt front, and pulled herself up to plant a

99

major kiss on his lips. "For one thing, no ring. You're not married, and I'm not leaving, so there."

She picked up a dishcloth, began to wipe the stove and countertops, and burst into the most off-key version of an old country-western standard he'd ever heard.

"If you love me, let me know. If you don't, please let me go..."

Bruiser howled along with her. Frasier stifled the urge to cover his ears. Emma Prescott was stuck in his life like a burr on a dog's tail. And after that kiss, pulling her out of it would hurt a whole lot more.

****

"*He's* not coming." Frasier pointed at the Pug sitting alert on the doorstep. "He'll stay here with Scout, who'll be guarding the place."

"But we'll be gone all day!" Emma's tone reflected the depth of her concern. "And he's wearing his camouflage gear! He'll be so disappointed!"

"That cutesy vest does not disguise his entire little white body or his doggie smell. He'll be safe with Scout. I'll leave food and water, and there's a dog door in the back that opens into a good-sized run. If you'd had a similar setup at your cabin, we might have been spared the skunk incident."

"I'm not about to go cutting holes in a rented cabin. So what's the itinerary for the day? A hike up the mountain, a drive on your four-wheeler through the bush?"

"A canoe trip across the lake. The Professor wants me to check that area asap. I'll be covering a lot of country. I won't have time for anyone who can't keep up."

"But wouldn't it make more sense to go back to where I saw those eyes and heard that awful scream?" Her forehead furrowed. "I don't understand..."

"The search has to be conducted in a systematic manner, one area at a time."

"But we might find tracks!"

"Last night's rain will have obliterated them. Anyhow, it's unlikely the panther, if it was a panther, stayed in the area. They're furtive by nature. You and your noisy car probably scared the beegeebers out of it."

"My car was stopped! I'd just changed a tire, remember?"

"Look, do you want to come with me or stand here arguing?"

"Fine. Come on, Bruise. The associate professor is getting cranky."

****

It doesn't get much better. Sitting in the stern of the canoe, he guided it across the lake's glassy surface. The surrounding hardwood trees featured their finest autumn kaleidoscope of reds, golds, and oranges against the rich dark greens of the conifers. Their beauty doubled with their reflection in the calm water. Overhead a cloudless blue sky provided a perfect canopy. The silence was so intense he could hear each droplet of water fall from his paddle when he raised it to let the canoe drift. Only a loon's haunting cry broke the stillness.

Bruiser, sitting amidships, burped.

"Ah, no, he's not going to be sick, is he?" Frasier's idyll shattered.

"Of course not." Seated in the bow, Emma raised her paddle and swiveled to face him. "He just had a larger than normal breakfast. I knew we'd be doing some serious traveling today. I wanted him to have lots of nourishment."

"You're sure? Because this is a state-of-the-art cedar canoe that belongs to the research project. Getting Pug puke out of its ribbing would be—"

"Oh, stop worrying." She swung back into

position and took a deep sweep with her paddle that sent the canoe lunging forward. "And stop talking. We don't want to scare our quarry."

Ah, man! Now she's including herself in my assignment.

****

"Exactly what should I be looking for?" Emma hissed after they'd beached the canoe.

"Big catlike paw prints and scat on the ground, any unusual tufts of hair caught on bark, and oversized felines up in the trees," he whispered.

Bruiser, his leash clipped to Emma's belt, sneezed. A startled partridge rose into the foliage with a frantic drumming of wings.

"Blast!" Frasier breathed.

"Sorry. Feather allergy."

Frasier stifled a rude expletive, hefted his backpack, and headed off up the trail. When he heard no sounds to indicate Emma and the Pug followed, he turned. With one arm through a single strap of her backpack, she struggled to get the other into a similar position. Failing, she lost her balance and fell over backwards.

Damn! Frasier turned back.

"Here, let me help you."

"Thanks," she smiled as he helped her to her feet and guided her other arm through the elusive strap.

When she started to tilt backward again, he caught her by her jacket front to level her on her feet.

"Try to lean forward," he advised. "But satisfy my curiosity. What have you got in there?"

"Just necessities. Sandwiches, cookies, chocolates, fruit, a novel to read while we're resting, a bottle of wine, dry socks..."

"Give it to me!" He jerked the pack from her back. Kneeling he released the buckles and began to sort through the contents.

"This stays here." He set aside the wine. "And this." The hardcover novel joined the bottle. "And these." He removed a box of gourmet chocolates. "And these." He couldn't believe the can of escargot and a tin of imported cheeses. "You can keep the trail mix, water bottle, and dry socks. Now." He refastened the sack and arose. "Turn around."

Her forehead furrowed as she gazed at the pile of rejects on the ground, but she did as she was told.

"Better?" He adjusted the haversack between her shoulders.

"Better." Her frown smoothed.

"They'll be gone when we get back...bears have good noses for treats, but it can't be helped. We'll need to leave it far enough from the canoe so that it won't get vandalized in a feeding frenzy."

The Pug sneezed again. Frasier glanced down to see the little dog wearing small, bulging saddlebags.

"What is *he* carrying, caviar?"

"Just a few of his own favorite treats, like cheese doodles and beggin' strips."

"Why didn't you just paint a big sign on him— Bear Snack?" Closing in on the end of his patience, Frasier removed the Pug's packsacks and threw them among the stack of discards.

"Let's go," he said, adjusting his shoulders.

"Go where?"

"Up there." He pointed at the peak of the mountain looming out of the forest in front of them.

Although he felt it was beneath his sense of fair play, he couldn't help but derive a bit of satisfaction when he saw what he took to be dismay flash across her face.

But it was only a flash.

"Should be a challenge...and fun," she said, her expression returning to one bright with enthusiasm. "Let's go."

****

Halfway up the mountain, at a point where a brook bubbled across the trail, he paused to look back at the pair following him. After the constant uphill two-mile hike, they should be exhausted.

Instead Emma's face was glowing, the Pug prancing energetically on his leash by her side.

"It's gorgeous." She spread her hands and looked around. "We have to do this more often."

"Can you keep it down? Remember there's a purpose in all this."

"Oh, sure, sorry." She lowered her voice, then drew a deep breath, her eyes widening. "Frasier, look!"

He turned in the direction she was indicating and saw a pair of deer, the buck sporting a magnificent set of antlers, just ahead of them in the stream.

The Pug sneezed.

Both animals did an instant heads-up, glanced about, sniffed the wind, then bounded off into the bush.

"Oh, Frasier, weren't they fantastic?" She came to his side. "I'm so glad you brought us along. Let's go. I can't wait to see the view from the summit."

She started off up the trail, leaving Frasier to follow, favored with a view of the Pug from the rear.

****

"It's magnificent!" Emma's words and expression mirrored delight when she stood on the summit of Mt. Carleton. She held out her arms and pirouetted. "Thank you!"

"For what? For leaving your gourmet treats to the bears, for leaving him down there?"

He pointed at the Pug tied to a tree twenty feet below. They'd had to leave him behind for the last few feet to the top. They'd scaled the last section up a perpendicular rock wall.

"For bringing us along, for showing us this wonderful place." She threw back her head, closed her eyes, and drew a deep breath.

As he stood watching her uninhibited joy in the experience, he was glad he'd brought her...yes, and even her troublesome little dog. Emma Prescott exuded a joyful exuberance that enhanced every experience.

The next instant he had to fight down images of her reaction to lovemaking...passionate, from-the-heart lovemaking. *Damn, damn, damn! Where had that come from?*

****

Twenty minutes later, as they settled to their lunch back on the plateau where they'd left Bruiser, Emma unhooked the little dog from his leash.

"I don't think that's a good idea." Frasier paused between bites of apple as he watched the Pug scampering about the small clearing.

"You don't know Bruise," she replied, peeling back the wrappings on a trail mix bar. "He never goes far when there's food available."

"If you're sure." Frasier stretched out long legs and leaned back against the trunk of a massive white pine, his head resting against the rough bark. "Man, I love the woods at this time of year," he breathed, gazing up into its wide branches. "And this day is perfect." Relaxing, he closed his eyes.

****

The Pug's screams jolted him alert. The little dog burst out of the bushes, darning-needle-sized black spears protruding from his snout.

"Oh, my God! He got a porcupine!" Frasier vaulted to his feet as Bruiser barreled into Emma's arms. "Be careful! Don't get them in your hands!"

"Oh, Bruiser, my sweet, sweet little Bruiser!" Emma began to rock the squealing Pug. "Frasier, help us!" She looked up at him, green eyes wide and desperate. "Please, please help us!"

"Take it easy." He spoke reassuringly as he fished a collapsible device that looked like a jackknife from his knapsack and squatted beside them. "I have a pair of industrial strength tweezers included in this contraption. We'll have the little guy out of his misery in no time."

****

Twenty minutes later, sweat trickling down his face, Frasier held up the last quill, clamped in the tweezers. "Done." He wiped his forehead with the back of his forearm.

Bruiser, panting in Emma's arms, looked over at him with sad, tired eyes and whimpered, bloody speckles dotting his snout where quills had been.

"Thank you." Emma's words trembled as she looked up at him, her cheeks streaked with tears. "Oh, Frasier, thank you so much!"

"No big thing," he said. He wiped away a final tear trickling down her cheek with his finger. "The little guy will be fine, but you'd better reattach him to your belt. Some dogs come out of these experiences hell-bent on revenge. They head right back into the bush to exact it, mega-mistake though it is."

"You're right." She fumbled for the leash and snapped it to the little dog's collar and her belt. "I'll never let that happen again."

Frasier stood and stretched tense, cramped muscles. The procedure of removing quills from the screaming Pug had been stressful. Seeing any person or animal in pain had always been emotionally draining for him.

Emma got to her feet. She looked up at him as she stood close in front of him, the snuffling Pug in her arms.

"We weren't much help, were we? We shouldn't have come."

"An accident, nothing more." The struggle began again, the struggle to resist Emma Prescott at her most vulnerable and appealing.

"Nevertheless, you're our hero...again, Frasier MacKenzie." She stood on tiptoes, leaned over the Pug, and kissed him so lightly and quickly on the lips that for a moment he wondered if it had actually happened. She turned away, cooing over the Pug. When the now all-too-familiar reaction slid down his body, he knew it had.

****

Frasier stepped out of the shower, toweled dry, and pulled on his best black underwear. Back in his bedroom, he opened the closet door and looked over his collection of shirts and pants. The tan Dockers with the green silk shirt? Or maybe the brown pants with the dark gold sweater? He didn't want to look as if he'd dressed up. Maybe he should go with a pair of decently new jeans and the L. L. Bean sweatshirt he'd bought last month in Maine.

Damn it! He was acting like a teenager on his first date. He was simply asking Emma over for supper...as a friend. After their adventure with the porcupine that afternoon, he figured she'd welcome a nice, quiet dinner accompanied by a bottle of his best white wine.

Then why the sexy underwear and the fine vintage?

"Argh!" He grabbed the jeans from their hanger and pulled the sweatshirt from a bureau drawer.

****

"Frasier." Her face lit up with a full-fledged smile when she opened the door to find him on her front step. "I was just about to go over to your place."

Words failed him. He gaped.

Emma Prescott stood before him in a short, shimmering emerald green dress held in place by sequined spaghetti straps. Her hair was caught up in some new kind of fancy coiffure with dangling gold earrings dancing above the most beautiful, smoothly tanned shoulders he'd ever seen. Her sun-kissed arm holding the door open sported matching bangles that caught the soft lighting of the room behind her and glittered out at him. She smelled sensational.

"Frasier, what's wrong? Aren't you feeling well? You look a little dazed."

"No, no, I'm fine." He struggled to recover, a warm glow beginning to wash over him. She was planning to spend the evening with him and had gotten all glammed up. *Wow!*

"I didn't expect..." He glanced down at his sweatshirt and jeans.

"Oh, I'm sorry." She reached out with a tinkling of bangles and drew him into a living room warm and romantic in the glow of muted lamps and a small fire on the hearth. "I wasn't going over to see you... Well, not to spend the evening, that is. I have a date in town, and I was wondering if you'd keep Bruiser. I could be late getting back."

"Oh...sure...no problem. Glad to help." A bucket of ice water thrown over him at that moment couldn't have killed the glow any quicker or more sadistically.

"Thanks." She crossed the room and bent to pick up the Pug snoozing in his basket by the fire. Revealing long, smooth, shapely legs that seemed to go on forever in sheer black pantyhose, Emma Prescott took her damn good time. Frustration ripped at his innards.

"Here." She handed him the warm, sleepy Pug. "He's fed and had his evening bathroom break, so he should be good for the night. Maybe, though," she turned back toward the fireplace, "you should take his bed."

"I'll get it." Frasier barely avoided knocking her

aside as he made a lunge for the quilt-lined basket. He didn't need her bending over in front of him again.

"Thanks, Frasier." She stopped him and planted a sisterly kiss on his cheek as he tried to bypass her, the Pug under one arm, the basket under the other.

"What are friends for." he replied gruffly. "By the way..." He paused at the door. "Who's the lucky guy? Brock the Rock?" Sarcasm dripped from the question.

"Frasier, it really doesn't concern you." She crossed her arms and stood looking at him evenly. "We're friends, but that doesn't mean we have to share the details of our love lives."

"No, definitely not. Sorry I asked," he mumbled.

Feeling like he'd just swallowed a lump of hot coal, he adjusted his cargo and went out into the clear moonlight of an October night already beginning to hint at winter's frosts. As he slumped off toward his cabin, he remembered Mildred Carter's remark about Emma's men having expiry dates and found himself hoping that Mr. Autumn, whoever he was, was on his way to the recycle bin.

****

Two a.m. Frasier looked over at her dark cabin again, another in a long line of so many glances he'd lost count. Then he strode to the refrigerator and took out a beer. It had to be a Bud, he thought bitterly as he opened the long neck. With an exasperated sigh, he dropped onto the couch in front of the fire languishing on the hearth. Bruiser awoke in his basket, looked up at Frasier, gave a lazy wag of his curly tail, yawned, and snuggled back to sleep.

"You'd think he'd be a little concerned, wouldn't you?" he addressed Scout who was curled up on the far end of the couch. "You'd be worried if I didn't come home, wouldn't you?"

Scout gazed at him for a moment, then stuffed

109

his nose back under his tail, fox-fashion, to return to sleep.

"Great! So I'm on watch alone." Feeling stiff, he pulled himself to his feet. He'd covered what he believed to be every square inch of the area in the last month. Jolting over rocks and roots was beginning to seep into his joints. About the only breaks he got were when Emma and the Pug interfered.

Emma.

"Argh!" He took a long pull on his beer, grabbed a map from the bookcase, and spread it out on the kitchen table. An image of her and Brock enjoying a romantic evening at the restaurant where they'd had lunch flashed across his mind. A grunt of frustration escaped. *Stop it. Just stop it.* He sat down and bent over an aerial survey of the region.

"Where to look next, where to look next—"

****

"Emma, are you awake?" Mandy Cooper knocked gently on her guest room door, then peered around its partial opening.

"Mandy, come on in." Emma was sitting up in bed wearing a pair of her friend's flannelette pajamas, reading a romance novel. "I was going to go down to put the coffee on, but I didn't want to disturb you."

"You wouldn't have." With a sigh the redhead sank down on the edge of the bed. She wore a filmy nightgown and fluffy slippers. "I didn't sleep very well. With Jeff away on some sort of secret assignment, I never really relax."

"Wish you'd never married him?" Emma teased, grinning.

"You know better than that. But I do wish he hadn't been shipped off two days after our honeymoon."

"You'd better get used to it, buddy." Emma

110

stretched and slid her feet over the edge of the bed. "Such will be the life of a law enforcement officer who's on his way up. Just thank your lucky stars he's got a career that is making a difference to society, not chasing a ghost cat through the woods."

"Come on now, Emma. You don't really feel that disrespectful of Frasier's work. You're just mad because he's placed it ahead of you...for the present. And because..."

Mandy's voice trailed off.

"Go on. Because..." Emma prompted, narrowing her eyes as she challenged her friend.

"And because he's the first man who didn't fall groveling before the charms of Emma Prescott."

"Mandy, really! You'd think I was some sort of femme fatale!"

"I know you don't see yourself in such a light, but, believe me, there's a lot of guys around Carleton who regard you as the uncatchable Emma Prescott."

"Oh, come off it! Let's go make some coffee."

"Are you saying you don't care all that much for this Frasier MacKenzie?" Mandy pressed, as the two friends headed downstairs in Mandy's new two-storey home. "Because if you are, I see no reason for the elaborate subterfuge you set up last night...letting him think you had a hot date, then spending the evening sharing a bottle of wine with me."

"I know you're lonely when Jeff is away." Emma avoided Mandy's eyes as they reached the kitchen and she headed for the coffeepot. "I thought I'd keep you company, that's all."

"Then why that sexy dress and Bruiser left for Frasier to babysit? You know that adorable dog is always welcome here." A cockatoo in a big cage near the garden doors squawked. "I'll feed you in a minute, Beauty," she quieted him.

"Okay, okay." Emma poured water into the

coffee machine, set the dial, and turned back to face her companion. "Maybe I would like him to notice me...well, more than notice me. I'd like him to at least acknowledge that I'm a desirable woman, someone he might have a taste for once his days of chasing phantom felines are over."

"Seems like a risky business to me." Mandy removed a loaf of bread from its box and turned toward the toaster. "Maybe he'll think you're a hopeless man-teaser and decide you're not worth the trouble."

"Yeah, well, we'll see." Emma sat down at the table, green eyes sparkling wickedly. "I'm thinking that by tonight I'll have the hermit at Loon Lake just where I want him."

****

The sound of Emma's car grinding and muttering up the trail awoke him. Morning was announcing itself, peering through his window in a shaft of sunlight. Feeling relief flood through him, he jolted up from where he'd fallen asleep with his head on the table, knocking over his beer. It gushed out over the map he'd been trying to study before he dozed. Cursing, he bolted toward paper towels on the cupboard.

As he sopped up the mess, a tap sounded at the door. Emma cautiously pushed it open.

"Are you decent?" she called. Then, seeing him mopping up the spill, the bottle beside it, she stopped.

Frasier stopped, too. And stared. Emma still wore the sexy green dress, but now her hair was down and, worst of all, she was barefoot in those strappy sandals.

"A little early for that, isn't it?" She indicated the long neck as the Pug leaped out of his basket and bulleted to greet her.

"It's from last night." He finished cleaning up

the spill and flung the wet towels into the garbage can with more than necessary vehemence. "Speaking of last night, where exactly were you?" He swung to face her. "The Pug was worried."

"Was he?" She scooped up the little dog cavorting about her feet.

"Yes, he was. He hardly slept a wink."

Damn! Lying again.

"Sorry, sweetie." Emma kissed the little dog's furrowed forehead.

"Aren't you going to reassure him, tell him where you were, promise that it will never happen again?"

"Frasier, what's wrong?" Emma stared at him, all emerald-eyed innocence. "I don't..."

"I'll tell you what's wrong." In two long strides he'd crossed the room and pulled her into his arms. Bruiser, sandwiched in between, squeaked as his sitter kissed his mom quick and hard at first, then, for a second time, long and deep.

"Oh, Frasier!" Emma breathed when he finally freed her lips. She looked up at him, green eyes soft and wide as she ran her free hand down his stubbled jaw.

Just what do you think you're doing? Snap out of it, idiot!

"Emma." He released her and backed away, rubbing his hands on the seat of his jeans. "Sorry. Sorry." His voice sounded gruff or squeaky or a bit of both, changing tone with each word. Battling emotions that threatened to force him right back into her arms, this time for much more than a kiss, he headed for the sink. "Coffee?" he managed to get out as he turned on the tap and reached for the pot.

"I hate you, Frasier MacKenzie!" The words flung at his back stung like buckshot. "I really, really hate you!"

The slamming of the door announced her

departure. Frasier was left alone, his shoulders slumped, head down, as he held on to the edge of the sink with one hand, heedless of the water overflowing the coffeepot in the other.

****

"You forgot this." Frasier thrust the Pug's basket toward her when she answered his knock on her door at 7:00 p.m. "I thought he might need it."

"Thank you." The two words reeked of cold civility. She took it from him and started to turn away, but his hand shot out, stopping the door she was closing on him.

"Emma, we need to talk."

"Really? I've always believed actions spoke louder than words." She paused and looked up at him, her expression hard and hurt. "Today yours yelled that you're only attracted to me physically...or maybe it's because I'm the only female human game at Loon Lake. It doesn't really matter which." She held up a hand to stop him when he started to protest. "Most importantly, you've told me your work takes precedence over anything that might develop between us. So, sorry, Frasier. I don't have time for a guy who's only capable of a knee-jerk relationship that he feels he has to apologize for."

This time she succeeded in shutting the door on him.

****

Frasier MacKenzie couldn't sleep. He kept tossing and turning, seeing images of Emma, her touchable, smellable hair a tousled chestnut mass, her feet bare in sexy sandals, her smooth shoulders taunting him to touch them, to bury his face against them, inviting his lips to her neck, her cleavage.

Then another image crashed across his roiling mind; an image of Brock Kelly kneeling before Emma, slowly and sensuously removing first one shoe, then the other. Of Brock Kelly reaching to remove those sexy black pantyhose. Of Brock Kelly...

He grabbed his pillow and pummeled it. The woman was driving him nuts. He had to think of all the reasons why a relationship with her would be a big mistake. First, there was his assignment. She had it in her power to ruin his chances of success and incite the Professor to assign someone else to do the job. Second, there was the suspicion that she might be involved in dealing drugs to students. And third, there was her aggravating little dog. The Pug had been nothing but trouble ever since Frasier had dived into the lake to rescue him.

He rolled over, stretched out on his back, locked his fingers behind his head, and heaved a sigh that bordered on a groan. *Get your hormones under control, my friend, or else accept the fact that you can spend the rest of your career shuffling papers in some office cubbyhole, feeling like a failure.*

The possibility brought him back to his senses. He closed his eyes, determined to get at least some sleep that night.

****

"What are you doing?" He was out of his cabin in a bound. It was 6:00 a.m. the following day. He'd awoken an hour earlier to see every light in her cabin blazing out into the darkness of the frosty fall morning. He watched, wondering what she was up to, but when he saw her emerge dragging a big suitcase, a bag of dog food under her arm, he could no longer contain his curiosity.

"What does it look like? I'm moving out." She looked up at him. In the shadows of the porch light, he saw her eyes were puffy. "It's what you've always wanted, right? Bruise and me out of the way so you can concentrate on your stupid project?"

"Yes...no...ah, damn it, Emma!"

"Would you mind either helping me or getting

115

the hell out of my way?"

"Okay, okay." He grabbed the suitcase and dog food and headed for her car. Like she'd said, this was what he'd wanted, what he needed to happen, right? Then why did he feel so downright sickly rotten?

"Where are you going to stay?" he asked, as she cracked the trunk and he swung both his burdens inside.

"With Mildred Carter, the woman you met in the office at school. She has a big house and needs to share expenses. Since she has two cats, another animal isn't a problem."

"But the woman's jealous of you, made nasty remarks about you!" He caught her by an arm as she started back toward the house.

She glared up at him. He hated the fact that she'd obviously been crying. "I don't have a lot of options with Bruise. Now I'll thank you to let me go." She shrugged free with a hard, decisive jerk and strode back into the cabin.

****

Late in the afternoon, Frasier braked his muddy ATV to a halt in front of the storage shed and dismounted. He opened the doors and wheeled the vehicle inside. After locking up, he turned to go up to his cabin, Scout at his heels.

Halfway there, he paused to look over at Emma's former home. The curtains were drawn, no smoke issued from the chimney, and no Pug sounds or loud music broke the silence of the cold, foggy day.

A wave of emptiness enveloped him, making his belly reach for his backbone. With an impatient jerk, he pulled off his gloves, stuck them under his arm, and headed for his cabin. There was a big, juicy steak in the freezer and a package of the Shepherd's favorite meal, liver. He'd fry himself and Scout up a meal fit for a couple of kings. That would cure that hollow feeling.

An hour later he was sitting on his couch in front of the fire, staring into the flames and nursing a cup of coffee in the bleak silence of the October twilight, when he heard a familiar sound. A car, a distinctive car, one that rattled and sputtered, was making its way up the trail.

He lunged to his feet and strode out onto his verandah to watch as the headlights of Emma's old Sundance flashed through the early evening darkness into the clearing. A rush of anticipation flooded through him like he couldn't recall experiencing since Christmas mornings when he'd been a kid. He vaulted over the railing and stood waiting while she braked to a stop near her front steps.

"You're back," were his inane first words as he opened her car door.

"Yes, I'm back." Her reply reeked of weariness as she climbed out.

She looked so spent, so dejected, as she stood in front of him, he had to fight the impulse to gather her into his arms, to hold her, to stroke her hair, to tell her how he'd missed her.

"What happened?"

"*This* happened." She opened the rear door, reached in, and re-emerged with the Pug in her arms.

"Oh, my God!" In the glow of the car's interior light, he saw the little dog's face and snout gouged with deep, ugly ribbons of red. A heavy smear of some sort of cream didn't improve his appearance. Between his little black ears that drooped in uncharacteristic sadness, a bandage crowned his head.

"Mildred's cats didn't like Bruiser any more than she likes me." Emma cradled the little dog close. Frasier saw tears glistening in her eyes.

"Emma, I'm sorry. This is my fault."

He reached out and gently ran a finger down her cheek. A pair of sad green eyes looked up at him over a pair of equally unhappy brown ones. His resolve to get rid of the pair melted like ice cream in a heat wave. He let his hand slip to his side, stepped back, and tried to continue matter-of-factly, "Let me help you unpack and get a fire going. Then you and the Pug can come over to my place while yours warms up. I'll heat some soup for you, and I have some liver left over from Scout's supper, for the little guy."

He headed for the back of the car. "Crack the trunk and let's get to work."

****

A half hour later Emma, wrapped in a quilt, sat curled up in a corner of Frasier's couch, her hands clasped around a steaming mug of coffee. On the low table in front of her were the dishes left from a thick chicken sandwich and a bowl of beef vegetable soup. In his basket, which Frasier had brought in from Emma's car, Bruiser lay curled up at her feet, snoring away his bad day, his small belly stuffed with fried liver.

"Feeling better?" he asked as he gathered up the dishes and took them to the sink.

"Much. And Frasier?"

"Yes?" He turned back toward her.

"I'm sorry, too. I didn't mean what I said about knee-jerk relationships. I'm pretty sure you're just a guy caught between a rock and a hard place...me and a job that requires peace and quiet, a job that means as much to you as mine does to me. So there's only one solution, and we've already declared it. We have to remain just friends. Do you agree?"

He leaned back against the counter, thought a moment, then nodded. "Agreed. But I can't say it's my first choice."

"Mine either." She leaned forward to place her cup on the table. "But, hey, it's not like we're in love or anything. We're just two people who are attracted to each other...two mature, responsible people. We can do it." She smiled brightly up at him.

"Sure we can." He turned back to rinse the dishes in the sink, the words "It's not like we're in love or anything" echoing in his brain.

"How about a tune?"

"What?" Her question snapped him out of it. He swung to face her.

"The guitar." She pointed to the instrument leaning in a corner. "What about a tune? You're not half bad, as I recall. I could do with a bit of cheering up."

"Okay, sure, fine." Anything to keep his mind off their relationship...or lack of one.

He picked it up and sat down in a chair across from her. "I have to warn you, though. I'm into classic country rock."

"Fine by me. Let me have it."

He strummed a chord and began to sing "Tequila Sunrise." When she joined him in the chorus, loud and off key, while Bruiser threw back his head and howled along, he realized he was a happy man.

Only Scout didn't seem to be enjoying their wild jam session. He lay down on the floor and put his paws over his ears. He ignored Bruiser as the Pug jostled around the room in Emma's arms while she danced.

Finally Frasier laid the guitar aside.

"Whew!" Emma sprawled on the couch, Bruiser busily licking her face. "Okay, okay, so you're still rearin' to go." She pulled herself to a sitting position and placed the dog aside. "I'm beat. That was fun...wasn't it?" She looked over at Frasier, and he grinned back.

"Yeah, it was. Care for some refreshment? Soda, water, coffee, beer?"

"Just water, thanks. I'll get it."

Brushing damp curls from her forehead, she headed for the sink.

"Emma, that deserted logging camp you mentioned... Any more ideas about where it might be located?" He tried to sound casual.

"As a matter of fact, yes." She swung back to face him, a glass of water in her hand. "I recall we turned off the trail to these cabins about midway. There was an overgrown road to the right, when you're coming from this direction, with two massive white pines on either side. Actually, it was right about the spot where I had that flat tire—and my encounter with the Eastern Panther."

"Interesting. I'll take a look tomorrow."

"Well, I hope you find that cat, and if it's a she and there's babies, that you'll be able to protect them."

"I hope so. Now I'd better get you back to your cabin. This is a school night, in case you've forgotten."

****

The following morning Frasier backed his ATV out of the storage shed and put on his helmet. It was a gray, overcast morning, the grass white and crisp with frost from a sharp overnight drop in temperature. Snow couldn't be far off, he reckoned as he climbed aboard and turned the key.

The powerful engine leaped into life. Not for the first time he recognized his good fortune in having state-of-the-art equipment. If he came upon his quarry in a hostile mood, it wouldn't do to have a shoddy vehicle as his only means of escape.

Heading down the trail in search of two tall white pines with an old logging trail between them, he heard Scout bark. Confined in the cabin, the dog resented being left behind on guard duty. Tomorrow, he vowed, he'd take him along, but this morning he'd packed a lunch in preparation of being gone all day, if necessary, in his attempt to locate that deserted lumber camp Emma had talked about in her wild tale of murder and ghosts.

He must be getting desperate. There was little chance the old place was still standing, never mind serving as a hideout. But if it had been made of logs... They had a long life span...

An hour later, after cruising up and down the midsection of the trail and finding nothing that even remotely resembled two ancient white pines with a road running between them, Frasier stopped his vehicle, pulled off his helmet, and took a thermos of coffee from his saddlebag. He'd never find that road with only Emma's faulty memory and directions to guide him. He poured out a mug of steaming dark brew.

Leaning back against his machine, he stared up at the lofty white pine beside which he'd stopped. *One with no partner. No partner now, but maybe...* The idea struck him like a flash. He strode into the undergrowth a few feet to the left of the tree.

"Yes!"

Hidden beneath undergrowth was the stump of another big pine. Someone had harvested it just inches above the ground.

He jogged back to his bike, stowed his thermos, started the engine, and headed into the bush between the two trees. As his wheels fell into a concealed rut, he muttered "Yes!" again. *Definitely on the right track!*

His exuberance didn't last. The trail soon became a tangle of undergrowth and thickets of burgeoning willows and alders. Annoyed, he abandoned the bike. Flinging his packsack over his shoulder, he started off on foot.

When he paused to get his bearings, he found himself surrounded in an eerie silence. Not the least breeze stirred the branches. Not a single bird sang. About a half mile farther on, he stopped again to listen. A slight rustle in the dead leaves behind him made him whirl, his hand going to the gun concealed in a shoulder holster.

"Partridge," he breathed as the little brown hen-like bird scuttled across the faint trail.

Get a grip. Emma's tale of mutilated ghosts must be working on my imagination. Wouldn't the Professor love to hear that! He hefted his pack and started off again. When he heard another scuffling behind him, he didn't bother to turn around.

An explosion rent the peace of the forest. Something slammed into his side. Frasier yelped.

And then nothing. For a long time, nothing.

Chapter Five

Frasier came back to consciousness in a murky mix of pain and confusion. His mouth felt as if he'd eaten sawdust. His side burned. Lying face down in the undergrowth, he vaguely remembered hearing a rustling in the dried leaves behind him before the blast.

He grunted when he eased his right hand from beneath him. His fingers came out red and wet. *Sweet Jesus! That explosion! I've been shot!*

Struggling against pain and weakness, he pulled himself to a sitting position to look down at his left side. It was matted with blood. Carefully he brought his right hand around to examine the wound. When his fingers found it, he yelped.

He willed himself to breathe deep and slow, to try to ignore the searing pain and convince himself it was only a flesh wound, that it hadn't broken any ribs or torn through any vital organs. All he had to do was stop the bleeding and make his way back to his vehicle.

Gritting his teeth, he grabbed the branches of a young spruce and forced himself to his feet. *Damn, it hurts.* Blood leaked down his side in a slow, ominous trickle. He had to get something to plug up the tear before he started to walk. He looked for his packsack but couldn't find it. Whoever had shot him must have taken it. His cell had been in it, although he seriously doubted if it would work at his present location. Someone had deliberately left him to die.

He clamped down on his lower lip and tried to focus. *Think, think.* Clutching his side, he eased down onto his knees and grabbed a handful of moss. Grunting, he stuffed it inside his jacket and shirt, over the wound.

I hope I don't get some kind of weird infection from this. That would be just too damned ironic.

He picked up a piece of fallen tree limb, used it to hoist himself back onto his feet, drew a deep breath, and started back in the direction he'd come, lurching and cursing as each step sent a shot of pain through his side. *Am I going the right way?* His wound disoriented him, made him doubt his ability to find his way to safety. He had no method of checking his location. His compass had been in his backpack.

Pausing to catch his breath, he leaned against a white birch. Emma. She emerged from the fog in his head. He'd planned to do something about their relationship as soon as his project was completed, as soon as the suspicion around her had been cleared up—she couldn't be involved with kids and drugs—but if he bled to death now, he'd miss out on something that could have been the best thing that ever happened to him. With renewed determination, he pushed away from the tree, grasped his improvised cane, and stumbled forward.

When darkness began to filter into the forest, he sank to the ground and rested his back against a massive white pine. *Lost. No doubt about it.* How long would it take for anyone to realize he needed help? How long would it be before a rescue operation was launched?

A thin, cold rain began to fall. He shivered. *Don't let me sneeze. Oh, God, don't let me sneeze.*

He eased the moss away from his wound. *No fresh blood. Got a chance...if someone finds me before I come down with pneumonia...or sneeze.*

****

"Frasier!" Her voice echoed around in his head.

124

Ah, damn! Now I'm hallucinating.

"Frasier! Oh, good Lord! Frasier!"

Scout stared down at him with wide, anxious eyes. In a dreamlike haze, over the dog's shoulder, he saw her running toward him, her face pale against an encroaching darkness, a darkness that was either evening or another bout of unconsciousness, he couldn't be sure. She waved a flashlight.

"Emma..." He mumbled her name just before the blackness washed over him again.

****

"Frasier, Frasier, wake up! We have to get you to my car. You're soaked and...oh, my God, bloody. Here, put your arm around my shoulders. That's it. See? That wasn't so hard. Now, one step at a time. We haven't got far to go. You must have a great sense of direction. You're only a few yards from the road." She was spewing words so fast he could barely comprehend.

"Emma, how did you know...?" Dragging along at her side, he knew he was leaning too heavily on her, but he had no choice. His feet felt as if they were filled with lead, and only Emma's determined body holding him upright kept him moving.

"I got home from school to find Scout raising a ruckus. I let him out through the gate of the dog pen and told him to find you, and he took off down the road like Seabiscuit. I followed him in my car until he took to the bush, and then I ran after him on foot...and found you. You'll have to buy the big guy a nice, juicy steak once we get you patched up."

"Yeah, yeah, a steak." Frasier's head swam. "Damn knees! They've turned to rubber."

"Here we are!" Emma's voice sounded optimistic and cheerful, as if they'd arrived at the beach on a fine summer's day, as if she hadn't just found and dragged a bloody man through the bush for farther

Gail MacMillan

than he'd thought her capable. "Lean on the roof while I open the door. I'll get you to the hospital in town in no time. Lucky I brought Bruiser along. We won't have to worry about rushing back to care for the dogs."

He grunted when she eased him into the passenger seat and moaned when she leaned across him to belt him in place.

"Sorry," she apologized, but his fuzzy mind was suddenly acutely aware of her closeness, of the soft, familiar smell of her hair.

"Emma," he breathed and hiccupped. His right hand, trembling and blood-stained, reached out to clutch her curls.

"Hey, big guy." She touched his cheek gently and smiled into his eyes. "Don't go starting anything you're not fit to finish. Lean back, relax. I'm taking you to the hospital, and damn the speed limit." She backed out and shut his door. "Bruiser, Scout, in the back," she called to the dogs. "We're heading for town. This time I hope the cops do stop me. I could do with a police escort."

****

"Is he going to be okay?"

Frasier came back to consciousness with the sound of Emma's voice.

"That bullet tore a nasty piece of flesh off his side but didn't touch any vital organs or even nick a rib," a man's voice reassured her. "He was mainly suffering from blood loss. Now, thanks to you, that's been overcome. Fortunately you're type O."

When he became able to focus, he realized he was in a hospital bed. Emma Prescott stood beside it, talking to a man in surgical scrubs.

"Hello," he croaked over parched lips. "I'm back."

"Frasier!" Emma clutched his hand, gazing intently into his half-opened eyes. "Bruise and I are going to take you to our cabin and nurse you back to

126

health. You have absolutely nothing to worry about."

He closed his eyes and groaned. What was that old saying about the cure being worse than the disease?

"Mr. MacKenzie." The doctor standing beside his bed was speaking. "I've reported your injury to the local RCMP, as I do all gunshot wounds. They'll be here to question you when I decide you're up to it."

"A hunting accident, pure and simple," he mumbled.

"A bit more than that." The doctor looked skeptical. "Whoever shot you didn't come to your aid. I'm no expert on the law, but I'd say that would add up to quite a few charges, with careless use of a firearm right at the top of the list."

"I don't want to make an issue of it." The anesthetic was wearing off, the pain returning. "But I'll talk to the officers when they arrive. Right now..." His eyelids drooped and his words trailed off.

"Come on, Emma. He needs to rest," Frasier vaguely heard the doctor say softly.

Emma. He'd called her Emma. Hadn't taken the guy long to get on a first-name basis. Frasier's last conscious thought was that the doctor had been about his own age and not entirely ugly.

****

"Good morning." Emma entered his hospital room looking as bright and cheerful as the sunshine flooding in at the window, a duffle bag in her hand. "Are you ready to come home? I brought fresh clothes." She waved the valise.

"Definitely." He couldn't wait to escape. He'd argued vehemently with the doctor the previous evening when Emma had been about to leave, but he'd been refused release.

"I want to keep you under observation for just a few more hours," Dr. Bradley had insisted. "You lost a lot of blood, and you're suffering from exposure."

Gail MacMillan

"Listen to the doctor," Emma had insisted. "I'll be back for you bright and early tomorrow. Right now, I have to take Bruiser and Scout home and feed them. See you in the morning, big fella." With a teasing grin crinkling her lips, she'd bent and kissed him lightly on the forehead. As she'd left the room with a wave and an encouraging smile, Frasier felt he'd never wanted anything so much as to go with her.

Now she was back with fresh clothes and the promise of their returning to the cabins together. He started to scramble out of bed, then fell back to sit on its edge as a wave of dizziness overwhelmed.

"Hey, take it easy." Emma was instantly beside him, her arm around his shoulders. "You've still got some recovering to do. Do you think I should help you dress?"

"No!" The word was emphatic as he managed to come to his feet and stand alone. "I'll be fine."

He took the duffle bag from her and headed more sedately into the washroom. When he turned back at the door to glance in her direction, he saw her repressing a smile.

"What?"

"From the back, those hospital gowns don't leave much to the imagination."

"Argh!" He shut the door on her chuckle.

****

"Emma." As he pulled on his jeans, Frasier recognized the voice of the doctor who'd attended him the previous night. "Good to see you again. Ready to take our patient home?"

"Ready and willing." Emma's reply was bright and bubbly. "Any special instructions regarding his care?"

"Just try to keep him quiet and well fed for a couple of days. After that, he should be fine on his own. Speaking of his being on his own, I was

128

wondering if you might like to have dinner some time after your friend is back on his feet."

Damn! Did the man have no sense of decency, asking out a woman when his patient, her... friend...had only recently been at death's door?

"Thanks, but it's a little early to make plans. Tell you what. Why don't I take your number and call you when I have some free time?"

Emma, what do you think you're doing? Frasier gave his zipper a yank, pinched himself, and bit his lip to suppress the resultant yelp. The quick, sharp pain brought him to his senses. Why shouldn't she make plans with a good-looking doctor? Did he expect her to live like a nun because he couldn't offer her more than friendship?

Trying to convince himself he was being unreasonable, he finished dressing and then went back out into the hospital room determined not to let Dr. Bradley notice his annoyance.

****

"Are you sure there's no one I should notify?" Emma drove carefully down the trail that led to their cabins, braking gently for each root and bump. "Family, friends...significant other?" She shot a swift glance over at him as she made the final suggestion.

"Only the Professor. I notified him from the hospital. There's no need to go around alarming people, since I am going to be just fine."

"Okay." She eased the car over a massive root. "I hope you like pasta. It's my specialty."

"Why?"

"I'll be cooking for you for the next few days. I've taken a compassionate leave to look after you."

He felt his breath desert his body in a gust. But, damn it, he wasn't sure if it was because of anticipation or exasperation. A vision of her giving him a sponge bath flashed across his mind, immediately followed by a vision of the Pug looming over him as he lay helpless on a bed. The little dog was burping, his small round belly heaving... *Ah, hell!*

He remembered the conversation he'd overheard between Emma and the doctor. Something about a blood donation.

"Did you donate blood...for me?" he asked.

"Yes." She grinned over at him. "I wasn't content just to get under your skin and in your hair."

"Well, anyway, thanks."

"No problem. I figured the Bruise and I owe you more than a bottle of blood."

He leaned back, closed his eyes, and tried to relax. But the thought of Emma Prescott's donation coursing through him gave him crazy ideas about her getting into his heart physically as well as emotionally.

Man, I'm getting weird. Has to be the painkillers.

He flinched when she hit a root dead-on. The sharp hurt revived the memory of another unpleasant sensation.

"Speaking of blood donations and hospitals and doctors, what about Dr. Bradley?"

"What about him?" Emma slanted him a sideways glance.

"Are you going to see him again?" Frasier heard himself snap. *Man, how many of those pills did they give me? I'm definitely losing it.*

"I haven't decided." She returned her attention to the trail. "Might be fun to date a doctor. I never have."

"Amazing." Sarcasm belched from the word.

"Frasier MacKenzie, stop it. Just stop it." She pulled over to the side of the trail and shoved the gear stick into park. "You!" She released her seatbelt and swung to face him. "You're acting like a jealous lover. You have no right, since you aren't prepared to assume the position. Or are you?" She met his gaze squarely, and he flinched inwardly.

"You know I can't."

"Well, then." She turned back to face front, rebuckled her seat belt, and put the car into drive.

"Emma, you know it's not what I want, what I'd do if things were different."

"But right now I'm second to the ghost of the Eastern Panther."

"Yeah, I guess."

He sounded like a spoiled little boy, and Emma burst out laughing.

"Sounds as if you're sulking because you can't have both your career and a hot number like me, as well," she said as she pushed a CD into the player.

She was pretending not to care. Pretending. Yeah, that was it. He hoped.

****

"Let me get you settled in bed." Emma was close behind him as he made his way to the spare bedroom in her cabin. She'd insisted he stay with her for at least a few days. Realizing he wouldn't win that battle, and not entirely sure he wanted to, he gave in. "I've brought over your pj pants and a couple of T-shirts you can wear in bed. I put fresh underwear and socks in the dresser drawers. Once you're feeling better, I'll bring over your jeans and shirts and stuff."

"Thanks." Surprised at how weak the short walk from the car had left him, he sat down heavily on the edge of the bed. "Man, I need a shave." He ran his hand over the two-day stubble on his jaw and chin. "And my teeth feel like they're wearing little fur suits."

"Got it covered." Emma opened the door to the bathroom between the two bedrooms and proudly displayed his toiletries set up on a shelf above the sink. "Why don't you climb into bed, and I'll shave you? Then I'll bring a glass of water and you can brush your teeth..."

"Hey, I'm not a complete invalid." He got to his feet, trying to exude more confidence in his physical capabilities than he was feeling. "I can make myself presentable. But," he continued, "I'm really hungry. I haven't eaten since yesterday. I could do with some lunch."

"Coming right up." Emma headed toward the kitchen.

With a sigh of relief, Frasier moved gingerly into the bathroom, dragging his pajama pants and a clean T-shirt. All he wanted to do was get cleaned up and fall into that comfortable-looking bed.

****

"Soup's on." Emma stepped into the room carrying a lunch tray. She placed it on the dresser. After his ablutions, Frasier had climbed gratefully into bed and was now dozing.

"You'll have to sit up," she said, bending to slip an arm beneath his good side and heap his pillows into a stack behind him with the other. "Couldn't quite manage the shave, right?" She grinned at his stubbled chin and jaw.

"Easy, easy," he grimaced. "I'll do it tomorrow."

"You've only got a flesh wound," she belittled his cringing. "When my brother came home from Afghanistan, he wasn't half the wimp you're being, and he was hurt a lot worse."

"You have a brother in the military?"

"Yes, and a twin sister we call Etta, although her real name is Henryetta. My mother was into old-fashioned names when we were born."

"You mean there's two of you?" He couldn't believe it. One Emma type was more than he could handle.

"You sound as if that's a bad thing." She cocked her head to one side and narrowed her eyes as she looked down at him.

"No...that is, not exactly. I never would have guessed..."

"That the world had been so blessed? But enough about me. Time for you to eat and get your strength back."

She settled him back on his pillows, then brought the tray to the bed.

"Minestrone with garlic bread," she said as he looked down at the meal she was placing in front of him. "Should be chicken, but I didn't have any stock."

"Looks great." He picked up the spoon. "You're a twin, you say?"

"Yes. Now what about your family? Who and where?" She sat down in a rocking chair and crossed her arms.

"Three brothers and a pair of happily married parents, who live in Halifax. My older brother Scott is a doctor at the cardiac care centre in Montreal. Colin is a member of the Royal Canadian Mounted Police...in Alberta, I think. I'm never sure where he is."

"And the last one?"

"Gareth, the youngest, is still in university, well on his way to becoming a permanent student."

"An impressive lot. What about your mom and dad? Are they retired?"

"You ask an awful lot of questions when a man's trying to eat." He took a big bite of garlic bread.

"That's such an old trick it's got a long, white beard." She looked over at him, narrowing her eyes. "I'll wait until you swallow."

"Okay, okay! Dad's a cop, RCMP Inspector, and Mom is a social worker. There, satisfied?"

He feigned annoyance as best he could, but the truth was the delicious soup and tasty bread were having a mellowing effect.

133

"Wow! You must be proud. And they'll be more than proud of you when you prove the existence of that big pussycat."

She arose, green eyes bright with gentle teasing, and started out of the room. "Eat up. I'll be back shortly with a dessert so good it's sinful."

"Emma." He stopped her. "Where's Scout?"

"Over at your cabin, guarding your research from I have no idea what." She turned back. "But since that's what you generally expect him to do, I've left him to it. Don't worry. He's been fed and watered and had a bathroom break. Tonight I'll get Bruiser to sleep over there with him so he won't be lonely."

"Thanks." He leaned back with a relaxed sigh. "I appreciate...everything you've done, believe me."

"Hey, I owe you a lot more than a bowl of soup." She grinned back at him. "You saved Bruiser's life...remember?"

She left the room humming tunelessly.

"God help me, so I did," he muttered, and returned his attention to the soup.

****

When Frasier woke from his next nap, the room had darkened. A thought struck him.

"Emma," he called. "Emma, where are you?"

"Right here." A moment later she appeared in the doorway and came to his bedside to snap on a lamp. "Are you okay? Do you need more painkillers?"

"No, no. It's time I did some drug-free thinking. Where is my ATV? I don't like the idea of it sitting out there in the woods where anyone might steal it."

"Steal it? The only things out there are birds and animals and maybe the ghost of Midnight Jim. Don't worry, Frasier. Bright and early tomorrow, Bruiser and I will go out and get it."

"But you don't know where to find it."

"It's got to be at the end of the tracks you made, right?"

"But you don't know how to drive one."

"Ah, ha! Now there you couldn't be more wrong. That brother I told you about taught me how to handle one of those critters when I was twelve. Like riding any bike, you never forget how it's done."

"I don't think you should go wandering around alone in the woods..."

"Hush and stop worrying. I'll have the Bruise with me." She gave his shoulder a pat and left.

Frasier looked down at the Pug standing beside his bed, his curl of a tail wagging vigorously, his wide mouth stretched in a good-natured grin. And groaned.

****

"Would you like me to read to you?" She came back into the room, three books under her arm. "Since we have no TV and you don't look up to making music, it's the only form of entertainment I can come up with. I have—" she held them up one at a time— "A nail-biting thriller, a cozy murder mystery, or—" she paused before swinging the provocative cover toward him and striking a seductive pose— "A steamy romance."

He flinched. "Not up to a thriller and especially not that." He indicated the romance cover. "Let's go for the murder mystery. It'll be a test to see if my brain is functioning again after the anesthetic and painkillers."

"Okay." Emma pulled a rocking chair close to the bed, adjusted the light, and opened the book. "You're sure about this?" she asked as she found Chapter One and paused. "That romance is really hot."

"Yeah, yeah, I'm sure. Just read."

****

He opened his eyes and blinked up at her. "Sorry. Must have nodded off. What?"

She was staring at him, transfixed. "I can't stop

thinking I've seen you somewhere." She closed the book and squinted at him. "Now, with that stubble and your hair all tousled…"

"Pretty unlikely." He moved and winced. "If we'd met, I know I'd remember you and…" he pointed at the Pug, "Definitely him." He let his eyelids droop. "Sorry, can't seem to concentrate…"

"A clear indication you need your sleep." She got up, placed the book on the nightstand, and began to adjust his pillows. "Do you have to go to the bathroom before I tuck you in?"

"No! Emma, I'm not five years old! I think I'm capable of knowing when I have to…"

"Okay, okay, but you did have two glasses of water with your supper. Don't blame me if you have to get up in the night. I helped nurse my brother when he came home wounded, so you don't have to feel shy."

"Thanks," he muttered avoiding her eyes. "That's very reassuring."

She finished tucking him in, then bent and kissed him on the forehead.

"If you do need to go in the night, just holler and I'll come." She paused at the door. "Can't have you tripping in the dark or falling headfirst into the toilet. I'm sure the Professor would never forgive me if I let anything like that happen."

"Argh!" he gritted between his teeth as she snapped off the lamp from the switch by the door. She went out, leaving him in darkness.

"Sweet dreams," she called back.

With a grunt, he yanked free the blankets she'd tucked about him, then stifled a yelp as his side lurched with pain.

Gorgeous Emma annoying him, teasing him, raging at him, amusing him, impressing him, making him laugh, constantly astonishing him, saving his life, and now mothering him. How was a man supposed to deal with all that and remain aloof and impersonal? Worse still, how could he possibly manage to plot a method of getting rid of her when all he wanted to do was...

Frustrated beyond his wildest dreams, he rolled over on his good side, stifling a grunt as his stitches pulled. *Damn it, damn it, damn it!*

****

"Rise and shine, cowboy."

Frasier awoke the next morning when Emma threw open the curtains to let a blast of sunlight hit him squarely in the face.

"Damn, Emma!" he muttered, shielding his eyes as Bruiser landed in a single bound on his bed. "What time is it?"

"Nearly 8:00 a.m., my man. Breakfast is spoiling even as we speak. I've already brought Bruiser over from your cabin and fed Scout. I would have brought the big guy over, too, but I wasn't sure you'd want your place left unguarded. Now let me get you into the bathroom and—"

"No, no, no!" Grimacing, he struggled to a sitting position, thrust his feet out onto the cold floor, and rubbed his temples. "I'll manage. Just give me a couple of minutes to get awake."

****

By 3:00 p.m. Frasier could stand no more of Emma's mothering and ordered her from the room while he got up and dressed.

"If you feel weak, call me," she said, leaving the room, undeterred by his refusal to allow her to help. "Put on those warm socks. Can't have you catching a chill."

"Sure, sure," he muttered, feeling like a belligerent six-year-old.

"And don't try to shave," she swung back on him. "You're still too shaky."

"Go." He eased his feet onto the floor. One day in

bed under Emma's smothering if well-intentioned care was about all he could handle in a platonic state.

"Okay, okay."

****

When he joined her in the living area twenty minutes later, he was glad to sit down on the couch, although he'd never admit it to her. Getting washed and dressed had made him realize he wasn't yet back in full working order.

"Good. You didn't try to shave or comb your hair. But you did wash. You smell fresh as a spring shower." She sniffed him appreciatively.

"You didn't bring my soap," he said. "I had to use yours."

"It is a lovely fragrance...not manly, just lovely."

"Fine, so I smell like a girl. At least I'm clean." He pulled back from her sniffing and looked down at the Pug who sat on the floor in front of him, staring and sniffing, tail wriggling. "No comments from you."

"How about some music?" Emma turned toward a small stereo on a table in the corner. "I had a great sound system in my apartment, but there was water damage and the insurance still hasn't come through. Therefore, this is a bargain store special."

"It'll be fine." He settled himself more comfortably. "What have you got?"

"Not much choice." She shuffled through a small stack of CDs. "Only my oldies that I kept in a plastic container in the basement storage unit survived. Now, let me see..." She paused in mid-sentence and stared down at the square plastic case in her hand, eyes widening.

"What?" Her startled expression brought the word out sharper than he'd intended.

"I thought I recognized you...with your hair all tousled and a stubble." She raised her gaze from the

CD cover to stare at him incredulously. "You're the Frase, Larry Hadlen's backup singer and guitarist for The Sound. Oh, my God! You really are the Frase!" She was all-out staring at him, her expression one he'd seen thousands of times on the faces of fans and groupies. His heart plummeted.

"You are, aren't you?" She crossed the room to stand in front of him, the CD clutched in her hands.

"Yeah, well, I guess you've got me cold. Yeah, I was Larry's backup a long—a very long time ago." He spread his hands in resignation.

"I had such a crush on you!" She sank into the chair opposite him and stared, wide-eyed. "You were the ultimate bad boy of my dreams."

"Yeah, well," he repeated uncomfortably. "The band's broken up. I'm a dull old associate professor of biology. Times change, people change, and stuff moves on."

"I guess." She continued to gaze over at him, the same star-struck expression on her face.

"Ah, come on, Emma." He shifted uneasily. "All that is long past. I'm the hermit at Loon Lake now, so shove your eyes back in place and put on some music that isn't by The Sound."

"Okay." She backed slowly away from him, still looking awestruck. "Okay."

"By the way, thank you for heading out into the woods to rescue me. That took guts, with an Eastern Panther in the vicinity, not to mention the ghost of Midnight Jim. I should have said it sooner, but I guess I was too wrapped up in myself. I'm sorry."

"No big deal." The star-struck look still dominated her features.

"I disagree. It was a very big deal."

"Oh, come on!" She snapped out of her hero worship mode. "Don't get too melodramatic! I had Scout and Bruiser with me. And I did take a self-defense course last year. Although how effective any of those moves would be against panthers or ghosts..."

"Okay, okay." He caught the twinkle in her eyes. "Nevertheless, I'm grateful. I regret I didn't say it sooner."

"Apology—and thanks—accepted. Now let me get back to our dinner." She went to the refrigerator.

"You never told me how you happened to take a job in Carleton," he said, as she rummaged through the crisper. "It's a long way off most beaten paths."

"We spent our summers at Loon Lake when I was a child, remember. I fell in love with the place. A few years ago when I was surfing the net for job prospects, I found one that suited my qualifications in Carleton. I jumped at the chance."

"Are you still happy with your decision? Seems you've had a lot on your plate, dealing with kids with drug problems."

She faced him, a bag of carrots in her hand. "It's been a challenge, but it's my job, what I hoped to do when I became a guidance counselor. Sometimes, though..." She frowned. "I wonder if I'm making any difference at all."

"It can't be easy. But don't give up. Never give up. It's a battle worth the effort."

****

An hour later he sat ensconced in a chair in front of the fire, reading one of the newspapers Emma had bought when she made (she told him later) a quick (the word made him cringe) trip to Carleton that morning while he'd (apparently) been dozing. A soothing instrumental wafted softly from the small stereo while Emma prepared a beef roast (another acquisition of her journey) that smelled so good he felt he could salivate like one of Pavlov's dogs. It wasn't only the meat. Emma Prescott in her jeans, plaid shirt, and moccasins looked a whole lot more tempting than any food as she chopped vegetables at the counter.

The fine weather that had begun the day had vanished. Now an autumn storm buffeted the cabin, with rain slashing at the windows while a gale howled around the corners. But inside all was cozy, domestic warmth. Emma, with Frasier's permission, had brought Scout from his cabin. The big Shepherd lay stretched out on the hearth, the Pug in his basket beside him.

I could get used to this real easy. Frasier put down the paper and stretched as best his stitches would allow. *A comfortable little wilderness cabin, the dogs, Emma making like a wife...*

"Broccoli or spinach salad?" She broke in on his thoughts as she opened the refrigerator door and bent over the vegetable bin. Bent. Yellow pantaloons, short green dresses, now super-fitted jeans. A series of frustrating images flashed through his mind.

"Frasier?" she half-turned to look at him. "Spinach or broccoli?"

"Spinach...yeah, spinach," he garbled and held up his paper to block the view.

****

"I didn't hear you leaving for town this morning," he commented an hour later as they ate their dinner. "Did you get a new exhaust system on your car?"

"No, I took your SUV." Emma didn't miss a beat as she cut into a slice of medium rare roast beef.

"You *what?*" His knife clattered onto his plate. "It's not *my* SUV. It belongs to the project, and—"

"Relax, Frasier." She looked up at him in mild exasperation. "It's still in A-1 condition. My car was low on gas. I didn't want to risk getting stranded on the road, with you incapacitated and all, so when I saw yours was full to the brim..."

"How many citations did you manage to rack up

on this cannonball run?" He looked over at her.

"None." She returned her attention to dinner. "I was careful. I brought back a container of gas for my car, too, so I won't be using yours again."

"Good." He heaved a sigh and shoved his fork into a mound of creamy mashed potatoes.

"But, wow, can that baby move!" She slanted a wicked glance over at him. "Do you know it can go from zero to one hundred and forty clicks in less than—"

"Oh, my God!" This time both of Frasier's utensils clattered onto the plate. "You didn't—"

"Just kidding." She speared a piece of carrot. "But it got your blood charging, didn't it? Good for the circulation."

She paused with the carrot inches from her lips, twirled it, and grinned.

He stifled the guttural moan rising in his throat and went back to his dinner. Annoying she might be, he thought, as he dug into his vegetables, but the woman was never dull. And she certainly could cook.

****

After they'd finished a dessert of apple pie and ice cream and were savoring a second cup of coffee in front of the fire, Emma asked him the question he'd known couldn't be far off.

"What happened to your band, Frasier? I mean, you were heading up the charts. Then suddenly The Sound just vanished."

He drew a deep breath and decided she could handle the truth.

"Larry died," he said, staring down into his cup. "OD'd one night after a show."

"Oh, my God!" Emma's hand flew to her mouth. "But there was nothing in the media about it."

"Larry's father had the kind of money that can muzzle the press," he said, still focused on his cup. "After that, the band went belly up."

"But you were good on your own." Emma was adamant. "I thought you were even better than Larry. You could have taken over...after a decent period."

"No, I couldn't." He looked up at her. "You see, when my father heard about Larry's death—it's hard to keep that kind of thing unnoticed by the RCMP—he caught the next flight to Toronto and pulled me out of the music business once and for all. You haven't met him, Emma, but, believe me, no one argues with Inspector Benjamin MacKenzie.

"He took me home, sent me back to university. I'd been in my third year when I joined the band. I completed my degree and, several years later, here I am, former rock musician turned backwoods hermit."

"So you do know about drugs and what they can do." She spoke softly as she placed her hand over his on his cup.

"Yeah, I do, first hand, up close, and way too personal."

"I'm sorry, truly sorry, about your friend," she said. Looking into her eyes, he knew she was.

"Thanks," he said gruffly over the thickness gathering in his throat. Again, in his mind, he was in that shambles of a hotel room, seeing Larry sprawled across the bed. He'd never be able to expunge that image. "He was a great guy. He shouldn't have been murdered by that junk he kept ingesting."

"Frasier." She removed her hand and sat back on the couch. "Would you come to school and speak to my students about drugs, tell them your experience with Larry? I know it will be painful, but they'd listen to you as a rock star. You could save some of them from a similar fate."

"No!" He got to his feet too quickly and grimaced as his stitches caught at him. "Former is the operative word, Emma. Those kids are too young to remember The Sound. Anyway, we never made the top of the charts."

"Still, you traveled the concert circuit, you witnessed first hand the horrors of drugs…"

"No." He placed his cup on the counter and strode as fast as his wound would allow into the bedroom.

****

"I'm going back to my cabin," he informed her the next morning over breakfast. "I can manage on my own now. Thanks for everything."

"Are you sure?" Emma looked up from her bowl of cereal. "Because you're welcome to stay as long as—"

"I know." He spoke softly. "You've been terrific, Emma, but I have to get back to work. And…" He paused.

"And?"

"And I'm sorry about bolting out on you last night. The idea of talking about Larry and his problems in front of a bunch of kids threw me for a loop. I'm just not ready…"

"Frasier, believe me, I understand." She touched his arm. "I shouldn't have asked. Now." She pulled back and stood, just as he was beginning to prickle with arousal. "I'll put our dishes in the washer. Then I'll run over to your place and get you a jacket. We'll take a little stroll around the yard before I put you back on your own. That should restore your sea legs."

"Sea legs?"

"Heard it in a pirate movie." She clattered her bowl and spoon into the dishwasher. "Eat up, matey. It's a gorgeous day and time's a-wastin'."

****

Frasier stopped abruptly in the "stroll" he and Emma were taking around the property.

144

"When did *that* happen?" He gestured at the hole dug beneath his dog run. It had been crudely patched with a stick laced through the chain link.

"Must have been on the morning I went to pick you up at the hospital." Emma tried to sound casual. "Bruiser wanted to come, but I left him penned up at your place with Scout. I guess he wasn't happy about it."

"Damn!" Frasier stared at the breached fence. "Next time I'm in town, I'll have to get some tent pegs to repair it. I don't want Scout enlarging it and getting out."

"Scout would never do anything like that!" Emma scoffed sarcastically. "He's too well trained."

"Yeah, well, your Pug does seem to have a way of corrupting him."

"Anyway..." She turned him back toward his front porch. "It's inside for you, my boy. I have to get your ATV. I don't plan to leave you wandering around alone outdoors while I'm gone."

****

Frasier heard them roaring up the trail in the sunny, previously quiet morning. He limped out onto the verandah to watch their arrival, Scout by his side.

"Oh, God, no!" he groaned as Emma careened into the clearing, his crash helmet on her head. Bruiser, secured in a basket behind her, sported a wide grin.

"Hey, Frasier!" She swirled to a stop in front of him, tearing up a chunk of lawn as she braked. "I'd forgotten how much fun these things can be." She swung to the ground and removed the helmet to shake her chestnut curls free. "We had a ball, didn't we, Bruise?"

She released the little dog and set him on the ground. He paused, looked up at her, gave a couple of sharp, happy barks, then cannoned off to play

145

with Scout.

"You do realize this bike isn't my personal property?" He hobbled down the steps, flinching as his stitches caught him with each drop. "It belongs to the project, and..." He inspected a mud-caked fender.

"Oh, lighten up, Frasier." She put her hands on her hips. "ATVs are meant to take rough treatment."

"Rough terrain, you mean. At a reasonable speed. Emma..."

He turned to her to continue his lecture, but she was gone, running up the verandah steps.

"Put your baby away, will you? I'm going to start lunch."

"Argh!" He flinched again as he swung his leg over the saddle. In his annoyance he'd forgotten his stitches.

****

Emma's cell tinkled as he stepped back inside her cabin. He sank onto a chair at the table.

"Hello. Oh, hi. This is a surprise. He's fine, just fine. Thanks for inquiring. Tonight?" She glanced over at Frasier and hesitated. "Thanks, but no. It's still too early to leave Frasier alone. Maybe a rain check? I appreciate the call. See you soon."

She placed the phone on the counter and returned to tearing romaine lettuce.

"A friend asking you out?" He couldn't suppress the question.

"Sort of. Dr. Kent Bradley. You remember. From the hospital."

She began to wash mushrooms. Something charged through his veins. Rising blood pressure had never been a problem, but he imagined it would feel like this. He began to drum his fingers on the table. "You could have gone. I'm perfectly capable of taking care of myself."

"Are you?" She turned to look at him. "I'm not

146

sure. In a week, you'll be right as rain and I can start accepting dinner invitations, but until then I plan to stick around. As a matter of fact..." She returned to her salad making. "I should call Kent back and ask him to chaperone the high school dance with me on Friday. I need a male companion, someone tall and impressive-looking, who will command the kids' respect. He fills the bill."

She reached for the phone.

"Dry your hands first." The words snapped out.

"What?"

"You could get a shock."

"That's only electrical plugs. Just how practically inept are you?" She wiped her hands on a cloth. "There. Satisfied?"

"I'll do it." *Damn, where had that come from?*

"Do what? Dry my hands, make the salad, place the call?" She quirked a corner of her lips at him, green eyes sparkling.

"Chaperone that dance with you."

"Ah, but you'll still be in recovery. I hardly think—"

"You shouldn't be asking a guy you barely know to take on an important responsibility like seeing that kids have fun in a safe environment." His fingers drummed harder on the table. "I'll be fine by then. With my experience at university socials, I come highly qualified."

"Well, if you're sure." She swung and went back to the kitchen counter, hips swaying in a fashion he saw as self-satisfied and smug.

She didn't trick me into this! No, no, no, she couldn't have. Did she?

****

"Hey, Miss Prescott. Cool guy. Has he got any brothers?"

A circle of teenage girls garbed in Goth getups formed around Emma and Frasier as they entered the high school gym decked out in a Halloween/horror motif.

"Yes, but fortunately they're in a land far, far away. Now shoo! Go pick on someone your own age."

Casting them a mockery of an annoyed look, Emma sent them off giggling and pointing back at Frasier.

"Seems you're a big hit with the jailbait set," she hissed sideways at him.

"Hardly a compliment." He rubbed his side. "I can't believe I volunteered to chaperone a high school dance a week after being shot."

"Well, you did. Anyhow, you're fine now. That's what Dr. Bradley told you when he removed your stitches this afternoon, didn't he? Or were you lying to me, Frasier MacKenzie?"

"Dr. Bradley, right," he grunted. "Rain-check Kent."

"Excuse me, you muttered?" She glanced up at him.

"Nothing, nothing."

"Well, then, fine. Get out there and mingle. Don't forget to check the washrooms for drugs and alcohol."

****

"Hey, guys, what's up?" Frasier stepped into the washroom to find four teenagers involved in a deal.

Amid the scuffle to hide the merchandise, a small packet fell to the floor. One dived for it, but Frasier was quicker, even though he barely managed to stifle a yelp of pain.

"Now what could this be?" He held it up. Three took a quick glance and, pushing past him, fled. The fourth, wearing black leather and a sneer, stayed, feet planted apart, hands on his hips.

"Give it here, man." He held out a hand.

"I don't think so." *Damn, this kid is nearly as big as me, and he looks like he works out. He might just take me, the shape I'm in.*

Frasier backed as the younger man approached. Backed until he was in a stall. With a quick flick of his wrist, he threw the packet into the toilet and flushed.

"Are you crazy, man!" He slammed Frasier aside to drop on his knees, too late, over the swirling water.

"Gone." Frasier rubbed his side, throbbing from the blow, as the small plastic bag vanished.

"Bastard!" The teenager shot to his feet, his face a testimony to how rage could distort even youthful features. "You'll pay for this—you and your Loon Lake piece of..."

"Hold it right there!" Frasier's hands knotted into fists.

The washroom door opened and two teenagers entered. They stared at the pair in the stall.

"Get stuffed!" Frasier's adversary gave him a last, enraged glare before pushing the new arrivals against the wall as he strode out of the room.

"It's okay, guys." Frasier stepped out of the stall. "A little trouble. Everything's fine now."

"You're lucky, sir," one of them addressed him. "Todd Stoddart carries a knife. No one, but no one, messes with him."

So that was the infamous Todd. Frasier headed back to the gym. *Good thing those kids came in when they did. I might have taken a swing at him for what he seemed to be winding up to say about Emma. And wouldn't that have made a nice headline: Chaperone punches out student over derogatory remarks about school guidance counselor.*

****

"Everything okay in the washrooms?" Emma asked when he rejoined her.

"Everything is fine...now." He clasped his hands behind his back, feet planted firmly apart.

149

"What do you mean 'now'?" She looked up at him as he stood scrutinizing the dance floor.

"Small matter of a drug sale in progress. Someone named Todd."

"Oh, no! Just when I thought I was making headway with him. Frasier, are you sure?"

"Emma." He looked down at her deadly serious. "I can recognize drugs."

"Yes, I suppose you can." Her words held disappointment.

"You can't save them all." He touched her hand. "You've done your best. That's all any of us can do."

"You're right." She blinked and drew a deep breath. "I'll live to fight another day, I suppose."

"I know you will."

"Dance?"

"Sorry." The corner of his mouth twitched up in a half grin as the DJ spun a hard rock number. "I'm not good at gyrating right now...on the dance floor, that is," he added hurriedly.

"Why, Frasier MacKenzie, I do believe you're blushing." Emma moved to face him, grinning. "I like that. It's sweet and old-fashioned and downright endearing."

Damn! Sweet and old-fashioned and endearing? What about hot and sexy and virile?

****

"Last dance," the DJ announced.

"You can't deny me this one." Emma turned to Frasier. "It's always a waltz—or something that's supposed to be, no gyrating required."

"Emma..." He started to protest, but she was leading him out onto the floor.

She placed both hands on his shoulders, leaving him no choice but to put his on her hips.

"Good Lord, where did that come from?" Emma breathed as the sensuous strains of "Moon River" floated into the air. "The last dance is usually a request. I didn't think anyone here was old enough to know that tune."

"I don't know, and I don't care." Frasier let his hands move to the back of her hips and drew her close. Adrenaline still active from his encounter with Todd Stoddart, he couldn't resist. He let his lips brush her ear. "Let's just relax and enjoy the moment."

Enjoy. Savor. Get lost in. Float off to the moon. The thoughts drifted around him as he moved slowly, fluidly, against her in the shadowy gym. Maybe he didn't gyrate very well on the dance floor, but for a guy who felt his face heat up at a verbal faux pas, he wasn't exactly bashful.

Like a glass of ice water in the face, the song ended, the gym was flooded with light, and the DJ was hollering, "See you next time!"

Emma stood looking blankly up at Frasier, who still held her in his arms. Blue eyes met green and locked.

"Well," he said finally, drawing a deep breath and stepping back. "I guess we'd better make sure everyone leaves in an orderly fashion." He headed for the main exit.

****

"Did you enjoy the last dance, Miss Prescott?" Penny Jamieson joined them as they left the building. Her brown eyes deep inside a rim of black makeup danced with mischief.

"Yes." Emma paused and looked into the teenager's face in the bright light over the main entrance. "But who on earth requested 'Moon River'?"

"It was my parents' favorite..." Penny's voice faltered. She became involved in zipping up her jacket. "I figured older folks like you would enjoy it."

"Oh, the geriatric crowd." Emma drew the girl into a hug and chuckled. "Okay, I forgive you.

151

Thanks for the thought."

"My treat." The teenager drew back from Emma, grinning. "Can't let all that go to waste."

She slid a sly head-to-toe glance over Frasier, then winked and skipped off the steps.

"That's quite enough, young lady!" Emma called after her, but the amusement in her tone negated any serious rebuke.

"I feel like some kind of trophy boyfriend." Frasier took her arm and hunched deeper into his rancher's jacket. Together they went down the steps. "But what did she mean 'was' her parents' favorite? Divorced?"

"Deceased. Both killed in a terrible highway accident." Emma slipped on a frozen puddle. He caught her back on her feet. "She's had a couple of really bad years. It's only recently she started to come out of it. Now she's hooked up with Jesse Jones."

"Damn."

"Yes, definitely damn. A girl in her fragile mental condition doesn't need a druggie boyfriend."

"But you're there for her, right? She seems to like you a lot. Right up to pimping me off to you as best she could." He put his arm around her shoulders as they headed toward the parking lot and gave her a squeeze.

"Yes, well, most kids are optimists." She slanted a sideways glance up at him. "They don't realize some things just aren't possible."

"Let's put that discussion on hold. Would you like to go for coffee...or a drink?" he asked as they walked toward his SUV. It was the last vehicle in the lot.

"Another time, thanks. Right now I'm exhausted. Mind if we head home?" She stifled a yawn. "Bruiser and Scout will be getting anxious."

"Sounds good to me. I've had a long day, too."

Home. Coming from Emma it sounded so good.
****

"Miss." A figure rose out of the shadows behind Frasier's SUV as he was unlocking the passenger door.

Frasier pulled Emma back and stepped between her and the stranger.

"Hey, it's cool!" Jesse Jones hissed as Frasier's hands knotted into fists. "I just came to warn you. Todd's in a rotten mood." He looked up at Frasier. "Says you'll pay for flushing his stuff. He's got friends...tough guys who know where you live."

"Jesse, Todd wouldn't send anyone to do us physical harm." Emma stepped up beside Frasier. "He's just talking big."

"Yeah? Like he was when he said he was going to torch your apartment? Like he was when my girlfriend disappeared for a whole day?"

"Penny was abducted? Jesse, why didn't you come to me? Why didn't you report it?"

The teenager shrugged. "Said his friends would hurt her real bad if I did. After what happened at your place, I knew he wasn't bluffing."

"Who are these friends?" Frasier asked.

"Don't know. I only met them once—when I got Penny back—and they were wearing ski masks. I gotta go. If you tell anyone I talked to you, I'll swear you're both lyin'."

He turned and ran into the darkness at the edge of the parking lot.

"Well, that was interesting." Frasier put his arm back around Emma's shoulders.

"We have to go to the police and tell them what Jesse said!" Emma looked up at him, her eyes wide and bright in the glow of security lights.

"They'd only pull the kid in for questioning, he'd deny everything, and Penny would be back in danger. No, all we can do is watch our backs and keep our eyes open for proof of what he said. Now, come on. You're shivering. Let me get you home."

****

"Where did you learn to dance like that?" she asked when Frasier had headed the SUV out onto the highway.

"I attended high school and university and played in a band. I wasn't always the hermit at Loon Lake."

"Who insists on keeping his lady neighbor at a safe distance?" Emma finished, sarcasm coloring her words.

"Sorry. The timing's just not right."

"Yeah, yeah." She pulled up the collar of her coat, slumped down in the seat, and closed her eyes. "Like I haven't heard that before. Wake me when we get home. And," she opened one eye to glance up at him. "Mind the speed limit. I understand the Mounties patrol this stretch of highway pretty rigorously."

"Look who's giving driving advice!"

He glanced over at her, but she'd shut both eyes again and cuddled deeper into her jacket.

****

Five minutes later he looked again. She appeared fast asleep, long dark lashes spread out on soft, glowing cheeks. She'd worn a simple white turtleneck and black pants to the dance, a pair of gold hoop earrings her only jewelry. Outdoors she'd topped it with a white, hip-length, double-breasted, belted wool jacket. The outfit suited her soft beauty to a T.

His attention flew back to the road as a tractor-trailer whizzed past. He'd better stop mooning over Emma and concentrate on his driving.

It would have been a whole lot easier if she weren't so beautiful. *Why couldn't she have been ugly, with a wart on the end of a crooked nose?* No, no, on second thought that probably wouldn't help, now that he knew her, now that he'd come to respect and admire (he wouldn't even think the word "love") her. Like the princess with that stupid frog...in role reversal...he'd probably kiss her anyway. *Blast it!* He hit the steering wheel a thump. She flinched in her sleep, then with a soft little sigh snuggled back into slumber.

Sorry, but you're driving me nuts.

****

Back at the lake, he swung the SUV around to illuminate the entire clearing before braking to a halt with the headlights focused on her verandah. *It doesn't hurt to be careful.*

"Emma, we're home," he said softly, touching her on the shoulder.

Blinking back to wakefulness, she pulled herself up in the seat. He got out and jogged around to the passenger door.

"Give me your key," he said holding out his hand. "I'll open up and start a fire."

Groggily she dug a key ring from her purse. "Pink one," she mumbled. "I had a color-coded one cut."

"Okay." He took it from her and headed toward the cabin illuminated in the headlights.

"Hey!" She came fully awake. "Isn't this the romantic part where Prince Charming gathers his lady fair up into his arms and sweeps her into his castle?"

"Didn't you read the sequel?" He fitted the key into the door. "Prince Charming ended up with a herniated disc. The princess had to rub disgusting, smelly ointment on it for months before he was well enough to hobble, never mind make love. Now come on. Let's get you inside before drowsiness brings on any more inane suggestions."

Emma fumbled out of the SUV. Grasping her

purse, she headed up the steps. When he turned from unlocking the door, she leaned against him and rose on tiptoes.

"Come here, Frasier MacKenzie," she murmured drowsily. "The least you can do is give a girl a decent goodnight kiss after dancing yourself into her dreams."

A whiff of a scent so delicate he couldn't be certain whether he smelled it or imagined it emanated from her hair. From against his chest, all the warm, sensuousness that was Emma engulfed him and drew every ounce of male instinct raging to the surface.

"Emma," he breathed and lowered his head.

When he drew her body close to fit into every curve and hollow of his, all thoughts of the project and an unrelenting Professor whisked off into the moonlight. A soft, sexy Emma was kissing him as he'd never been kissed before; an overwhelmingly sensuous Emma, who washed all rational thoughts from his mind with the power of a tsunami.

"Emma," he breathed again. Kicking the unlatched door open, he made a move to gather her up in his arms. The wound yanked at his flesh, and he grunted.

"No, no, no!" She stopped him. "I was joking. You're not physically fit for anything more than a kiss. And," she continued more slowly, "I'm not ready for anything more than a kiss from a guy who puts me second to his cat-chasing career. Good night, Frasier MacKenzie. I'll see you in my dreams."

With a coy smile she eased herself out of his arms and backed into the cabin. When she closed the door gently in his face, he wanted to roar up at that stupid full moon like a frustrated werewolf.

"Lock your doors and windows and keep your cell by your bed," he managed instead. "Call me if you see or hear anything in the least suspicious."

****

When Frasier awoke the next morning, he hoped Emma Prescott had seen him in her dreams every minute of the past six hours. He hoped she'd felt at least half as frustrated as he had. She'd danced around in his head all night, just out of his reach, until he'd awoken to find himself rolled up in knotted sheets.

Rubbing his head, he shut off the alarm and got out of bed. He'd be glad when this project came to a successful conclusion. Hopefully successful. The words reared out of his subconscious and, much as he wanted to, he knew he couldn't entirely disregard them. What if Emma was in some way involved with students and drugs? Crazy as it seemed, absurd as it appeared, he had to keep an unbiased outlook. He couldn't go letting his inclinations and body rule his brain.

He showered, shaved, dressed, and made a pot of strong coffee. With a steaming cup in his hands, he went onto his veranda to admire a bright new morning sliding in over the mirror-still lake. A familiar gossamer mist was rising off the calm water, the first rays of the sun peeking over the rim of the mountains turning it to a veil of transparent gold. He drew a deep breath and wished he were free to enjoy this fantastic place with Emma. He leaned pensively against a verandah post, watching a pair of loons cavorting and hooting happily just beyond the dock.

Some birds have all the luck.

His cell vibrated against his hip. He pulled it out, snapped it open, and groaned. The Professor.

"Frasier?" His supervisor's authoritative voice brought him up straight.

"Good morning, sir."

"How are you making out with that woman? Convinced her to leave yet?"

"No, sir, actually I haven't. But I don't think she poses any threat to our project." *Man, now he was lying to his boss.*

"I'm not so sure. I need to meet with you to discuss strategies. She could be in serious danger when you close in on those Eastern Panthers."

"I've had no evidence of their presence, sir, not for some time. I'm wondering if they've moved on to safer territory. They may have spotted me."

"I don't think so, Frasier. You've been doing a good job, in spite of that woman. I'm confident they're still in the area. Now to the point of this call. I need you to come to Fredericton today for a meeting. The Project Executive has gathered and wants responses to questions I can't answer without you to back me up."

"Fredericton! But, sir, that would mean leaving Emma...Miss Prescott...alone here at the lake. I hardly think that's a good idea."

"Don't worry. I'll see to it that one of the rangers keeps an eye on her. She'll be perfectly safe. Furthermore," he continued, his tone brooking no refusal, "your coming to Fredericton is an order, not a request, understood?"

"Understood." The word was a reluctant compliance. I'll leave right away...sir."

****

"Emma."

An hour later he knocked at Emma's door. "Emma, I've been called to Fredericton. May I leave Scout with you?"

"Coming, coming. It's Saturday, by the way. Counselors' sleep-in day." He heard her voice from the back of the cabin. Shortly she opened the door, wearing a pink, knee-length flannel nightshirt with two bears hugging on its front. Her hair was tousled, her feet bare. His breath clumped in his throat.

"You're leaving?" She looked up at him, rubbing

158

sleep from her eyes.

"Meetings at the university. I won't be back until Monday around noon. I was going to leave Scout with you for protection, but on second thought I believe it would be better if you moved into town while I'm gone. Can you stay with a friend?" The Professor's promise of a ranger's protection hadn't assured him of Emma's safety.

"Frasier, I'll be perfectly okay. And I'll be happy to babysit Scout. No need to find an excuse for leaving him with me."

"Emma, I'm serious. I don't think you should stay up here alone."

"Go." She made shooing motions with her hands. "Come in, Scout. You're just in time for breakfast."

As the big Shepherd followed her inside, she planted a quick kiss on Frasier's lips.

"Safe journey," she said, and vanished into her cabin.

Hell and damnation! He headed toward his SUV. He knew the Professor would have someone watching out for Emma; still, he felt a long way from comfortable at leaving her.

"Call me if anything strange happens," he called back. "You have my cell number."

"Go!"

****

A desire for a coffee for the road hit when he drove into Carleton. The sandwich shop displayed the "open" sign in its window. He pulled into a parking space and strode inside.

"Good morning, Professor MacKenzie." Mildred Carter joined him at the counter while he waited for his coffee. "You're away from Loon Lake early on a Saturday morning. I would have thought you'd be spending Emma's time off with her."

The snide implication in her words made Frasier turn to face her, annoyance muddying his mood.

"Miss Prescott is my neighbor. We don't plan our days around each other's activities."

"Really? You chaperoned our dance last night with her, didn't you? And school rumor has it you recently shared a romantic lunch at Pine Lodge."

"We're friends. Now if you'll excuse me—"

He picked up his coffee, dropped payment on the counter, and started to turn away.

"Be careful, Professor." She caught him by the arm. "Emma Prescott may not be what you think she is."

Vindictive, jealous wench. Nevertheless there's an opportunity here.

"What do you mean, Miss Carter? Is there something about Emma Prescott I should know?"

"Not for me to say." She stuck out her chin and shrugged. "It wouldn't do any good anyway. Once Emma gets her hooks into a man, they become deaf, dumb, and blind to reason."

The waitress placed Mildred's coffee and muffin on the counter, and Frasier dug in his pocket and shoved a bill across to the other side in payment.

"My treat." He smiled down at her. Her prim lips loosened as she flushed. *Apparently I can still charm some women.* "Let's take a seat, and you can tell me all about the infamies of Emma Prescott."

"Well..." She let him guide her to a booth near the front of the restaurant. The place was empty except for themselves and the waitress, who'd retreated into the back. "On the surface, Emma is all sunshine and flowers. But she's had way too many men friends and is way too friendly with the dark element of the student population for my taste."

"Isn't dealing with troubled students a big part of her job?" Hating himself, he sat down across from her. He didn't want to hear anything negative about Emma.

"Of course. But she often spends her noon hours

with them and remains later than any other teacher after the final bell. When she and Brock Kelly were an item, well, we knew what was going on. After that affair ended, one could only suspect what she was up to. And poor Mr. Worth, our English literature teacher! Broke his heart and never even paused to look back. Why, when I offered her and that ugly little dog of hers a place to stay, she wouldn't even invite him and Mr. Kelly over to dinner. She was afraid that seeing us together Mr. Worth would realize I was the woman for him, not some flighty girl with eyes for a big, dumb, muscle-bound creature like that gym teacher!"

"You and Mr. Worth have a lot more in common than he and Emma?"

"Oh, my, yes. Mr. Worth and I have a deep appreciation for Lord Byron. Do you know what she fancies? The poems and songs of that alcoholic Scot Robert Burns. Why, Professor, some of his works are enough to make any decent woman blush! Promise me you'll be very careful around Emma Prescott. You'd be an easy target for her, living way up at Loon Lake all alone."

"Actually, it's Associate Professor." He picked up his coffee and stood. "Thanks for your time, Miss Carter. And your warning."

Man, that woman has a venomous tongue! He strode out of the restaurant and climbed back into his SUV, slamming the door harder than necessary.

****

Emma shoved The Sound's CD into her stereo, cranked it up, and, gyrating to the beat, began to clean her cabin. When Frasier's voice came in to back up Larry Hadlen's, she paused in her dusting, a dreamy smile sliding across her features.

"Isn't he great, Bruise!" she yelled to the little dog sitting beside Scout on the couch. "And he lives right next door! How lucky is that!"

A loud knocked startled her. She whirled to see a man in a forestry uniform peering in through the screen. She crossed the room, turned off the music, and smiled at the visitor.

"Come in, Officer," she called. "It's not locked."

"'Morning, miss." The man pulled off his hat and stepped inside. "Beautiful morning, isn't it?"

"Sure is. Would you like a coffee? I just made a fresh pot."

"Thanks, but I can't stay. I'm just making my rounds, warning campers of a big, rogue bear that's roaming the area. Seems he's attacked a dog and chased a hiker. They don't often behave that way, so we figure this one may be sick, possibly rabies. We're asking everyone to evacuate the region around Loon Lake until we can capture him. I can help you pack up, if you'd like."

"Thanks for your concern, Officer, but we'll stay." Emma flashed him a smile. "We've got good sturdy doors and windows, and I'll be vigilant when I go outdoors. Just keep me posted, will you? Let me know when you've gotten the situation under control."

"But, miss, I really must insist. If you're worried about finding a place to stay, I know a decent motel up on the highway that accepts dogs. And," he continued, "these guys," he indicated Bruiser and Scout, "will have to go outdoors from time to time. I'm sure you don't want to risk their safety."

"Well..." Emma looked at the pair on the couch, gazing over at her with wide, trusting eyes. "When you put it that way... Okay, give me a minute to pack."

"Allow me to help."

****

Emma lay on the bed in the motel room and flipped idly through the pages of a magazine. She was bored, and she longed to be back in her cabin

162

where she could work on her files, clean house, and enjoy the beauty and tranquility of Loon Lake.

Her mind wandered back to the ranger's visit and his insistence on her leaving. Rabies. She hadn't heard of a case in the area for years. She turned to her laptop beside her on the bed. Google search. Rabies. Loon Lake region.

Ten minutes later Emma was in her car, the dogs in the rear seat, headed back to Loon Lake. As near as she'd been able to ascertain, there hadn't been a reported case of rabies in the area in nearly two years, and never among regional bears. She found it difficult to believe that the Department of Natural Resources had seen fit to evacuate the entire area because of a single suspicious case. Something definitely didn't smell right about the situation, and she was going to find out why.

****

She braked to a stop close to the front steps of her cabin and paused to peruse the area. Nothing suspicious that she could see.

"Stay," she ordered the two dogs in the back seat, then eased herself out of the vehicle, shutting the door behind her. Again, she scanned the clearing. She started up the steps, keeping a watchful eye for anything that might signal trouble or danger of any kind. With the car parked at the foot of the steps, she could make a dash back into it at the first indication of a problem.

She tried the door. Locked as she'd left it. She inserted the key, turned it and opened the door, and stepped apprehensively inside. During her drive back to Loon Lake, she'd grown more and more suspicious of the man who'd identified himself as a forest ranger. She'd trusted him on his uniform alone and hadn't asked for ID. Not a wise move. Anyone could fake or steal one of those getups. The more she thought about it, the more implausible the rabid bear story had become.

Gingerly she began to inspect the cabin for signs of anyone having been inside. The door might have been locked, but she knew keys could be stolen, copied, and used. She'd never been overly careful with hers, not even around the school.

Just when she was feeling reassured that everything was in order and that she'd been paranoid, she saw it. Her stack of CDs weren't in the same place. Thinking about fingerprints, she went into her bedroom, took out a pair of gloves, pulled them on, and examined the collection.

She searched through them, trying to handle the cases as little as possible. A third of the way through, she stopped, puzzled. She flipped through the CDs again, this time looking for something specific. They definitely weren't there...her two CDs by The Sound.

Puzzled, and with an eerie feeling of having had her personal space violated, she sat down beside the stereo, an unpleasant quiver invading her stomach. She remembered the Goldilocks fairy tale. She arose and tiptoed toward the bedrooms and was relived to see whoever he or they had been, they weren't sleeping in either of her beds.

She pulled her cell from her pocket and started to dial Frasier's number. Then she paused. What if he'd taken her CDs? He'd made it clear he didn't want any reminders of his days with the band.

She dropped the cell onto the coffee table and went to let the dogs out of the car. She would allow them only a quick run before shutting them up in the cabin with her, just in case that ranger had been genuine and there really was a very sick bear wandering around nearby.

****

Frasier found his mind wandering in the meetings that weekend as he waited for his cell to vibrate against his hip. Several times the Professor had to bring him back to the moment with a sharp remark. He was relieved when the conference ended on Monday morning and he could head back to Loon Lake.

He was passing through Carleton when his phone finally did ring. He pulled into the supermarket parking lot and answered.

"Frasier?" Emma's voice. "Where are you?"

"In Carleton. Are you okay?"

"Yes...well, sort of. Will you drop by the high school? It's important. I'll explain when you get here."

****

Ten minutes later, Frasier entered the principal's office at the high school. Emma and Jesse Jones occupied chairs in front a big man seated behind a cluttered walnut desk. The expressions on all three faces were grim.

"Frasier." The relief in Emma's voice told him something serious was underway. She got up quickly and went to draw him into the room, toward the desk and the man behind it.

"Frasier, this is our principal, Thomas Pentland. Mr. Pentland, this is Frasier MacKenzie, the man I was telling you about. He's my neighbor up at Loon Lake, a biologist working on a research project for the University of New Brunswick."

"Professor MacKenzie, good of you to come." The man arose and extended a hand.

"Associate Professor." Frasier modified the title as he shook hands. "No problem, Mr. Pentland. I was passing through town when Emma—Miss Prescott—called. What's this all about?"

"Take a seat." The principal indicated a third chair in front of his desk and sat down again as Frasier accepted his offer.

"Now." The principal steepled his fingers. He

was a tall, balding man with broad shoulders and a protruding belly. A former athlete losing muscle tone, Frasier decided. "Some serious charges have been laid. Miss Prescott believes you may be able to shed some light on them."

"Certainly, if I can." Frasier glanced over at Emma. Her expression reflected tension and distress.

"Miss Prescott claims she gave Jesse here two thousand dollars in cash to purchase sports equipment for the school. Jesse says the only money Miss Prescott gave him was a couple of hundred to purchase marijuana for a bachelorette party she hosted up at her cabin. Which story can you support?"

The accusations hit Frasier like hailstones. He glanced from the apparently complacent principal to the sneering teenager to Emma. Suddenly he knew how Jesse had gotten Penny released. Aside from agreeing to keep his mouth shut, he'd handed over Emma's two thousand dollars.

"First, let me say the charge against Miss Prescott is so ridiculous as to defy addressing." He drew himself up in his chair and spoke with authority. "I saw Emma...Miss Prescott...give this young man a thick roll of bills on October fourth when I came to pick her up for lunch. As I opened her office door, I overheard her explaining to him that he was to purchase sports equipment with it, that she and the students had worked hard to raise the cash, that he was to get the best deals possible, and bring back receipts. I don't know the exact amount, but from the size of the roll, it could easily have been two thousand dollars in twenties."

"What do you say to that, Jesse?" The principal looked calmly over at the teenager, but his hazel eyes behind steel-rimmed glasses were penetrating.

"He's lyin'." Jesse stared at the floor. "He's

playin' house with her up at the lake. He'd say anything not to lose his main squeeze. Hey, he even tried to buy a few joints off me at the dance last Friday night, and then threw me out when I said I didn't have any."

"Jesse!" His name was a shocked gasp from Emma. "You know very well Mr. MacKenzie did no such thing!"

"I have to believe Miss Prescott and Mr. MacKenzie, Jesse." The principal drew himself up in his chair with a sigh. "I can't envision an associate professor from the University of New Brunswick attempting to buy drugs from a student at a high school dance. I also believe Miss Prescott gave you a substantial sum of money to purchase sports supplies. What you did with it I have no idea. Therefore, I see no other solution than to suspend you. I'll discuss the duration with the superintendent."

"Great! Just great! This place sucks anyway!" Jesse flung back his chair as he bolted to his feet. "Happy hunting! You'll never find proof that I did anything wrong! It's them who should be gettin' the boot! She had a big drug party up at her cabin last month! She even had a male stripper...just ask her!"

He stormed out, slamming the door behind him.

"Well." Principal Pentland drew a deep breath and leaned back in his chair. "I wonder how many more crashes that poor old door can weather."

A twinkle brightened the man's eyes.

"Quite a party, was it, Emma?" Thomas Pentland stretched as he sucked in a deep breath. "Gave Mandy a proper sendoff, did you? Good. She's a fine teacher who works hard and deserves some fun. By the way, my wife enjoyed the shindig immensely. She needed a night away from the kids. She described Mr. Roc Hard and his performance in some detail, but I can't recall her mentioning any pot being involved."

He grinned over at Frasier. Associate Professor
MacKenzie relaxed and grinned in return. But how
did Jesse know about the stripper, he wondered,
unless the drug dealers, those peeping toms, and the
kids at the school were somehow connected.

"If there's nothing more, I'll be going." Frasier
stood. "I've been away for a couple of days. I'd like to
get home."

"Of course. Thanks for coming in." Thomas
Pentland got up and extended his hand. "I knew
Jesse's accusations were false, but I had to give him
a hearing. I only wish Emma and I could come up
with a solution to that boy's problems. We'll meet
with the superintendent this afternoon, Emma, and
get his opinion. Wish us luck, Associate Professor
MacKenzie."

****

"Emma, check and see if Penny is in class."
Frasier caught her by the arm after they'd left the
principal's office. "That kid was definitely under
duress."

She nodded and hurried away.

Five minutes later she was back.

"She's in class, but she's white as death. Maybe
they threatened to abduct her again if Jesse didn't
do as they instructed."

"Keep an eye on her, but I'm sure she'll be okay.
Jesse obviously did exactly as he was told."

"Oh, Frasier, those poor kids! What a mess
they're in."

"Don't worry. They've got us on their side. Now
what about Scout and the Pug? Do I pick them up at
Doggie Day Care?"

"No, they're both in my cabin up at the lake. You
said you'd be home this morning."

"Fine. I'll head up there and let them out for a
run. Thanks for looking after my boy while I was

away."

"Frasier, don't try to con me. You left Scout with me as protection." She looked up at him and smiled. "I appreciate your caring. Really I do. Maybe you were right to be concerned. A curious thing happened up at the lake while you were gone. I'll tell you all about it tonight."

She gave him a quick kiss on the cheek and hurried off down the corridor.

What had gone on in his absence? Had the professor made a not-too-subtle attempt to get rid of Emma on his own?

****

Frasier waited in his SUV until he thought Emma had had time to return to her office. Then he got out and went back into the school.

"May I see Principal Pentland?" he asked the secretary.

"Just a minute, I'll check." He could see she was puzzled as she went to the door behind her desk, knocked, then stepped inside, closing it after her.

Wondering why I'm back so soon, I guess.

She emerged from the inner office. "You can go right in, Mr. MacKenzie."

"Thank you." Frasier furnished her with a smile. She blushed and lowered her gaze.

He wished he had that effect on Emma Prescott.

"Associate Professor MacKenzie." Thomas Pentland indicated a chair in front of his desk. "Didn't expect you back so soon. What can I do for you?"

"What do you know about the fire at Emma's apartment last month?" he asked, taking the proffered seat.

"Not much, but the fire marshal did say it was of a suspicious nature. His findings were in the local newspaper. Emma chose to ignore the implications. She's a trusting young woman, as you no doubt have come to understand." He spread his hands in a gesture of resignation. "Don't get me wrong. I admire trusting people. I just wish Emma would be a little less so, with some of these students."

"So you think maybe Todd Stoddart or some of his drug-involved friends might have torched Emma's apartment?"

"That's too serious an accusation to make without sufficient proof, but, between you and me, I believe it's highly possible. I was relieved when Emma chose to move out to Loon Lake. At least there she's far enough away to keep most of that crowd from bothering her on a regular basis." He looked over at Frasier, and his lips tightened. "Frasier, I'd be grateful if you'd keep an eye on Emma. She's a special woman, not to mention a good friend to both my wife and myself. We worry about her."

"No problem. I've been trying to do just that, but she doesn't make it easy. She's like a butterfly, never staying put very long." Frasier arose to leave.

"And just as pretty?" Thomas Pentland looked over at him, his eyes twinkling.

"And just as pretty." Frasier grinned over at him and extended his hand. "I'll do everything I can to keep her safe...short of putting her in a cage."

****

"Mr. MacKenzie?" A tall, thin man wearing thick glasses and clutching an armful of books stopped him when he stepped out into the corridor. The books were held tight with one arm against a sweater vest worn over a white shirt while the other hand nervously smoothed wisps back from the man's receding hairline.

"Yes?" Frasier paused.

"I'd like to talk to you...about Emma." He swallowed, his Adam's apple bobbing in his thin neck. "We could go to the cafeteria. It should be

170

empty just now."

"I don't know that we should be discussing the lady." Frasier had to stifle his desire to learn more about Emma. It wouldn't make him appear much of a gentleman if he appeared too eager to gossip about her. But he did want to hear what this man had to say.

"Please. It involves her safety. Oh, I forgot to introduce myself. I'm Brandon Worth, one of the English literature teachers here at Carleton High. Emma and I have been...colleagues for several years."

"Very well, Mr. Worth. Lead the way."

When they were seated in the deserted cafeteria, Brandon Worth deposited his books on the table between them, took off his glasses, and began to polish them.

"Mr. Worth, if this interview is making you nervous..." Frasier had to make the opening statement.

"Yes, yes, it is, but I feel I'd be less than fair to Emma if I didn't talk to you. She's a wonderful woman, Mr. MacKenzie...or is it Associate Professor MacKenzie?"

" 'Frasier' will do just fine. Please. Continue."

"Well, Emma and I have been friends for several years. Just friends, mind you. She's much too wonderful to be romantically involved with me. She and I share an enjoyment of the romantic poets. Sometimes, when we both had a few spare minutes, we'd come down here when the room was empty, and I'd read to her." He hesitated, then continued, looking down at his hands and blushing, "Believe it or not, I do read poetry rather well. At least Emma said so."

"I believe you must. Emma isn't a lady who throws around false compliments."

"No, she isn't." He paused, a wistful smile

171

drifting over his features.

"You said you wanted to talk to me about something involving her safety." Frasier brought him out of his reverie. He understood how a man could easily get lost in thoughts of Emma Prescott.

"Ah, yes." Brandon Worth blinked and looked over at Frasier. "Getting back to the business at hand. Emma is a really good woman. She works hard here at the school trying to help troubled students, some of whom, in my opinion, are well beyond anything she can do for them, no matter how much effort she puts into it or how optimistic her outlook. Worse still, some are downright dangerous."

"You're referring to...?"

"Jesse Jones and Todd Stoddart. Well, mostly Todd Stoddart. I believe he's involved with a serious criminal element in the area, by whom Emma's efforts to stop drugs in the school aren't welcomed. While she was living in town, she had the police nearby in case of an incident, but way up at Loon Lake..."

"I understand your concern, Mr. Worth. Trust me, I'll keep a sharp eye out for any suspicious activity. I admire Emma, too, and wouldn't want to see her come to any harm."

"Well, then, good." Brandon Worth gathered up his books and stood. "Thank you, Associate Professor."

He started to lead the way to the door, then paused and turned back to face Frasier.

"They call you the hermit of Loon Lake." He looked squarely into Frasier's eyes. "Does that mean you've abandoned interest in women?"

"No, Mr. Worth, it most certainly does not. Currently my work requires that I live alone and undisturbed, but I assure you I have a healthy interest in the opposite sex."

"What about Emma?" He shifted his feet but

didn't lower his gaze. *It's taking all his courage to face me about her. Poor guy. He really cares. Is there a single guy on the planet who hasn't got the hots for Emma Prescott?*

"Emma and I are friends. As I've told you, Mr. Worth, the nature of my work requires I remain dedicated to it."

"Fine." He lowered his penetrating gaze while he readjusted his books. "You're an attractive man, Associate Professor, and, I would venture to guess, a worldly one. You just might be the type that could seriously interest Emma. I wouldn't want to see her hurt if you weren't about to honor any commitment you may have led her to believe existed."

"I appreciate your concern." Frasier extended his hand. "You can feel confident I will never do anything that won't be in her best interests. I will take special care to make certain no harm comes to her...from any quarter."

Brandon Worth hesitated only a moment before grasping Frasier's hand. "Thank you, Associate Professor." He shook it vigorously. "You're a gentleman as well as a scholar. I feel much better now that we've had this talk."

On his way out of town, Frasier remembered a bookstore beside the sandwich shop on Main Street. He parked and went inside. When he left fifteen minutes later, he carried a volume entitled *Songs and Poetry of Scotland: Robert Burns* in a brown paper bag.

Poor Brandon Worth, reading her romantic poetry when she really loved the earthier works of a Scotsman. She'd probably been too kind to tell him the difference.

"Frasier MacKenzie?" Her voice made him turn to face a pretty redhead in jeans and a rust-colored sweater that set off large brown eyes.

"Yes?"

"I thought so, when I saw you get out of your SUV. I felt reasonably sure it was the one Emma told me about. I'm Mandy Cooper." She extended her hand.

"The lady of the antebellum wedding." He accepted her introduction and smiled. "A pleasure, Mrs. Cooper."

"Just Mandy, please. Professor MacKenzie, do you have a minute? There's a coffee bar at the back of the shop. I'd like a few words with you."

"Certainly." He let her lead the way to the rear of the store. While she took a seat in a booth in a corner, he ordered two coffees.

"Thanks." She smiled up at him when he rejoined her. *Jeff Cooper is one lucky man.*

"I want to talk to you about Emma."

"I guessed." Didn't everyone! But still another prime opportunity to learn more about the lady at Loon Lake had just fallen into his lap. "What did you want to say, Mrs. Cooper?"

"Mandy. Well, I've known Emma for a very long time, ever since she and her family came down here for vacations when she was a child. She's a wonderful person...bright, generous, funny, loving, trusting, and a whole lot more adjectives I can't even come up with at the moment. When she's dedicated to anything, she gives her all to it. That's why..."

"That's why...?" He urged her gently on when she paused.

"That's why I don't want to see her hurt."

"What makes you think she's going to be hurt? And by whom?"

"I'm afraid she's going to get hurt by you, Professor MacKenzie." Her brown-eyed gaze met his, full force. For all her delicate beauty, Mandy Cooper was not a woman to be trifled with.

"We're just friends." A sudden constriction wrapped around his chest. "I don't know why you'd have any reason to think—"

"Because..." She looked down at her hands. "I've known men like you."

The tightness worsened. "You have?"

"Yes." She raised those penetrating brown eyes. She spoke with conviction. "I have. Men who put their work ahead of everything else, even that one all-important personal relationship that could change their lives. Professor MacKenzie, don't let that happen to you. Emma is a wonderful woman. You'll never again find her equal."

"Thank you." He stood. He had to escape her innuendoes. "I promise I'll consider what you've said. I also promise that I'll do everything in my power to see to it that Emma Prescott doesn't get hurt...at least not where I'm concerned." He extended his hand. "It's been a pleasure, Mandy. Oh, by the way." He turned back. "Why didn't Emma go to live with you when she left Loon Lake? Why would she choose to move in with Mildred Carter?"

"Because of Bruiser's feather allergy. I have a cockatoo."

"Ah, yes, the feather allergy." The partridge incident flooded back.

"Pretty severe. Do you have any suggestions, Associate Professor? I understand you're a biologist."

"A biologist, yes. A vet, no. By the way, my name is Frasier."

"Okay, Frasier." She got up and faced him squarely. "Just one more thing. Emma is an expert at reading body language. She has to be, in her line of work. What she's reading in yours isn't disinterest."

"So this is a heads-up about my blatant male interest in your friend and a warning to tone it down?"

"Definitely, if you're truly not interested. But if you aren't, you're a truly exceptional man, Frasier

MacKenzie."

"I've been well informed I'm not the first man in her life."

"I don't like what you seem to be implying." Mandy's dark eyes suddenly flashed. "Emma is a truly old-fashioned girl. One night stands and purely physical attractions aren't for her. She's got a lot of romantic notions about heroes and happily ever after. She just hasn't found the man of her dreams...yet."

Her tone moderating, she gave him a sly wink. "I wonder if you'll be the one who finally sweeps Miss Emma off her feet. Be warned, if you are. Your life will never be the same again. Good afternoon, Associate Professor."

A smug smile on her lips, she turned and sashayed out of the store.

Ah, man! More confusion.

Back in his SUV, he took the book he'd purchased from its bag and turned it over in his hands. What was he doing? And just exactly what had Mandy Cooper meant, that she'd known men like him? A sardonic grin quirked up the corner of his mouth. It couldn't be. But maybe it was. Damn. He had to decide, and soon. He laid the book on the seat and turned the key in the ignition.

While Frasier drove out toward Loon Lake, he pondered what Thomas Pentland had told him. What he'd learned from the principal bothered him. Was Emma involved with her students in some way that made her a risk to them? What wasn't she telling him? And all that money. Could anyone be so trusting as to hand over two thousand dollars to a student with a shaky reputation? But, most of all, what had happened at Loon Lake over the weekend? Had drug pushers been involved?

Drug pushers. The term sent a red haze of anger washing over him. One of them had murdered Larry as surely as if he'd stuck a knife in him. He flashed back to memories of the good days with the band, when every concert had been a wild adrenalin burst of energy and excitement. He remembered the roaring crowds, the late nights, sleeping on busses, never enough clean clothes, fast food that had eventually given him acid reflux.

He grimaced as his recollections grew darker. Larry popping more and more pills, getting more and more moody, paranoid, unpredictable, forgetting lyrics, storming off stage in the middle of a concert, being forced to fill in. Larry yelling at him, taking a swing at him when he'd tried to get the bottle of tablets away from him. Larry lying dead across a hotel room bed in a puddle of vomit. Larry, who'd been his best friend.

He banged his fist on the wheel and flinched. *Damn it, damn it, damn it.* Now a lady he was starting to feel a whole bunch of stuff for looked bad. He didn't need this, not any of it. Maybe if he weighed her pros and cons he'd see the light, realize she wasn't worth the anguish she was causing him.

Okay, first the pros. The lady at Loon Lake was clever, resourceful, kind, generous, funny, and brave, sometimes to the point of ridiculous. He couldn't remember spending a single dull moment with Emma. She was also a great cook and loved animals. Somehow the fact that she was drop-dead gorgeous had fallen to the end of the list, now that he knew her.

Now to the cons. He thought hard. Well, she did drive like a Nascar contestant, and she couldn't swim or carry a tune. Then nothing. He couldn't come up with any more cons, no matter how he racked his brain.

Damn it, no wonder everyone loves Emma Prescott, from muscle-bound hulks like Brock Kelly to bookishly mild Brandon Worth to Nigel whoever-he-

was, male stripper. Where do I fit in? Or do I? Or am I just slated to be Mr. October?

He reached the point where he had to leave the highway for the secondary road to Loon Lake. Traffic was light to non-existent along the upcoming stretch of chip seal. *Time to call for assistance.* He pulled out his cell and punched in a number.

"Scott?" he responded to the voice that answered. "Yeah, it's me. How's everything?"

"Great. Fine. Haven't heard from you in a while, little brother. What's up? The old man finally loosen your reins?" His brother's friendly voice instantly made him feel better.

"No, nothing like that. You know what he's like. Anyhow, I'm not calling you about him. I need some advice in the romance department."

"You? The rock star? You're asking me, the mild-mannered cardiologist, for advice?"

"Come on, Scott. You know that's all in the past."

"Sorry. I forgot that era ended on a painful note. What can I do for you? Remembering, of course, I'm no expert."

"You have Jenny. You're going to marry her. I'd say that qualifies you as at least a minor authority. And you are a heart specialist."

"When you put it like that, I guess maybe I am. It's not every guy who could land a terrific woman like Jenny. Okay, let me have it. How can I help?"

"There's this lady who came to live in the second cabin at Loon Lake."

"Ah ha! Hit the hermit a blow in the sexual plexus and thickened the plot, did she?"

"That's pretty much the bare bones of the situation."

"And the old man wants you clear of personal involvement for the duration of the project?"

"Right. But now it looks as if she may be

involved."

"In the project? Damn. What's your gut feeling?"

"That she couldn't possibly be."

"Then go with your instincts. You always were astute in that department."

"But I can't get involved with her now...she shouldn't even be at the lake."

"Well, then, you'll have to get rid of her."

"Hey, I've tried! Believe me, I've tried. Even made a total fool of myself in the process."

"Okay. If you can't get rid of her, you'll just have to try to keep her safe...and interested...until the project wraps up." There was no response. "Frasier, are you there?"

"Yeah, yeah. You're right. But keeping her safe and interested, not to mention clearing her of any involvement, won't be easy."

"It never is. I chased Jenny all the way to Australia, remember? But, let me tell you, little brother, it's been well worth the effort. Now she's shopping for a wedding dress, and Mom is visualizing a granddaughter. Living with four men hasn't been easy for her, you know. I'm thinking whichever one of us gives her a little girl will go right to the top of her maternal charts."

"As usual, you'll get there first."

"Sibling rivalry? Frasier, I'm disappointed."

"Sorry, Scott."

"Now about this lady...what's her name, by the way?"

"Emma. Emma Prescott."

"Emma. Nice, old-fashioned name. What are your intentions toward Miss Emma?"

"That's part of the problem...a big part. I don't know. Sometimes she and her crazy little dog irritate me to the bone. At other times I'm attracted to her like iron filings to a magnet. When she's not around, I find myself waiting for her to come back like there's no tomorrow. When she does, it's like Christmas morning when I was seven."

"Serious stuff."

"Could be. Maybe. I guess."

"Scared?" Scott laughed.

"No...yes."

"Man, you've got it bad. Keep her in your sights. When the project ends, go for it."

"You think?"

"I know."

"You would. Thanks, brother. I'll be in touch."

Frasier punched End as he slowed to turn into the trail leading to the cabins. He was humming "Annie's Song."

****

He was sitting on his top step with the dogs when Emma arrived home from school that afternoon. As the Pug and Scout rushed to greet her, he got up and forced himself to come down the steps at a more reserved pace even though, had he been as uninhibited as the dogs, he would have rushed to meet her.

"Frasier, hi." She got out of her vehicle, smiled at him, and the overcast day brightened. His brother had been right. He did have it bad.

"Emma, I need to talk to you." He stifled the return smile threatening to curl up his lips and spoke seriously. "What exactly happened while I was away?"

"Nothing much. A ranger arrived to tell me I had to take the dogs and move to a motel because they'd discovered a rabid bear in the vicinity."

"What? Are you serious?" Frasier stared down at her. The professor was scraping the bottom of his barrel of tricks with this one.

"Yeah." She started up the steps to her cabin. "But no big deal. I only stayed away a couple of hours before I decided that was no real reason to deny myself a great weekend here at the lake."

"Then what happened?" He followed her inside.

She kicked off her shoes, and shrugged. "Nothing much. No bear, peaceful couple of days. Guess he decided to stay away. Or got caught by a ranger."

"No one around when you came back?"

"No, Frasier, I didn't see man or beast all weekend." She looked quizzically up at him. "You sound concerned. Is there some reason why you should be? Some reason I'm not aware of?"

"No, no." He backed toward the door. "Just puzzled, that's all."

"Actually, me, too. I've never heard of an entire area being evacuated because of the very slim chance of a rabies threat. Warning residents, yes. Ordering them from their homes, no. Maybe I should call the Department of Natural Resources and check up on that ranger. I probably should have done it immediately, but I didn't think of it until now. Where's my phone?"

She picked up her purse and began digging through its contents.

"No!" Frasier's response was quick and abrupt. In two long strides he'd crossed the room and was grabbing it from her.

"Frasier, what's the matter with you?" She stared at him, her eyes wide.

"Nothing, nothing. It's just that I know most of the rangers. I wouldn't want to get any of them in trouble by calling to check on them."

"How can my inquiring about the validity of their visit possibly hurt them? Whoever he was, he was just doing his duty. Unless..." She stopped abruptly.

"Unless?"

"Unless he was bogus, unless he was trying to get me out of my cabin so he could rob both of us!

Frasier, was anything taken from your cabin?" She caught at his arm and looked up at him.

"No, nothing. You?"

"Nothing except..." She stopped.

"Except?"

"Well, if you must know, my two CDs of The Sound are gone."

"Nothing else missing?"

"Nothing. Crazy, right?"

"Well, not so crazy." He stared down at his sneakers and shuffled them. "I took them the last evening I was here. After Larry died, I destroyed all our CDs. Now I'm sorry. When I saw your copies, I had a sudden urge to play our songs again...when I was alone."

"No problem." She put a gentle hand on his arm. "Keep them. I understand. And," she continued, her tone lightening, "I'm relieved to know I didn't have an intruder. I bought us a couple of juicy steaks. Why don't you take the dogs for a run while I slip into something comfortable and start cooking?"

"Would love to, but I have to take another drive into the bush. I missed a couple of days. The Professor won't be happy if I let any more time elapse without a surveillance report. I'll be back in time for dinner, never fear. Scout, stay with Emma and the Pug."

He turned and strode out into the darkening afternoon.

Thank God Emma didn't ask for the return of those CDs. He recognized the Professor's work in their theft.

****

His drive took longer than he had anticipated. He returned to the cabin clearing using the ATV's headlights. As he pulled into the yard, he ground the machine to a halt and leaped to the ground.

"Dear God!" he choked.

Illuminated by her porch light, Emma stood on her front verandah, the Pug by her side, facing a snarling coyote the size of a German Shepherd dog. She brandished a barbecue lighter. From inside his cabin, Scout barked and howled but the coyote appeared undeterred.

The situation baffled him. Coyotes were generally reticent animals that avoided human contact. Striding toward them, he saw the white froth rimming the animal's snout. His gut knotted.

Sliding his hand inside his jacket, he closed cold fingers around the thirty-eight in his shoulder holster and eased it out. Heart hammering, he leveled the gun at the animal's head. When it crouched to spring he took a chance.

"Hey!" he yelled.

The coyote turned on him. With a gurgling snarl, it sprang. Frasier pulled the trigger. The animal died in mid-leap.

"Frasier!" Emma started to run to him but he waved her away.

"Take the Pug and get inside! This animal has rabies. I'll need to bag the body and take it to the DNR office in town."

"Frasier..."

"Emma, just do as I say, okay? We can argue later."

****

Three weary hours later Frasier drove up the rutted road to Loon Lake. Although the Department of Natural Resources people hadn't been able to definitely declare the coyote carcass rabid, they agreed it was highly likely.

What if he hadn't arrived when he did? What if the animal had gotten to Emma? Right now she could be desperately ill, maybe dying. A sick, hollow feeling encompassed him. Scott had been right. He had it bad. Worse still, right now there was nothing he could do about it.

He braked to a stop in front of his cabin. He'd disinfect, then join the most terrific woman he'd ever met.

****

"Emma, it's Frasier," he called when he reached her verandah. "I've cleaned up. You can let me in."

"Frasier, are you okay? I was so worried!" She threw open the door and caught him by an arm to draw him inside. "Did that coyote really have rabies?"

"Looks like it." He shrugged out of his jacket, comfortable to make himself at home in her cabin. "They'll run conclusive tests in the morning, but all signs point to it. I assume the Pug has had his rabies shots?"

"Of course. Scout?"

"Of course."

"Seems you're always rescuing me, Frasier MacKenzie," she said, softly, looking up at him with those resolve-melting emerald eyes.

"You did a fair job of lifesaving yourself, when I got shot." He let a slow grin curl his lips.

"Maybe we make a good team," she said her tone so warm and appealing Frasier repressed a groan. He wanted this woman like nothing he could remember.

"I didn't know you carried a gun," she said, her voice suddenly snapping to normal. "Is it really necessary?" She took a step away from him.

"Yes, it is. I'm on the trail of a large cat that can be dangerous. Now I'm starving. Any food left from that supper you promised, or did you feed it to our four-legged companions?"

"Definitely lots of food. I'll warm it up. Of course, the steaks won't be what they once were, before I found that coyote about to take them off the barbecue, but the potatoes and salad should be

184

decent. But about that gun... Wouldn't a hunting rifle be more appropriate?"

"I don't want to kill the Panther. A revolver blast would be enough to scare it off." He strode past her to stir up the embers in the fireplace. "Good Lord, woman, don't you ever clean out your ashes? Remind me tomorrow, and I'll do it." He wanted to get her off the subject of the gun.

"Regarding the gun, I'll accept your explanation for now, but I'm not convinced." She headed for the refrigerator. "Supper will be ready in a flash, my knight in the white SUV."

"Fine." He cleared his throat as he shoved aside the ashes to make way for firewood, relieved to have disposed of the gun issue so easily.

"But you know, Frasier MacKenzie, you're an amazing shot for an ex-rock star, present-day associate professor of biology."

Was this woman part fox terrier? Once she got a scent of something that interested her, she just wouldn't leave it alone.

"A hobby. Used to do skeet shooting with my dad when I was a teenager."

"Ah, ha! Sergeant Sam Steel of the Northwest Mounted. I should have guessed."

She began to set the table, and he returned to building a fire, hoping that this time she was satisfied with his explanation.

Chapter Six

"Ahoy, me hearties."

The following evening Frasier opened the door to find Emma wearing a white off-the-shoulder peasant blouse, wide black belt, and flowing, floor-length crimson skirt, a knapsack slung over her left shoulder. Her hair was tied back with a yellow kerchief, revealing the largest hoop gold earrings he'd ever seen. A black eye-mask covered the upper portion of her face. Under her right arm she carried Bruiser wearing a tiny tricorn, eye patch, and frock coat. A belt around his middle held a little plastic sword in a small scabbard.

"Trick or treat." Emma grinned.

"What...?" he began.

"Don't tell me you aren't aware it's Halloween?" She stepped past him as he continued to gaze slack-jawed at the pair.

"I did notice it's the end of the month," he said, staring in utter amazement at the pair. "But I never thought I'd get trick-or-treaters way up here."

"Well, ya do, matey. Now fork over your goodies, or I'll have to unleash my Dutch Mastiff. Fierce, Bruise, fierce!"

In response the Pug quivered his wide lips, showed a few overcrowded teeth, and let out something that sounded more like a grunt than a growl.

"Dutch Mastiff?" Frasier couldn't help grinning.

"Haven't you heard the legend of the Pug who saved the life of William the Silent of Holland in 1572? When William was surrounded by Spanish troops, his Pug cried and scratched and leaped into the face of the sleeping prince. He awakened him just in time."

"Now, that I can believe…annoying the daylights out of someone." Frasier chuckled as he took a box of dog biscuits from the cupboard.

"I'll have you know Pugs are amazingly courageous when the safety of someone they love is at stake." Emma threw back her shoulders indignantly.

"Sure. Moving on." He flipped a couple of biscuits to Scout and the Pug.

Man, Emma Prescott has to be the sexiest pirate wench ever.

"What's your pleasure, mistress?" Frasier left the pair of dogs munching contentedly and turned to her. *Don't stare, don't goggle.* "Coffee, tea, a beer?"

"Milk, if you've got it, kind sir." Emma placed the knapsack on the table and pulled it open. "I've brought cookies."

Frasier stared down at the plate of plastic-wrap-covered sugar cookies with jack o' lanterns at their centre.

"You baked these?" he asked.

"Right out of the frozen cookie dough section of the supermarket," she grinned, pulling off her mask. "My humble way of thanking you for saving Bruiser and me from that coyote." She smiled coyly. "Until maybe some day when I'm allowed a better way."

She sashayed off across the room to get glasses from the cupboard. He watched her go with a frustration level so high it would have blown the top off a thermometer if it had been mercury.

****

Ten minutes later they were seated at the table, the remains of tall glasses of cold milk and the cookies in front of them. Emma was telling a story about a wild major miscalculation she'd made early in her counseling career. Frasier was laughing harder than he could recall having laughed in months. This past summer if someone had told him he'd be having a great time over milk and cookies he'd have called them crazy.

Scout growled and jumped to his feet. He'd been lying in front of the fire with Bruiser. Now he stood, head lowered, hackles raised, staring at the door.

"What is it, boy?" Frasier swung toward the dog.

The door smashed open. Two men dressed in black and wearing ski masks burst into the room. One brandished a deer rifle, the second a baseball bat.

Accompanied by Scout's snarl, Frasier jolted to his feet.

"Stifle that dog if you want to keep him alive!" the rifleman ordered, pointing the gun at the German Shepherd.

"Scout, at ease," Frasier ordered. His adrenalin racing, he could barely restrain himself, never mind his dog.

"And, you, sit down!" the intruder bawled. "Sit down or I'll put you down."

Slowly Frasier obeyed.

"What do you want?" Out of the tail of his eye, Frasier could see Emma staring wide-eyed at the pair. *Don't challenge them, Emma, please don't!*

"We want you both gone from Loon Lake," the rifleman growled. "It's hunting season. You're scaring away game."

"We are not!" Emma bolted to her feet. "This is our home! We're not about to leave just so you can murder the local white-tailed deer population!"

"Emma, sit down!" Frasier hissed out of the corner of his mouth.

"I refuse to be driven from my home by a pair of backwoods bullies!" she snapped. "Now get out of here, both of you, before I call the RCMP and have

188

you arrested!"

"Emma!" Frasier felt a sick feeling welling up in his gut, a bilious sensation of terror for her safety. "Sit down!"

"That your dog?" The man pointed his gun at Bruiser who stood braced beside Scout muttering nasty Pug sounds.

"Yes." The word faltered from Emma's lips.

"Well, sit down and shut up, or he'll become a memory real fast."

Frasier saw Emma blanch, then sink back onto her chair. *Bastards.*

The bat wielder advanced slowly toward them. Mentally Frasier crouched. *If that guy makes a move toward Emma...*

The invader paused at the table and looked down at the remains of their snack. His dark eyes glistened. He drew the bat over his head with both hands and brought it down on the table. With a resounding crack, it snapped in two and crumbled, centre first, to the floor. Milk, cookies, plates, and glasses splattered and shattered, flying in every direction.

Emma's hands flew up to protect her face, Scout snarled, and Bruiser let out a strangled yelp.

"Shut those dogs up, MacKenzie, or it'll be their heads next time." The rifleman swung in the direction of the dogs.

"Scout, at ease. Pug, be quiet," Frasier ordered.

"Now you're being smart." The man turned and headed for the door. "Come on, buddy. I think they got the message."

The pair turned and vanished back out into the blackness of the Halloween night.

****

"Stay where you are!" Frasier ordered Emma as he bolted to the cupboard drawer. He yanked it open, grabbed the .38 and strode toward the door.

189

"Frasier, no! It's dark! You can't see them! And you're outnumbered!" Emma was instantly beside him, grabbing his arm. "Don't be crazy!"

"Just shutting the door," he reassured her. He closed it, slid the deadbolt into place, and drew a deep breath. "If I hadn't forgotten to lock it after you came in, I would have had major repair work to do."

"Frasier, do you keep that gun handy...always?" Emma released him and stared wide-eyed at the weapon in his hand.

"Is that your major concern? In case you've already forgotten, we were just threatened by a couple of masked men."

"Your responses with that weapon are beginning to get to me, that's all. You seem way too adept with it for a biologist, even one who was trained in firearms by a policeman father."

"We're living pretty much in isolation. It's only sensible to have protection and know how to use it."

"Do you also have condoms in that drawer?" She giggled wildly.

"Emma..." Her inane response startled him. She'd begun to shake. Not just tremble. Outright shake. Her teeth chattered.

"Emma!" He dropped the gun onto the counter and gathered her into his arms as she stood staring at the destroyed table, the remains of their Halloween snack scattered around it on the floor. "Emma, don't. It's over, and they won't be back. They're not stupid enough to try anything like that again."

"Frasier, I was terrified they'd shoot the dogs or beat you with that bat." Her words, muffled against his shoulder, tumbled out.

"Threats, nothing more," he muttered into her rainwater-soft, sweet-smelling hair with a lot more confidence than he felt. "No one's stupid enough to kill dogs or inflict serious bodily harm for the chance to bag a couple of deer. Anyhow, it was probably only a Halloween prank that got out of hand as a result of too many beers."

"You think?" She drew away and looked up, green eyes so innocently hopeful of reassurance he felt his heart lurch.

"Yeah, I think." He kissed her on the tip of the nose and forced a grin. "In fact, I know. Those guys stank of booze. But I also know you'll feel safer staying here tonight. You and the Pug can use the spare bedroom...again."

He released her and went to stow the gun in the drawer. He had to. He couldn't chastely hold a sweet, vulnerable Emma any longer.

"Okay." She forced a shaky smile. "Hope the neighbors don't gossip."

"Haven't yet met an indiscreet bear or bunny." He matched her teasing tone. "Come on. I'll lend you a T-shirt to sleep in."

She started to follow him into the bedroom, then stopped short.

"Frasier, one of them called you MacKenzie! They know you!"

"Not surprising." He turned back to face her astonished expression. "It's no secret. I've been living up here for a while. Remember, I am famous locally as the hermit at Loon Lake."

"I suppose that makes sense," she said slowly. "Do you have any idea who *they* were?"

"None." He shrugged and turned back toward the bedrooms.

"Frasier." She stopped him again. "What if one of them was the person who shot you? What if...?"

"Do you seriously think the person who confused me with a deer would show up on my doorstep after he's apparently gotten away with it? Come on, Emma. I know those guys aren't mental giants, but think about it."

191

"I suppose," she said doubtfully.

"Just try to put the whole thing out of your mind. Let's get that T-shirt. Do you want to take a hot shower? Might help you relax. You'll find clean towels on the bathroom shelf."

But as he headed into his bedroom, he wondered why the bat wielder hadn't spoken. Was it because he feared they'd recognize his voice? Was it because he perhaps had a distinct British accent? Maybe Nigel, alias Roc Hard, hadn't seen anyone running away from Emma's cabin. Maybe he'd invented the story to try to frighten her and possibly even Frasier away.

****

"Frasier?" She was tapping on his bedroom door. He hadn't been sleeping even though the dial on his clock radio indicated it was 1:33 a.m. The evening had left too many unanswered questions racing around in his mind.

"Yeah?" He rolled onto his back and hoped he wasn't about to hear the response he suspected.

"I can't sleep. Can I come in?"

"No!" He bolted from the bed and fumbled for his pajama pants. "Wait there. I'm coming out."

Damn, what does the woman think I'm made of? He couldn't imagine anything more resolve-shattering than a bed-tousled Emma, wearing only a too-large T-shirt, coming into his bedroom.

"I'm sorry, Frasier," she looked up at him apologetically when he stepped out of his bedroom pulling a sweatshirt over his head. "I thought I'd be okay, but I had this awful nightmare of those men shooting Bruiser and then Scout and then you and…"

"Okay, okay." He was relieved to see that she'd wrapped herself in a quilt. "I'll make some hot chocolate, and we'll sit up for a while. I wasn't enjoying a peaceful night's rest either."

192

Afterwards he wasn't quite sure how it began. He only remembered an impression of Emma suddenly with her arms about his neck, her lips on his, her warm body pushing him back into his room.

"Emma." He came up for air as the back of his legs hit the edge of his bed. "Emma, I..."

"Frasier MacKenzie, don't you dare say this isn't a good idea." Her hand slid up under his sweatshirt, over his chest, touching him with an intimacy that caused a fantastic flinch to shoot down his entire body.

"Kiss me, Frasier. Like you did before. Take my breath away. Make me forget what just happened."

Coming from Emma, soft and sensuous, the words sounded like the most erotic he'd ever heard. When her roaming hand slid lower, to the top of his pajama pants, where it released the tie, common sense and reason vanished. He covered her mouth with his in what he hoped was the best kiss he'd ever given.

As her soft, warm body melted into his, he reacted instantly and completely, but when he shifted his feet to pull his hips tighter against hers, his pants dropped and tangled around his ankles. In an effort to regain his balance, he staggered. Emma gave him a quick shove and he toppled onto the bed.

"Seems I've got you right where I want you, mister." In a shaft of moonlight, she gazed down at him, green eyes twinkling wickedly.

"Damn it, Emma." He struggled to sit up, but she pushed him back.

"Don't struggle, and I promise to be gentle." She pulled the pants from around his ankles. "Can't have you at a disadvantage, now can we?"

"Emma..." Words stuck in his throat as she pulled the T-shirt over her head. She stood in front of him, the most gorgeous woman he'd ever seen.

Tangling himself with the sudden desperation of

his effort, he sat up and struggled to pull the sweatshirt over his head.

"Let me help." Emma knelt on the bed beside him. The instant she'd pulled the shirt free, he had her in his arms and they were together in his bed— like he'd dreamed, only it was better, so much better, than he'd fantasized.

He kissed her lips, her neck, her shoulders, and on down to her breasts. His hands slid over hips as soft as silk. Her fingers in his hair held his mouth to her.

But when she moved to be on top, he pushed her back and took the position. She'd instigated their lovemaking. Now he'd show her it had been worth the effort.

As he positioned himself between her legs, she took him into her hands.

"Frasier, oh, my!" Emerald eyes opened wide in the moonlight. Then, "Oh, my!"

When he entered, when he made love to her with a sincerity he'd never before experienced, the tangled words and sounds of pleasure gasping from her lips told him he must be doing something right.

"Emma." Her name was an exhale as he climaxed. *Oh, my God!*

When he rolled away to gather her into his arms, a magnificent sense of peace and fulfillment enveloped him. This was what he'd been waiting for all his life, through those years of hard work and struggle. There'd been other women, but none to compare to his beautiful, smart, funny, bold Emma. He wanted to stay with her forever, to make love to her again and again.

With a sigh, she snuggled up against him, drew him into her arms, and settled her head on the pillow next to his.

"Emma." He breathed into her hair. Her reply was a soft sigh, then the gentle, regular breathing of sleep.

He planted a gentle kiss on her cheek. *Soft, warm, beyond-comparison Emma.* He wanted to hold her forever, to protect her forever. *To hell with the Professor.*

He slept.

He woke and rolled his shoulders like a contented feline. Something had left him feeling totally relaxed and mellow. Emma! Emma had made love with him. He rolled to his right. His bed was empty. *Damn, don't let the entire thing turn out to be a dream!*

"Emma?" He pulled himself to a sitting position and rubbed his eyes. "Emma!"

"Yes?" She appeared in the doorway in the pirate wench outfit she'd worn the previous night.

"Come here...please." He leaned back against the pillows and held out his arms. He couldn't wait to have her back in his bed, back in his arms. And this time he'd do the undressing.

"Frasier, I'm sorry. Last night was a mistake brought about by a near-death experience." Her words hit him like a whip lash. "You were right. You shouldn't get involved with me."

"Damn it, Emma! You can't push a man into his bedroom, pull off his clothes, make love to him, and then say it was a mistake! What kind of tease are you?" He jumped out of bed to stand beside it naked. "Or..." His words slowed and deepened as the thought struck him. "Today is November first. Was I just Mr. October?"

For a moment she stared at him. Then she drew a deep breath that made her breasts swell against the thin cotton of her blouse. "If that's what you think, Frasier MacKenzie, then I've made the right decision. I'm sorry I ever got carried away and made love with someone who thinks so little of me and my values."

She whirled and went out, banging the bedroom door shut behind her.

"Idiot!" he labeled himself. "Absolute idiot!"

****

"Frasier, let's be absolutely honest." She turned from making oatmeal at the stove to face him twenty minutes later when he came into the kitchen, fresh from a shower and shave.

Good. She's cooled down. "Okay." He leaned back against the counter and crossed his arms on his chest. "Let me have it."

"Okay." She heaved a deep sigh. "Last night showed we're both way too attracted to each other to cohabitate platonically in comfort. So until you're ready to be more than my friend, to make a commitment to our relationship, it's only sensible we keep our sleeping arrangements as separate as possible."

"Emma..."

"Oh, come on, Frasier!" She strode across the room to stand a foot in front him. "How much actual rest do you get when I'm sleeping over here? And don't even mention last night. It's not included. About as much as I got when you were injured and sleeping at my place, I bet. That isn't healthy for either of us. We've both got jobs that require us to be alert. We can't do them justice if we're running on sleep deprivation."

"You didn't sleep when I was staying at your cabin?" He felt a rush.

"No, I didn't. And last night was a perfect example of things getting out of hand before their time. So I'm moving home...alone."

They faced each other, the sexual tension between them so intense he felt it like an elastic band stretched to the snapping point.

"Damn it, Emma." He made a move to reach for her, but she ducked away and headed for the door.

"Not until you're ready to put me ahead of that big, elusive cat, Frasier MacKenzie. Come on, Bruiser. We're going home." At the door she paused and cast him a sly glance over her shoulder. "Enjoy the oatmeal. Oh, and by the way, you're definitely not Mr. October. You can fill up my entire calendar anytime."

****

"Frasier, I had a great idea." Emma only knocked once on his door before opening it and coming into his cabin the following evening.

"What might that be?" He looked up from the maps he'd been studying. "Didn't you put me on hold until I started placing you ahead of an Eastern Panther?"

"Frasier MacKenzie, you totally misinterpreted what I said. I was referring to our romantic relationship, not our friendship. Now do you want to hear my idea, or are you going to do your boring associate professor act?"

"Okay, let's have it. What's the idea?"

"We'll have jam sessions." She fetched his guitar from its place beside the fireplace and handed it to him. "You'll play and sing and I'll provide the backup vocal."

"You'll what?" He stared up at her.

"Provide the backup vocal...you know, like you used to do. I know all the songs you and your band used to play. Come on, it'll be fun. Bruise and I will dance."

"Okay." He heaved a sigh and strummed a chord. Trying to change any idea Emma had was like trying to change the weather.

****

Emma was singing and dancing around the room with a happily howling Bruiser in her arms while Frasier belted out rock classic, his sock feet tapping time on the hardwood floor, when a knock sounded on the door. It hadn't been easy, watching Emma gyrate around in front of him, but he knew making any romantic overtures to her now would be exactly the wrong thing to do. He was getting to know her character and personality and understand how he would have to proceed if he ever hoped to have anything more than a friendly relationship with this sexy, astonishing woman who was his neighbor.

Frasier broke off his tune and laid the guitar aside.

"Frasier." Emma caught him by an arm as he headed for the door. "What if it's those same men who threatened us? What if...?"

'They'd never be stupid enough to try that twice." He looked down into her concerned face. "And they definitely wouldn't knock."

"Maybe not, but..." Clutching Bruiser under one arm, she went to the drawer, pulled it open, and gingerly pointed to the gun. "Maybe you should take this."

He hesitated. Maybe she was right. He returned and hefted the .38 as another knock, this time an impatient one, sounded on the door.

"Frasier, I can hear you talking. Open the door."

"The Professor." Frasier breathed the recognition. He replaced the gun in its hiding place, then went to open the door.

Amid a swirl of dead leaves and blustering wind, a tall, broad-shouldered, silver-haired man stood silhouetted against the blackness of the wilderness. He wore a plaid mackinaw, khaki bush pants, and hiking boots.

"Professor." Frasier narrowly avoided snapping to attention before the older man's steely stare. "I wasn't expecting you. I didn't hear your vehicle because of the wind."

"Or maybe because of the music?" The man

advanced into the room and closed the door on the inhospitable night. His penetrating gaze swept the room, taking in Emma, the Pug, and the guitar.

"Professor?" Emma came back to animation. "You must be Frasier's supervisor. I'm Emma Prescott." She settled the Pug under her left arm and extended her right hand. "And this," she jerked her head in the direction of the little dog, "is Bruiser." She flashed him a dazzling smile.

There was a static hiatus as the newcomer looked Emma up and down. Frasier held his breath. Then the Professor let a smile curl up the corners of his lips as he took her hand.

"Good evening, Miss Prescott...and Bruiser. I'm Benjamin Taylor." He took her hand in a firm grip.

"What brings you up here tonight, sir?" Frasier suddenly understood the expression "sweating bullets" all too well.

"I had a few concerns about the project I needed to discuss with you. Since I was in the area this evening, I decided to visit. Haven't come at an awkward moment, have I?"

"No, sir, of course not, sir."

"Bruiser and I have been looking after Frasier since he was shot," Emma said. "He's almost completely recovered now. It wasn't all that serious anyway. In fact, he moved back here only three days after the accident."

"Moved back?"

"From my cabin next door. Frasier had been taking such great care of the Bruise and me, the least we could do for him was to let him move in with us so we could look after him while he recovered."

"I see." The Professor turned penetrating, blue eyes on the younger man. Frasier had to struggle to keep from fidgeting like a guilty child. "Well, I do thank you, Miss Prescott. Frasier is a valuable

199

member of our staff. We'd hate to lose him. But now, if you don't mind, I'd like a few words alone with him."

"Of course." Emma reached for her jacket. "Bruiser and I were about to head off home to bed anyway. See you tomorrow, Frasier. Good night, Scout. Nice to finally meet you, Professor Taylor."

"I'll see Emma to her cabin." Frasier sat down and pulled on his boots. "Help yourself to coffee, sir. We just made a fresh pot."

"Thank you." The man nodded a polite acknowledgement.

Something like jealousy shot through Frasier as he caught Emma looking up at the Professor with open admiration. Even at fifty-something Benjamin Taylor was still a good-looking specimen.

****

"Are you in big trouble?" Emma asked as they hurried toward her cabin, hunched together against the wind and swirling leaves. A gale howled and moaned through the trees. The wilderness was pitch black.

"Probably." On her verandah he paused. He hated the idea of leaving her alone. "Give me your key. I'll go in and turn on some lights."

"You don't need to. Bruise and I will be fine." She snuggled the Pug more securely against her. "I think it's important that you don't antagonize your supervisor any further by making him wait."

"And I think it's important I make sure you're safe and sound. Now give me the key."

In the darkness he felt her warm hand slide into his and deposit a piece of cold metal.

"Thanks." He drew a deep breath and took it, fighting the urge to hold onto her, to pull her close, to...

"Frasier, are you going to open the door or what?"

Her words snapped him out of it. He shoved the key into the lock, turned it, then pushed open the door. He proceeded through the cabin, snapping on lights as he went.

****

When he headed for the door ten minutes later, in the shadows of the fire he'd started blazing on the hearth, she caught him by the arm, raised on tiptoes, and kissed his cheek.

"Thanks, Frasier," she said softly. The expression in her green eyes took his breath away. She wanted him to stay.

He swallowed hard and hated his body for not accepting the reality of their situation.

"Gotta go," he muttered hoarsely and made his escape.

****

"Got her home safely, did you?"

The Professor was lounging in a chair by the fire, a cup of coffee in his hands when Frasier stepped back into his cabin.

"Yes, sir. I thought it the right thing to do...under the circumstances."

"Ah, yes, the circumstances. Let's get down to them, shall we? Bring out your maps and show me what range you've covered."

He stood as Frasier went to the bookcase to pull out the maps.

"By the way..." The Professor replenished his coffee while Frasier spread the papers over his repaired table. "I'm glad I came. It gave me a chance to meet the unshakeable Emma Prescott. Quite frankly, my boy..." He turned back to Frasier.

The younger man sucked in too much air and coughed.

Here it comes.

"In spite of the fact that she has to be one of the worst singers I've ever heard, I'd have serious doubts about your sexual preference if you *weren't* having difficulty getting rid of a charming beauty like her." A slow grin relaxed his features, and Frasier exhaled. "But," he continued, "you still have to make her leave Loon Lake. I have a feeling we'll be wrapping up this project sooner than expected. We don't want that nice young woman involved. Fortunately, while I was driving up here, I came up with the perfect solution. Andrea."

"Andrea? Not Andrea Morgan? Hey, look, I'll try harder. I'll come up with a foolproof plan. Just don't send Andrea Morgan up here."

"Sorry, my boy. While you were depositing Ms. Prescott back at her cabin, I called her on my cell. She'll be here in the morning. I'd advise you to make her welcome—you know what I mean. Now bring me up to date on the project. Any new developments?"

"Nothing you don't already know. I phoned you the details about those two who broke in on Emma and me. Aside from that..."

He hesitated. The Professor looked over at him sharply.

"Go on," he said evenly, blue eyes so intense Frasier felt he could look right down inside him.

"Did you send someone up here posing as a forest ranger to get Emma to leave the lake?" Indignation bristled. "If you did, I think that was going too far. I've already told you she's okay. There was no need..."

"There was and is every need to make sure she leaves this area, as you well know." The big man drew himself to his full height. Frasier, as always, felt himself backing down. "First, she's interfering with your work, and, second, she could be in serious danger. Under these circumstances, I did see fit to send Kevin Smith in the role of forest ranger in an attempt to move her along."

"But did you also order him to search her cabin,

invade her privacy?" Frasier was all-out fighting anger. "There was no need…"

"There was every need. Her job puts her in a perfect position to inject drugs into the town high school. Although our preliminary investigations turned up nothing suspicious in her past, we had to be sure."

"This Smith saw fit to take a couple of her old CDs of The Sound. Why?"

"An accidental discovery. Kevin found them and thought it best he take them in case she recognized you from the cover."

"She'd already done that. It was no problem."

"No? A case of rock-star-worship, or whatever they call it these days, could enhance her desire to stay near you."

"It didn't. By the way, where did Smith get a key to Emma's cottage?"

"Kevin helped her pack her car to leave. He saw to it that a window was left unlocked. He's adept at pushing himself through small spaces."

"Leaving not a single trace of his visit and finding absolutely nothing."

"I suggest you modify your tone, Frasier. It's not impressing or pleasing me. No, for your information, he didn't find anything…aside from those CDs."

Frasier drew a deep breath. "Very good, sir, but I have to tell you. When this project is finished, I plan to try to establish a relationship with Emma Prescott…if she can bear to look at me by then."

****

Frasier was finishing his breakfast when he heard a vehicle coming up the trail at a faster speed than the condition of the rough woods road warranted. She'd wasted no time. *Hell!* He got up from the table and went out onto the verandah.

"Frasier, sweetie, there you are!" The beautiful brunette swung out of the shiny black SUV and waved to him. With a figure that had caused more than a few male heads to swivel, the vision of Andrea Morgan in enough black leather to make a rock video, her shining ebony hair swinging down to just above her waist, would have been almost any man's idea of a really wild dream. Frasier muttered an expletive. He could have handled the Emma situation without this intrusion. In fact, if he knew Emma, it would only make things worse.

But he couldn't go against the Professor's instructions. He suppressed a cringe when she came up the steps, threw her arms around his neck, and pulled his head down to bury his lips in a deep kiss.

"Come on, come on, Frasier," she hissed against his mouth. "Put a little something into it, will you? You're supposed to be my significant other, for God's sake."

"Sorry," he muttered, pulling back. Glancing over her shoulder, he saw Emma coming out of her cabin, briefcase in hand, Bruiser on his leash. She stopped short when she saw the pair on the verandah, stared for a moment, then hurried down the steps and scrambled into her car.

As she gunned the motor and spun out of the yard with a backlash of grass and earth, Andrea released him and stepped back.

"Damn it, Frasier!" she snapped as he stood staring after the vanishing old car. "I've seen monkeys at the zoo give a better show of affection. You'd better be a lot more participative tonight when Miss Pain-in-the-Butt comes home, or I'll be stuck in this Godforsaken hole forever...which means the rest of the week."

Hell and damnation! Frasier followed her inside the cabin. He watched as she splashed coffee into a cup and drank it black.

****

"Emma!" Frasier stood on his verandah,

according to Andrea's instructions, when his neighbor arrived home from school that afternoon.

"Yes?" She paused in letting Bruiser out of his seatbelt.

"Will you come over here for a minute? There's someone who'd like to meet you."

"Really?" She placed the Pug on the ground. The little dog scampered off to join Scout, who'd come out of the cabin with Frasier. "Well, certainly, of course, why not?"

He barely avoided flinching at the coldness in her words.

She placed her purse and briefcase on the top step of her cabin, drew a deep breath, then swaggered across the yard and up his front steps.

"Come in," he invited holding the door open. Emma entered, shoulders back, spine rigid.

This was going to get nasty.

"Well, you must be Emma." As Emma entered, the brunette got up from the couch where she'd been curled like a contented feline. "Frasier's told me a lot about you. I wonder if he's told you about me."

"And you would be?" Emma's words held all the warmth of a January midnight.

"Andrea Morgan, Frasier's..." She allowed a suggestive pause before she continued, "significant other. Actually, more than that. He hopes to marry me as soon as he can convince me I'm hopelessly in love with him."

"Really?"

That word again! Damn and double damn!

The look in her emerald eyes told him he was about to experience Emma Prescott in action as never before.

"How strange! I take it you haven't been a frequent visitor to Loon Lake. Otherwise, how would you explain the sobriquet the locals have for him...the hermit of Loon Lake?"

Score one for Emma!

"I'm a career woman." Andrea narrowed her eyes. Frasier could sense her preparing for battle. "Frasier understands that careers have to come first."

The woman can be one nasty piece of work, no doubt.

"Really?"

This REALLY isn't going to be good.

Emma continued, "Well, if I had a significant other like Frasier MacKenzie, there wouldn't be a career in this world important enough to keep me away from him for two entire months."

"You think not?"

"I know it. Now if you'll excuse me, I have case files to update. You see, Ms. Morgan, I have a career, as well, but it didn't stop me from caring for Frasier when he got shot. I guess he knew you wouldn't come running to his side—that's why he didn't ask me to call you. He didn't even mention you as someone I should notify. Frasier?" She turned to him, her bellicose expression dissolving. The hurt overlaid with disappointment in her expression wrenched at his gut. "I assume I won't be seeing much of you for a while. Or at least not for however long *she* plans to stay."

Narrowing her eyes, Emma smiled at the brunette. "But once *she's* gone, I'll go back to making you a whole bunch more great breakfasts." She caught Frasier by an arm. Rising on tiptoes, she placed a soft, lingering kiss on his lips while she ran the fingers of her right hand down his cheek. His breath knotted in his chest. Every natural instinct in his body yelled, goaded him to take her into his arms, to kiss her until the dragon lady could have no doubts about his feelings.

Just in time, she released him and headed for the door. Before she stepped outside, she struck a seductive pose, winked at him, and murmured, "Until later, Frasier MacKenzie."

"Argh!" Andrea Morgan gritted the exclamation between clenched teeth. "What a little…"

"Don't say it, Andrea." Frasier was quick to warn her. "You might just be talking about the woman I love."

Now where had that come from?

****

"Frasier, breakfast."

Frasier awoke to Emma's voice. She was at his door. He flinched as he pulled himself out of bed and into a robe. Rubbing his head, he remembered the woman sleeping in the next room.

Blast the Professor for sending Andrea Morgan to Loon Lake.

"Quiche and coffee." Emma, in perfectly fitted jeans and peach-colored angora sweater, brushed past him with a basket and a thermos, heading for the table, Bruiser at her heels.

"Emma, I don't think…" he began, but suddenly Andrea was in the room wearing a short, black, semi-transparent nightgown and stiletto slippers. Her mane of hair was tousled.

"So you couldn't wait until my bed was cold before you made your move." She glared at Emma. "Well, Miss Emma Prescott, let me tell you…"

"No, let me tell you, *Ms*. Morgan. I don't know who you really are, but I can hazard a guess. The Professor sent you up here to get rid of me. No way are you Frasier's significant other. I've come to know him in the past few weeks, and no way would he get involved with a hard bit like you."

She thumped the thermos down on the table and went to the cupboard to remove the quiche from the basket. She appeared full of confidence, but Frasier saw her hands tremble when she lifted the pie from its nest of careful packing.

Man, she's terrific.

He suddenly knew what he'd said to Andrea about loving Emma was the truth, the whole truth, and nothing but the truth. Now if he could just keep these two women from open warfare...

"Really?" Andrea mocked Emma as she stood staring at her.

"Yes, really."

Green eyes challenged brown.

Frasier braced for the worst. A man would have to be a complete fool to get between them.

"Well, fine. You can have him with all his crazy dreams about finding an Eastern Panther and his stupid, softhearted ways."

The brunette whirled and headed back into the second bedroom.

"So she didn't sleep with you." Emma's voice sounded cool and confident. She turned on the oven and slid the quiche inside.

"No, she didn't."

"I was right...about the Professor sending her up here?" She straightened up and swung to face him squarely.

"Yeah." He looked down at his bare feet.

"Did you tell him we've made a pact to remain friends?"

"Yeah."

"But apparently that didn't satisfy him?"

"No." He felt like a guilty kid.

"He can't know you very well, or he wouldn't have sent that woman up here to convince me she was your lover." Emma took two mugs from the cupboard and returned to the thermos on the table. "A man as good and kind as you, Frasier MacKenzie, would never get involved with her."

"Don't worry, he won't." They turned to see Andrea Morgan standing at the end of the corridor, suitcase in hand, once more dressed in black leather.

"You two deserve each other. Ugh!"

She broke off abruptly and stared down at the lower left side of her thigh-high boots.

Bruiser slowly lowered his leg and looked up at her, round eyes innocently wide as the puddle spread out around her feet.

"Filthy little beast!" she hissed. "Your time would be much better spent, Emma Prescott, in housebreaking this mutt than in making breakfasts for your neighbor!"

She strode across the room and out to her vehicle. A moment later they heard the SUV gunning off down the trail.

"What a dragon lady!" Emma breathed. She headed for the counter and paper towels.

"Don't demean her," Frasier responded. "She's a top-notch professional at her job."

"Just exactly what might that be? Or is it not polite to ask?" Emma bent and sopped up the puddle. Frasier fancied he saw Bruiser give her a sly, conspiratorial wink when they were at eye level.

"Not what you think. She's a researcher connected with my project. She's one of the best in her field."

"Ah." Emma slanted a skeptical glance up at him. "She could have fooled me. I would have pegged her as an escapee from a rock video, or..." She paused and looked him squarely in the face. "A secret agent."

"Let's just put your colorful ideas away for the time being and concentrate on the breakfast you thoughtfully provided." He turned back toward his room. "I'll pull on some clothes."

"Don't take too long," she called after him as she threw wet paper towels into the garbage. "I have to leave for school in a half hour. Lord, I'm glad it's Friday. I'm really looking forward to the weekend. I do declare, going one-on-one with Miss Hell-Bent-for-Leather has quite exhausted me."

Stopped by her last sentence uttered in her feigned southern belle drawl, he turned back to see her fluttering her hands in front of her face.

"You're a wicked woman, Emma Prescott." He couldn't help grinning. "I can only hope you didn't train that Pug to pee on her."

"Hardly." She stopped abruptly and pulled out a slim volume that had been hidden behind the coffee maker. "What's this, Frasier? Porn?"

"Give me that!" He lunged, but she swung away, perusing the cover. "'Songs and Poetry of Scotland: Robert Burns.' Frasier, I had no idea you were a fan of the Scottish bard."

"It's Andrea's." As soon as the explanation was out of his mouth, its utter ridiculousness hit him.

"The Lady in Leather? I would have thought she was more the James Bond type, visualizing herself as one of his most fabulous mistresses. Or were you perhaps trying to woo her with words and couldn't find any of your own?"

"Come on, Emma. Woo her with words? Anyhow, I have a taste for it myself. The MacKenzie name is pure Highland Scot, after all."

"I never imagined you as having an interest in your heritage. But then, that's one of the things that intrigue me about you. I'm never sure about anything." She brushed a quick kiss over his lips before sashaying toward the bathroom, the Pug wiggling his bottom behind her. "Must wash up before I get our breakfast. After cleaning up poor Bruiser's little accident, I need to give my hands a good scrub." She turned back at the door, eyes wide and innocent. "I do hope Miss Andrea remembers to wash those fancy boots."

****

"Mom." Emma leaned back in her office chair, the phone to her ear. "Good, caught you at home.

How is everything in Ottawa? How's Etta? Have you heard from Andy?"

"They're both fine." Her mother's tone held concern. "You don't often call me on what I assume is your lunch break. Emma, is something wrong?"

"No. Yes. Well, just kind of." She squeezed out the last. "Remember I told you about the man who's living in the other cottage at Loon Lake?"

"Yes." Maude Prescott's tone oozed suspicion. "What about him? He hasn't been bothering you, has he? Because if he has, it won't take Andy long to drive down there. He's back with his regiment here in Ottawa, but he won't be shipping any time soon."

"No, no, Mom, nothing like that. In fact, maybe the opposite is happening. I may be making a nuisance of myself with him."

"I find that difficult to believe." Her mother's voice relaxed into a chuckle. "The wily Emma Prescott pursuing a man? He must be very special."

"Oh, he is, Mom. He may not have ridden in on a white horse, but he does drive a white SUV, and he's... Oh, Mom, do you remember that rock group I was so crazy about, called The Sound? Well, he was the Frase, the guy I had that incredible crush on. Only now he's out of the band, and he's an associate professor of biology at UNB, and he's up at Loon Lake working on a project to prove the existence of the Eastern Panther, and—"

"Emma, slow down! Is it safe to assume you still have a crush on him...or is it more than that?"

"I don't know, Mom. All I know is I can't wait to see him again, and when I'm with him I'm incredibly happy, but..."

"But?"

"He's kind and thoughtful and all that, but he just wants to be friends. His supervisor doesn't want him distracted from his work by anything, and that includes me. Do you know that man actually sent this dragon lady up to the lake to pretend she was Frasier's significant other?"

"Ah, so it seems Emma Prescott, heartbreaker extraordinaire, has finally come up against a man she can't wind around her little finger. And fallen in love with him."

"In love! No, Mom, the man has gone to incredible lengths to keep us apart. He's..."

"Been kind and thoughtful, and don't I recall your texting me he saved Bruiser's little white hide on more than one occasion? All that hardly reeks of a man who doesn't care about you."

"You think? Mom, what you just said, I'm getting afraid that it might be true. I'm afraid he might be the one. He bought a book of my favorite poetry."

"Maybe he just happens to like Robbie Burns."

"The price sticker was still on it. A man who carries a .38 automatic isn't prone to reading 'My Love is Like a Red, Red Rose.' "

"He carries a gun? Oh, Emma, I don't know—"

"For protection, Mom. He is tracking a big wildcat that has a bad reputation with people. Tell me. How did you know Dad was the one?"

"I listened to my heart, sweetie. That's what you'll have to do."

"And if it tells me he's the one? He's not exactly about to come to me on bended knee."

"Just be your usual charming, vivacious, disarming, unpredictable self. If the man has an ounce of testosterone in his body, he'll come around."

"Mom, I'm sinking here. I need more than that."

"Well, my darling, unless you can think of some way to make all his dreams come true—"

"What did you say?"

"Make all his dreams come true. But—"

"Maybe I can."

"Now, honey, I'm not advocating anything erotic

or—"

"No, no, nothing like that. Mom, do you remember the way to Midnight Jim's camp?"

****

"Frasier, my place or yours for supper? I brought Chicken Kiev from town, but if you'd rather we do something from scratch..."

Her voice made Frasier start. He hadn't heard her car churning up the trail. He got to his feet and strode to the door.

"How did you get home?" He bypassed a greeting. "I didn't hear your car."

"Ta-da!" She stepped back and swept out her arm to indicate her car, its sunroof back in place and its coat gleaming with a new wax job. "I got the old girl a facelift. With snow predicted tonight, I couldn't very well drive with the top open, so I decided to go the whole nine yards and get all her ailing bells and whistles fixed. Pretty, isn't she?"

"Yeah, I guess." He peered out at the old car.

"So what is it, my place or yours?" She looked up at him and smiled. "We should celebrate my car's rebirth, don't you think?"

"Yeah, I guess."

"Frasier, you sound absolutely disenchanted with the wonderfulness of my vehicle. And you're repeating yourself. Oh, okay, my place. I can't wait around while you gape and stammer. I have another bottle of Dad's wine..."

"No, none of your father's wine." The words scrambled out reflexively.

"But I have chicken. White meat, and all that."

"You can have wine, but none for me. I have an early start in the morning."

"Men all turn into farmers when they're afraid of being seduced into staying the night." She tossed him a saucy smirk before she scuttled back down his steps.

213

"See you in a half hour," she called over her shoulder. "I promise I'll be a perfect lady, no matter how much wine I consume."

Frasier watched until she and the Pug disappeared into her cabin. Then he turned back inside his own, an uneasy twinge starting in the pit of his stomach. Where had Emma suddenly gotten the money to rejuvenate that old buggy of hers? *Damn!* He'd be glad when this project was at an end and he wouldn't be haunted by suspicion at every turn.

****

"I've realized something, Frasier." Emma sat curled up on the couch, a cup of coffee in her hands. They'd finished their meal and were sitting in front of the fire.

"And what would that be?" He looked over at her, a whimsical grin quirking up the corner of his mouth.

"That I know next to nothing about your project. You've told me a history of the creature called the Eastern Panther but nothing about your work. Care to fill me in?"

"What would you like to know?" He took a sip of coffee and leaned back in his chair. Here was a subject he would feel comfortable discussing with her.

"Well, for instance, when was the last verified sighting in New Brunswick?"

"Verified? There never has been such a thing. At least, not one documented by photographs or a live specimen." Frasier settled into his role as biologist. "Bruce Wright, a biologist who studied at the same university I'm representing, worked from 1938 until his death in 1975 to establish the existence of what he called the Monarch of Mularchy Mountain. In the 1960s, this province still contained some of the finest unspoiled wilderness in northeastern North

America, and Mularchy Mountain would have been an inviting location for the big cats.

"Wright wrote a series of stories about this legendary cat and was convinced of its existence. Local legends he collected claimed this giant feline probably weighed about two hundred pounds and was seven feet long from tip to tip, although these are generally believed to be exaggerations."

"Wow!" Emma's eyes goggled. "I had no idea it was such a monster."

"It isn't. My research tends to point to a weight of about one hundred pounds or a little more. The latest and most convincing piece of evidence comes from findings near Juniper in this province. Tracks and scat from a panther of some type were found there on November 18, 1992 and later documented by the Canadian Museum in Ottawa. The question remains, however, was it a genuine, native Eastern Panther?"

"What else could it possibly have been?" Riveted by his story, Emma leaned forward, clutching her cup.

"Some biologists argue that it was a released or escaped panther, cougar, or puma brought here from some other part of the world. Although the provincial Wildlife Branch issued a press release at that time proclaiming evidence of a panther, the exact origin and lineage of the animal is still a question mark."

"Interesting. These cats had been found in this province in earlier years?"

"There's one mounted specimen believed to be of the Eastern Panther variety that was trapped in Somerset County, Maine in 1938. Bruce Wright purchased it during his years of researching the big cat. It measures seven feet one inch from its nose to the tip of its tail and is estimated to have weighed about a hundred pounds. It's in the New Brunswick

Museum in Saint John."

"So there's some evidence that they do, or at least did, roam these forests." Emma's excitement was mirrored in her face. He felt inspired to continue.

"That's my premise. But they're creatures of the deep woods. Farming, roads, logging, and summer homes have drastically reduced the terrain they would normally inhabit. They're reputed to avoid people and are not the predators of humans they're often depicted to be. However, it's best to give them a wide berth. They're unpredictable and perfectly capable of being savage if they feel threatened."

"Don't worry." Emma suddenly yawned. "I don't plan on bagging one to help you complete your project."

"Well, good." He finished his coffee and stood. "Now I'm heading home. You've had a long day and it's catching up with you. Try to put all thoughts of ghosts and Eastern Panthers out of your head and have a good sleep. I'm right next door if you need me. You can either holler or give me a call on your cell."

"Thanks." She yawned again. "Really, Frasier, I'm sorry. As the old saying goes, it's not the company, it's the hour."

"Sure, sure." He headed for the door. "Come on, Scout. We've heard that old chestnut before. See you tomorrow."

****

The following morning Frasier awoke to the first snowfall of the season. As he stood and stretched, he glanced out his window to see big, gentle flakes drifting down to join those already forming a three-inch ground cover. It all looked so innocent and peaceful no one would ever guess—

A dull thud on his front door ended his reflections. Someone, and it didn't take an Einstein to figure out who, was pelting his cabin with snowballs.

Pulling on a robe, he padded barefoot into the living area. Scout was leaping about the room, whining and running eagerly to the door.

"Okay, okay, you can go out and play with the Pug," he muttered as he crossed the room. "Only be advised, this will do nothing to enhance your credibility as a guard dog."

Scout gave an impatient yelp. The moment Frasier opened the door, the big dog darted out to join Bruiser. The Pug, dressed in a bright red turtleneck and fake-fur-trimmed boots, cavorted in the fresh snow.

"Howdy, neighbor!" Emma, her cheeks pink from the crisp air, stood at the bottom of his steps in a snowsuit, boots, and the most ludicrous Elmer Fudd-style hat he'd ever seen. "Ready to come out and make snow angels?"

"I'm just getting up. I haven't showered or shaved." *Man, he sounded grumpy.* "And I haven't eaten. And," he continued, gaining focus, "I haven't time to fool around. This new snow is perfect for tracking. I need to get to work."

"Don't be such a killjoy! You've been working seven days a week since I came here. You know what they say about all work and no play. Can't have Frasier becoming a dull boy."

"Emma..." he began, but a big soft ball of snow hit him full in the chest, where his robe hung open, and slithered downward. In an effort to get rid of the ice-cold thing, he flapped the robe open and yelped.

"Emma Prescott...!"

"Wow! So it is true what they say about guys and cold."

With a smug smile, she turned away, leaving him to pull his robe shut and blush like a startled virgin.

"Come over to my cabin as soon as you're decent," she flung back over her shoulder. "I'll have a stack of blueberry pancakes waiting for you."

****

"Today we find Midnight Jim's camp." Emma got up, shoved back her chair, and began to gather their breakfast dishes.

"What? I thought you didn't know where it is." Exasperated, Frasier looked over at her. He still smarted from her "guys and cold" innuendo.

"I told you the trail that led to it started between two huge white pines about halfway down our road," she said, putting the plates into the sink.

"But from there? I was trying to decipher a path beyond that point when I was shot. I've been back a half dozen times since, with no better luck. What makes you think you can do any better?"

"Because I've actually been there, and you haven't." Emma looked loftily over at him, her nose in the air. "Have you got a map of the area? Let me show you."

Ten minutes later he straightened from bending over the map on the table and looked across at her.

"Are you sure?"

"Well, not a hundred percent, no-room-for-error sure, but just about. Now gather up your gear while I make sandwiches and settle the dogs. I think we should leave them here today."

She was out the door before he could stop her.

****

Twenty minutes later Frasier pointed at her headgear and chuckled. "Where did you get that thing?" A shower and a good breakfast had mellowed his mood.

"At a state-of-the-art outdoor store." She looked up at him, first in surprise and then in outright annoyance. "What's so funny?"

"It looks like the latest Elmer Fudd model."

"Oh, and I suppose wearing a dead animal on your head is much better," she snapped, indicating his fur hat. "Or did you simply mug a Mountie to get that thing?"

"Hey, not funny." He adjusted it carefully. "For your information, it's synthetic. I'm an anti-kill type of guy."

"Sorry." She let a grin twitch her lips. "Neither of us is exactly haute couture in the millinery department, but at least we're warm. Let's go."

"You're not coming."

"What!" She put her hands on her hips and stared up at him, lips pursed, forehead furrowed.

"Look, Emma, I got shot trying to find that camp. Maybe someone has a reason not to want me to discover it. Maybe they're using it to hide carcasses of deer meat...deer meat they've poached and are planning to sell. Poachers can be dangerous people."

"So you'll go alone. Real smart, Frasier MacKenzie. Is finding that Eastern Panther worth that kind of risk?"

"It is if I can prevent those guys shooting it as a trophy. You and the dogs enjoy the day."

He bent to put on his snowshoes. "If I'm not back by dark, feel free to call out a search team."

"Frasier!" she called after him as he started off down the trail through the unmarked snow, her tone full of annoyance.

"Emma," he paused, turned and looked back at her, his breath forming a fog in the frosty air. "I said stay here. I mean it."

"Killjoy!" she yelled as he strode away.

****

Frasier had turned off the vehicle road and down the old logging trail between the pair of pines when his cell vibrated against his hip.

"Frasier." The Professor's voice cracked over a

219

faulty signal. "Where are…"

"I'm heading down the logging road where I was shot. This fresh snow has provided an excellent tracking opportunity. Any new developments I should be aware of?"

"…more information about …Prescott …arrested four years ago …assaulting a …officer."

"What's that? Emma was arrested for assaulting a police officer? Under what circumstances?"

The phone snapped and buzzed.

"Professor!" he bellowed but the connection had been severed.

Damn these cellular phones! He shoved it back into his pocket. Why had it taken the Professor so long to come up with this gem? Usually information like that came to the top of an investigation like cream on unprocessed milk.

There had to be some mistake. A sick feeling rolled into his stomach. What if it wasn't? Had Emma been trying to seduce him simply to use him? Could she be involved with students who dealt drugs? Had what he'd witnessed in her office that day been a drug deal, the story about buying gym equipment simply a smoke screen? Suddenly her explanation seemed ridiculous. What person in their right mind would trust a kid like Jesse Jones with two thousand dollars in cash? Sure, Emma had said she believed you had to give trust to get it, but still…

He drew a deep breath and looked around. If all that were true, was he walking into a trap? Strange how she'd suddenly remembered the camp's location.

Only one way to find out. Keep going. Keep alert. Keep alive.

Chapter Seven

Someone was following him. Each time he paused he was sure he heard a slight sound in the trees behind him, as if someone else had stopped short, as well.

He made a sharp turn into a thicket, crouched, and waited.

For a few moments all was quiet. He was about to chalk one up to his imagination when he heard the soft swish of snowshoes. His heartbeat quickened. His tracks would lead to his hiding place. He would have to take whoever it was down fast and demand an explanation later.

From his crouched position he saw only the legs of his stalker. When he lunged, he went for the knees.

"Frasier, what do you think you're doing!" Emma's voice hit him like that snowball in the chest two hours earlier. "Get off of me, you big brute! I'm going to suffocate in the snow!"

"Emma!" He'd fallen on her, his snowshoes tangling with hers.

"Frasier, I said get off!" She struggled to shove him away.

"Damn it, Emma!" He fell back into a squat beside her. "I told you to stay at the lake."

"Are you crazy!" she muttered, pulling herself to a sitting position and brushing snow from her face with a fuzzy mitten. "Just who did you think would be following you? You should have known it would be me."

"Yeah, I should have known." He got to his feet

and held down a hand to pull her upright, but she slapped it away. He looked directly into her eyes. "Why didn't you tell me you'd been arrested for assaulting an officer?"

"What?" She stared up at him. "Who told you...?"

"It doesn't matter who told me. Is it true?"

"Would it matter if it was?"

"Yeah, probably. I guess. Hell, Emma, I don't know. Just tell me, is it true?"

"Yes, as a matter of fact." Her gaze didn't waver. "Would you like to know the circumstances, or don't they matter? It appears you've already judged me and found me guilty of some heinous offense."

"Tell me."

"Fine." She sat down on a tree stump and slanted an angry glance up at him. "I was arrested four years ago for protesting the Newfoundland seal hunt. When a Department of Fisheries and Oceans officer tried to stop me from protecting a baby seal, I hit him...with my open hand. Subsequently I was arrested." She paused, then asked again, "Who told you? That was supposed to have been expunged from the records...my lawyer got it done in view of my career and the fact that this was my first offense."

"You were protesting the seal hunt?" Frasier felt as if a gigantic weight had been lifted from his shoulders. How could he have been paranoid enough to suspect her of anything truly violent or criminal? "Yeah, I can believe it." He chuckled. "I hope you didn't leave a mark on that officer. Were you wearing those mittens?"

"Damn it, Frasier MacKenzie!" She lurched to her feet. "I'm tired of explaining myself to you. First it was my past love life, now it's my so-called criminal record. Will you never learn to take me exactly as I am?"

He saw tears filling her eyes.

222

"Emma, I'm sorry. It's just that sometimes you seem hell bent on driving me nuts. I...like you, really like you a lot, and when you hide things from me..."

"Hide what things? Like an ancient arrest for trying to save adorable seal pups? I would have told you if I'd thought it was important, but you and your precious Professor had to go prying into my past, even setting that Lady in Leather against me. My God, Frasier, how important can finding an Eastern Panther be?"

"Very." He drew a deep breath and waded deeper into her contempt. "Where did you get the money to repair that car of yours?"

"Oh, my God, Frasier! You can't be thinking... No, I won't believe you're wondering if it was drug money."

"Emma, believe me, I don't want to ask. I have to."

"Have to? Why? There's only one reason. That's because you don't trust me, not even after all we've been through together. You're despicable, Frasier MacKenzie!"

She tried to shrug away from him, but he caught her arm. "Damn it, Emma, you can't despise me any more than I loathe myself right now, but I do need answers. Please. I promise when this is all over you'll understand."

She stopped struggling and looked up at him, tears brimming in her eyes. "Okay. I got the money from the insurance settlement for damages caused to my apartment by the fire. Now, are you satisfied?"

"Yeah, of course, right. I should have thought of it." A tsunami of relief flooded over him. He caught her into his arms and kissed her quick, and harder than he intended.

"Ouch!" She pulled back and scrubbed a mitten over her mouth. "What was that?"

"Sorry. It was meant to tell you I'm one relieved, happy critter. I knew in my heart you weren't guilty of anything worse than being way too desirable to a man who can't follow through, but I had to hear the words. You'd better head back to the cabin. I've got a lot of territory to cover today if I hope to come anywhere close to finding Midnight Jim's camp."

"Go back? No way! I'm going to show you exactly where it is." She wiped her eyes with a mitten and beat snow from the seat of her pants. "It's a good thing I caught up with you when I did. You took a wrong turn about a quarter mile back. Come on, follow me."

****

"Come on, come on," Emma urged him a half hour later. "I think it's just beyond this ravine."

"Think," he muttered. This was his first big hike since he'd been shot. The weariness of being out of shape was taking a toll on his energy and temper.

"What was that?" She rounded on him.

"Nothing, nothing. It's just that this makes the fourth time you've said the same thing. I'm beginning to wonder if you're leading me on a wild goose chase."

"Well, if you can find someone, anyone, else who has even the vaguest notion of where to find Midnight Jim's camp, I'll gladly resign my job as guide. Anyway, what possible reason would I have for attempting to lead you astray? Lord knows I've tried often enough and failed." She looked over at him, her eyes narrowing suggestively.

"Don't get huffy." He tried to ignore her innuendo, but his body tensed. "Lead on, Macduff."

"Aw, Shakespeare." She put her mittened hands on her hips and grinned back at him. "Nothing like it to turn a girl on."

She resumed making her way gingerly through the underbrush.

"Yeah, right," he muttered.

****

"Don't move!" Frasier hissed the words. His hand shot out and seized Emma by the arm.

"What...? She glanced up at him.

His gaze galvanized on the branches of a huge cedar about twenty yards ahead of them.

Draped over its branches about halfway up its height lay a big, tawny cat, the end of its long tail twitching intermittently as it sniffed the air.

"Frasier, is that...?" Emma's words came out in an incredulous whisper.

"Behold the legendary Eastern Panther," he breathed, barely able to believe what he saw. He eased his hand toward the pocket where he kept his digital camera, scarcely daring to breathe.

"He's magnificent," she whispered.

"Crouch...slowly," he whispered, adjusting his camera setting. "We don't want to alarm him."

Together they melted down into the snow. Frasier turned off the flash and lined up a shot. Even though he knew it wouldn't be as good as he wished in the poor light of the forest, he didn't want to risk a blaze of light scaring off the big cat.

****

It began to snow again. Frasier was grateful he'd been able to get a few shots. The snow would obliterate tracks and make hair and scat difficult if not impossible to locate.

The big cat roused itself and stood on the branch.

"He's huge!" Emma breathed in Frasier's ear.

Quite a woman. They'd been crouching in the snow for the better part of an hour, yet she remained enthralled by the situation. *Yeah, she probably was arrested in an effort to protect a seal pup.*

"Shhh!" he cautioned as the panther swung its head, sniffing to left and right. "The wind's changing. It's caught a scent...hopefully it's not ours. It's getting ready to make a run for it."

He decided he had to risk it. He turned on the flash, got a clear shot, and depressed the shutter.

At the jolt of light, the Panther opened its mouth and let forth its legendary, blood-curdling roar. *Like a soul trapped in Hades.* The scream echoed through the quiet forest. The next instant it leaped from the tree. With another hellish roar, it bolted into the forest.

"What an experience!" Emma brushed snow from her clothing as they got to their feet. She looked up at him, her face bright with excitement. "Frasier, we've actually seen an Eastern Panther!"

"Yet there's only the slightest of chances he left anything behind that will prove his presence," he muttered, as big, soft flakes of snow fluttered over them. "These pictures—" he held up the camera— "will probably be the only surviving evidence of what we've just seen. Come on, we have to try to follow and see if it will lead us to its den."

****

Frasier's hand shot out to stop Emma fifteen minutes later. At his silent signal, she crouched with him and stared ahead as he parted the branches of the bushes that concealed them.

Ahead in a clearing stood a long, crumbling log structure. Beyond it another, probably a stable, tilted into the ground. From a tree at the far end hung a pair of deer carcasses, one of which the Panther was tearing into shreds and gobbling.

"A poacher's lair," Frasier hissed. He aimed through the branches. Again the flash, again the outraged roar. The big cat dove into the forest.

"He probably won't return." Emma arose and stretched stiff muscles. "We should start back. It gets dark early among the trees, never mind the fact that this light snowfall is wiping out our tracks."

"In a minute." Frasier had an inspiration. "I want to take a look inside."

The clearing was well trampled. He knelt and removed his snowshoes. Camera in hand, he started to cross the clearing.

"Be careful." He glanced back to see her following him.

Ruts made by ATVs led around back. He followed them, Emma close behind.

"Look!" he breathed into the frosty air. "A new road leading to the camp. Someone is definitely using this place, maybe for more than poaching."

"What are you talking about?" Emma caught him by an arm, stumbled over her snowshoes, and turned him back to face her. "Frasier MacKenzie, what...?"

"I can't explain now, Emma, but soon, very soon, I hope. Come on. We have to go inside."

His heart pounded, his pulse rate soared. His gut told him this was it, the end of his quest.

With Emma following, he returned to the front of the camp and pushed open the scarred plank door. The stale, cold air of an unheated building gushed out, but as they advanced into the dilapidated structure the odor left by greasy cooking and burning wood indicated recent habitation. When his eyes became accustomed to the gloom, Frasier saw an old woodburning stove in the centre with a battered plank table surrounded by a half dozen abused ladderback chairs. In a far corner were built-in bunks that must once have held lumbermen, and a crooked bookshelf that held an assortment of liquor bottles and beer cases.

"Someone's been using this place recently," he muttered. He slid back the cover of the stove to peer inside.

"But why? They're obviously not very good poachers." Emma came close to his side and looked up into his face. He could see her astonishment beginning to take on a tinge of fear. "If they were, they wouldn't have left those carcasses where every passing scavenger could get them. Oh, my God, Frasier, I'll bet this place is being used by drug smugglers!" The last sentence burst from her in an epiphany of words. "We're not far from the American border. It would be easy! We have to get out of here before they come back! We have to call the police!"

"Hold on just a minute." He tried to minimize her conclusion, even though he was ninety-nine percent certain she was right. "We have no evidence of that. We may just have stumbled on the stash of a couple of greedy hunters. I don't see any evidence of drugs, do you?"

"No." The word held a note of uncertainty. "But..." Her tone picked up. "They'd hardly leave their illegal imports just lying around, now would they? Come on, let's search the stable. That's a lot more likely a place than this. After all, no one goes there anymore."

She turned awkwardly on her snowshoes and headed outside. *Ah, damn!* He turned and followed her. When he got to the cabin door, she was staggering through knee-deep snow toward the sagging horse barn about fifty yards away.

"Emma, wait." he risked calling out to her. His words echoed into the quiet of the snowy afternoon, and he cursed. *Not a smart move, MacKenzie.*

"Come on, come on." She turned back to him, her face bright with anticipation.

"Quiet!" he hissed. "Voices can carry for miles in this silence."

He had to help her push open the jammed stable door. When they had succeeded in forcing it ajar, all that greeted them was a series of long-deserted stalls with pole dividers and a faint long-ago odor of horses, manure, and shavings.

"Nothing here." Emma's tone reflected disappointment.

"Yeah, well, what you see is what you get," he said wearily gesturing at the deer carcasses. "We didn't set out to be Holmes and Watson, now, did we?"

"No." She drew a deep breath. "But it would have been a treat to have found a drug dealer's hideout and put him out of business."

"Agreed." Frasier looked around the clearing but saw only an ancient privy, its broken door hanging on one hinge. "Need to use the facilities?" He gestured toward it and grinned.

"Funny." Her reply was an absent-sounding comeback.

"What?"

"There is one other place they could hide stuff," she said slowly. "Every camp had one."

"One what?"

"A root cellar. A room dug into a hillside or rise in the ground where they kept root vegetables in winter to prevent them freezing." He watched as she let her gaze roam over the area.

"Ah-ha." She gestured to a slight rise. "Over there. Behind those bushes. That has to be it."

Stumbling on her snowshoes, she made a clumsy run toward it and hunkered down to begin digging through the spruce and cedar branches that had been used to cover its entrance. Within moments she'd unearthed a heavy plank door, a gleaming new padlock on its hasp.

"Good going!" Frasier knelt to examine the lock. "Someone definitely has something of value here. From the amount of camouflage used, I'd say it's a lot more than deer carcasses."

"But how do we find out for certain?"

"Like this." Frasier pulled a collection of small tools from inside his jacket and began to work at the lock. He knew it was exactly the wrong thing to do; he should take Emma back to the Lake and call for backup, but he'd come this far, had worked so long and hard, he had to vindicate his search without any further delays.

"Wow! Before you were a rock musician, were you a cat burglar?"

"Not exactly, but I do know how to pick a lock."

A click marked its release. He eased it open, then grabbed the edge of the thick door and pulled.

They entered a small, square room with another door at the back. Unlocked, it yielded when Frasier pulled on the rope handle. They stared. Inside were rows of shelves lined with packages of a white substance. On the floor were clear garbage bags full of plant-like material.

"Hold it right there. We've got two rifles pointed at the middle of your backs. Turn around real slow and careful."

"Hell." Glancing at the shock mirrored on Emma's face, Frasier cursed himself for a fool.

"Frasier?" His name breathed in a question from her lips made him hate himself even more. She'd depended on him to keep her safe. Was still depending on him.

"Do it," he hissed at her.

She swallowed hard, blinked, then nodded.

Together they turned to face two black-masked figures holding hunting rifles.

"We've had it with you, Mountie." The spokesman leveled a gun at Frasier's chest, his words a guttural snarl. "You and your girlfriend have interfered with us for the last time. Now get outside." He jerked his rifle toward the door, then nudged Frasier with its barrel.

"Mountie?" Emma, her face pale, eyes wide, stared up at him as the group moved out into the falling snow.

"Meet Constable Frasier MacKenzie, Royal Canadian Mounted Police, sweetheart," the masked figure growled. "Lied to you, too, did he?"

"Frasier?" She kept gazing up at him with those beautiful, innocent green eyes. He'd botched everything. He should have driven her away from Loon Lake. He should have caught these guys weeks ago.

"Let her go. She doesn't know anything about your operation."

"Yeah, right," the potbellied speaker snapped. "She's another narc like you. Women don't move up here alone. Anyway, she knows way too much. Now toss that camera over here. We saw it flash."

"Frasier, no!" Emma hissed. "It has the only pictures of..."

"The only pictures of what, cutie? Of our cache? Of the trail leading into it? Come on, Constable. Toss it or I take a shot at your lady friend's kneecap."

Frasier tossed it.

"Great." The man stepped forward and stomped on it, sending it into pieces. "There. That takes care of that."

"Don't forget the memory stick," his companion spoke for the first time in a hoarse rasp that Frasier guessed wasn't his natural voice. *Someone either Emma or I know.* The thought flashed through his mind.

"You're right." The first speaker shuffled through the snow until he found the small blue chip. With a grunt, he cracked it in two.

"I thought you had more sense, MacKenzie," he said. "Coming here alone."

"You're sure about that, are you?" Frasier tried a bluff. "Backup is moving in right now."

"Don't try playing mind games with us, Mountie," the man sneered. "We know you two live alone at Loon Lake. Since you hadn't found anything before you started out, you wouldn't have called for backup."

"What makes you think I didn't have this place in mind when I started out this morning?" *Keep them talking, play for time...although what good it will do...*

"If you'd been expecting to find anything, you wouldn't have brought her along, now would you, Constable? Not unless she's one of you. RCMP never involve innocent members of the public. You're such big heroes, aren't you?"

"I *am* an RCMP officer." Emma drew herself up and faced the pair brazenly. "Corporal Emma Prescott, undercover, posing as a guidance counselor at the local high school to get inside information. So you see, if you're thinking of doing away with Constable MacKenzie, you'll have to kill me, too. But let me tell you, killing not one but two RCMP officers will put a very big period at the end of your story. Our members won't rest until they've hunted you down like the scum you are."

"Is that so?" the man with the disguised voice snarled.

"Emma, be quiet," Frasier ordered out of the side of his mouth.

"Yes, it is so," she continued, cocking her head defiantly to one side. "As a corporal, I'm the ranking officer in charge of this operation. I'll guarantee you a fair day in court if you hand over your weapons immediately."

"Don't make me laugh. You're no more an RCMP corporal than I am. The pair of you are as alone and defenseless as a couple of babes in the woods."

"Actually," Emma looked up at him and smiled her most enchanting smile. "We're not alone. There's also...Bruiser! Now!" she yelled.

A small white streak flew out of the trees behind the two men and cannoned into the back of the speaker's knees. The man's legs buckled. As he staggered, he discharged his rifle upward into the cold, clear air. It echoed through the silent forest.

The other man, distracted by the attack, lost his focus. It was enough. Frasier leaped forward, taking him to the ground as his gun also discharged impotently up into the tree branches. The first attacker recovered his balance, raised his rifle, and brought the stock down on the Pug's head.

Bruiser squealed and went tumbling into the snow.

"No!" Emma lunged, tripped over her snowshoes, and plummeted into the man's protruding belly. With a grunt, he tumbled backward, his head hitting a stump with a dull thud.

"Hot damn!" Frasier witnessed the pair's efforts as he swiftly subdued his prisoner.

"Are you all right?" he called above his captive's shouted obscenities as he pulled out handcuffs and snapped them on the man's wrists.

"Fine, just fine." She stumbled to her feet and glared up at him. "But mad as hell, *Constable* MacKenzie."

Bruiser staggered up to her and she gathered him into her arms, kissing him. "Brave boy, good boy."

"Hey, I'm the one who ought to be mad. What was with that crazy story about your being an undercover cop, a narc at the high school, no less? Damn it, Emma, it's a crime to impersonate an officer."

"And just how would you have kept them talking long enough for Bruiser to get into position?" she snapped back.

"Oh, yeah, right, like you knew he was coming."

"No, actually, Constable MacKenzie, I glimpsed him almost as soon as those two ordered us out of the root cellar. You were so busy watching our would-be killers you couldn't see the rescuer for the criminals."

"Yeah, well, I will admit I missed out on that aspect." His tone moderated. He shoved his prisoner down to sit in the snow, then went to examine the man Emma had rendered unconscious. "He'll be okay," he said, as the man groaned and tried to sit up. Frasier handcuffed him, too, then straightened and pulled out his .38 from the shoulder holster inside his jacket. "Don't try to run," he advised both men. "I'm a good shot. There's also an irritated Eastern Panther in the area that's just been chased away from his dinner. Two shackled meals on legs like you pair would make up for his inconvenience."

"So you weren't really looking for an Eastern Panther. You were looking for drug smugglers." Emma's facial muscles tightened. "Is there anything you've told me that is the truth?"

"Not much," he said. Something like a lead weight sank in his chest.

"Well, fine, just fine!" Tears filled her eyes. "Apparently you've never trusted me, not once, not for a minute. Well, you can just take your suspicious mind and get out of my life, Officer. My hero is a man who will trust me completely, who won't lie about who he is and what he's doing, my hero is…"

"Emma, come on! I had no choice! I was under orders…and for a while, you were under suspicion yourself, and…"

"Don't, Frasier." She wiped her eyes with the back of one mitten and sniffed. "You can't fix things. It's way too late. You mistrusted me. You even used me to find this place. There's nothing you can say that will change the facts."

"Emma…"

With a final sniff and wipe of her mitten, she turned and plodded back the way they'd come, into the darkening forest. The Pug cast him a disappointed look, then limped after her.

Frasier watched them go.

Hell! Bloody Hell!

He turned on his prisoners. He had to finish the job. Frustrated, he yanked the ski mask from the one nearest to him, the one who'd worked to disguise his voice.

Brock Kelly, the gym teacher, glared up at him.

"Ah, nice," Frasier breathed his exasperation. "A great role model for the kids, aren't you?"

"Your girlfriend knows how to pick 'em," he sneered.

"Shut up! Just shut up!" Frasier's hands knotted into fists.

He turned to the other hooded figure to pull the mask from his face. With a deep sense of relief he recognized a well-known drug smuggler from wanted posters. After revealing Brock Kelly, he'd feared his pot-bellied accomplice might be Thomas Pentland, the school principal. That would have hurt. He liked the man.

"Emma will be really proud to have known you," he muttered, turning back to the gym teacher. "I bet sports events were a blast, with you supplying Todd Stoddart with junk to pass along to the kids. Into the cabin, both of you."

He held the gun leveled at the pair with one hand and pulled out his cell with the other. "Work, damn you, work!" he cursed as he punched in a single digit, held it to his ear, and followed the shuffling pair inside.

****

"Emma!" he bellowed desperately. He followed her tracks as fast as his snowshoes would allow. He'd managed to call reinforcements on his cell. He'd left his prisoners handcuffed to a couple of posts inside the old camp, the door securely shut against predators, then set out after her.

He hadn't been lying when he'd told the two men there was a hungry Eastern Panther in the area. He'd used precious minutes to make sure his prisoners were safe inside the cabin before he took off after Emma. No matter what the pair had done, he couldn't leave them outside, helpless to be mauled or killed by the big cat if it returned to finish its meal.

By the time he'd buckled on his snowshoes and set out in pursuit, twilight had gathered among the trees. His heart hammered a tattoo against his ribs. He had to find her, and quick. Somewhere in the thickening shadows was a hungry, frustrated cat.

He knew something else, as well. There could be no doubt about it. He, Constable Frasier MacKenzie, former rock musician, fake associate professor of biology, a.k.a. the hermit of Loon Lake, loved Emma Prescott with every ounce of body and soul. If he got thrown off the force for leaving prisoners unattended to go running after her, then so be it. He had his degree in biology to fall back on, and he still played a mean guitar. At least Emma said he did. He felt a corner of his mouth tugging upwards.

"Emma!" he bellowed.

She couldn't be more vulnerable. Trailing along behind her, tired and injured, was a carnivore delicacy in the guise of a Pug. He remembered how the little dog had managed to buckle the drug smuggler's knees with his small head, then withstood a vicious blow from a rifle butt before Emma had inadvertently rammed the man. *Tough little guy*. Tough and with a lot of guts Frasier hadn't thought he'd ever be acknowledging. Just like Emma. But she and the little dog would be no match for the big cat that might be stalking them.

****

The unmistakable screech made his breath clog in his throat. His body froze in midstride. The

Panther! Dear God! Emma! Pulling his gun, he plunged into the darkening bush.

"Emma!" he yelled.

"Frasier!" Her cry sent him charging forward.

He rounded a small thicket to see her huddled against the trunk of a pine, the Pug clutched in her arms. Stalking toward her, bird-dog fashion, its belly dragging on the snow, was the Panther.

He raised the gun. His hand shuddered. *No, please, God, not now!* Taking aim, he fired.

The report rocked the silence of the forest. The big cat screamed as the bullet whizzed inches over its head. Roaring, it whirled and vanished into the shadowy bush. The silence of the winter twilight returned. The hand holding the smoking gun dropped to his side, every ounce of strength drained.

"Thank God you missed." Emma recovered her speech. "It would have been awful to have killed him."

"Damn it, Emma...!"

"Well, if he hadn't run away from that warning shot, you would have got him with the next one, right?"

"Right." Her absolute confidence made him choke out the word.

Still clutching the Pug, she suddenly sank down on her haunches in the snow. "Frasier, I was so scared," she hiccupped.

"Anyone would have been." He hunkered down beside her. He cupped her chin in his hand and turned her to face him. "I love you, Emma Prescott," he heard himself saying.

"Frasier?" She looked up at him, emerald eyes round with surprise. "Are you sure? This isn't just a knee-jerk reaction after a near-death experience, is it?"

"No." He stood and helped her to her feet. "Definitely not. I couldn't say it before because..."

"Because you were working undercover with a secret identity," she rushed ahead of him. "But, Frasier, you should have trusted me. You really should have."

"You make it sound a lot more cloak-and-dagger than it actually is," he grinned. "I'm just a cop on the trail of drug smugglers, two of whom are now handcuffed to a bunk in Midnight Jim's camp. Believe me, I wanted to tell you the whole scam more times than you can imagine. It's lonely with no one to confide in, no one to love and trust."

He took her face in his gloved hands and kissed her lightly on the lips.

"Is that the best you can do?" Green eyes glinted wickedly up at him. "You've just said you love me, Frasier MacKenzie. Make like you mean it."

"Look, I've tried kissing you with him in your arms," he gestured at the Pug. "It's not a very satisfying experience."

"I can't put him down," she said. "He may have a concussion. Frasier, he saved our lives. We owe him."

"Okay, okay, give him here." He took the little dog into his arms. The Pug looked up at him, wheezed a weary sigh, and snuggled into his chest. "Now let's go. I've got to meet the reinforcements I called on my cell. For once the bloody thing worked. But rest assured, Emma Prescott, once he's safely in his basket by the fire and those jerks back at the camp are on their way to jail, I will kiss you. I'll kiss you until your toes curl."

"Okay. Deal."

****

Emma took a sip of her hot chocolate and glanced again at her watch. 11:45 p.m. and still no sign of Frasier or the group of RCMP he'd summoned nearly five hours ago. One of the officers had brought her and Bruiser back to her cabin and remained on watch outside while Frasier returned to the site of their drug bust at Midnight Jim's camp.

"What can be taking so long?" She turned to Bruiser, curled up under a small, soft blanket in his basket, an ice pack tied to his head. "I know Frasier would have to make a statement, explain all we did, but still..."

The sound of a vehicle approaching broke in on her words. She ran to a window to see an RCMP jeep pull up in the illumination of her verandah light. Frasier and the man who'd been introduced to her as the Professor got out. They paused to talk to the man on duty in the yard.

Emma could barely contain herself until her guard, with a wave and a nod, had climbed back into his own vehicle and headed back down the trail, his headlights piercing beams into the inky blackness of the wilderness night.

"Come in," she called. "I have hot chocolate and cookies."

"Just the thing." The Professor turned toward her with a smile. "Come along, Frasier. I'm sure you're cold and hungry."

They came up the steps and into the warm cabin.

"Let me take your hats and coats," Emma offered.

"Thank you, but I won't be staying," the Professor declined her offer. "I have a lot of work to do."

"Work?" Emma looked at him in surprise. "It's nearly midnight. Surely you don't plan to look for the Eastern Panther tonight?"

"Emma, let me introduce you correctly to this man." Frasier straightened from removing his boots and began to open his coat. "This is my father, Inspector Benjamin MacKenzie of the Royal Canadian Mounted Police Drug Squad."

"What?" Emma was aghast as she stared at the tall, broad-shouldered man crossing the room to hunker down beside Bruiser's basket. "Inspector...your *father*?"

"It's a fact." Frasier grinned at her. "He may not be Professor Benjamin Taylor, but he is my boss, and a darned exacting one, at that."

"Come, now, Frasier, I didn't expect any more of you than I'd expect of any of my men." The Inspector was gently stroking the little dog's back. "Brave little lad," he continued, smiling up at Emma. "You can be proud of him."

"I am." Emma, coming out of her astonishment, managed to curl her lips in response. "And he likes you." She indicated the blanket area over his tail. It was wiggling.

"Beware, Dad." Frasier hung his jacket and hat on a peg by the door and headed for the couch. "Being his friend can be hazardous to your peace of mind." With a sigh he sank down on the couch and stretched his sock feet out to the fire on the hearth.

"Emma." The older man arose and extended his hand to her. "It's good to meet you, really meet you."

"Inspector MacKenzie." Emma accepted his hand. "There's still so much I don't understand..."

"I'll let Frasier explain it to you." He glanced over at his son and winked. "I have a feeling he has a lot to say and he'd rather I left before he gets started."

"You're welcome to stay for hot chocolate and cookies." She smiled up into blue eyes she now realized were a perfect match to Frasier's.

"Not tonight. I'm guessing we'll have lots of opportunities to enjoy food together in the future, Emma." He went to the door. "Frasier, I'll see you bright and early tomorrow in Carleton. We'll need a full statement describing your work, including how you ended up at that old logging camp."

"Ah, come on, Dad…bright and early?"

"Inspector MacKenzie, please," the older man addressed him sharply. "Remember you're a constable in my squad."

"Yes, sir." Frasier bolted to his feet. "Sorry, sir."

"Much better." A twinkle came into his eyes. "At ease, Constable." He turned to leave. With his hand on the doorknob, he paused and swung back to face them. "Well, maybe not bright and early." He grinned. "But no later than noon."

"Yes, sir. Thank you, sir."

"No, thank *you*, son. You, and Emma, did a great job. Don't let her get away, my boy. She's a definite keeper. I'll let your mother know. She'll be pleased. We'll be expecting you for Christmas, young lady."

He slapped on his hat, winked at Emma, and left, shutting the door firmly behind him.

"Well!" Emma put her hands on her hips and heaved a sigh. "So that's your father. I can only assume that after he pulled you out of The Sound, and after you finished your degree, he recruited you into the RCMP."

"No, I recruited myself," Frasier said, sinking back onto the couch. "During the year it took to finish my degree, I had time to think, to consider how I could best keep other people from ending up like Larry. Dad was an RCMP officer who'd been on drug squads off and on for years. The idea to join the force just naturally fell into place. Dad's been working on a special trans-Canada drug busting squad for quite a while," he continued. "When he and his bunch zeroed in on this area last summer, he decided I was the man to go undercover as the hermit of Loon Lake. He knew I was itching to get into the drug squad, so here was the perfect opportunity."

"I wish you'd told me about Larry," she said

softly.

"I did."

"But not that what you were trying to accomplish was because of him. I'd have understood why you couldn't offer me anything more than friendship until you'd finished the job. Frasier, stopping drug smugglers is so very important. You must have known that, given my job, I'd have supported you."

"I know you would." He looked over at her ruefully. "But I couldn't betray the other officers working the case. That's what I would have done if I'd told you."

"When Constable Roy stopped me for speeding... He wasn't an old college friend, he's a colleague. You gave him some kind of signal to keep him from revealing your true identity... Wow! This sounds really cloak-and-dagger, doesn't it?"

"Yeah, well, not nearly as cloak-and-dagger as it should have been once you and the Pug got involved." He grinned. "My father chose my cover as an associate professor for the University of New Brunswick, researching the Eastern Panther, because with my degree I could talk the talk if I had to. It also gave me an excellent excuse to go searching through the bush."

"What will happen to Todd and Jesse? I assume they either are or will be caught up in this operation."

"Todd will be in major trouble. He's eighteen and no longer protected under the Young Offenders' Act. We can put in a good word for Jesse. He's seventeen, and he did try to warn us. Maybe he'll get off with a slap on the wrists and a lot of community service work. Like you, I think there's a good kid under that punk exterior."

"And the drugs? I assume that's what was hidden in the root cellar at Midnight Jim's camp?"

"Yes. The reason we didn't see any evidence of traffic from this end of the trail was because they were bringing that junk in by a new, well-hidden trail through the undergrowth at the base of the mountains. Even our aerial surveillance didn't spot them."

"I can't believe I never suspected who you really are. But then, I was blinded by the fact that you were...are...the Frase."

"Your friend Mandy Cooper spotted me."

"What do you mean?"

"I met her in the bookstore in Carleton, the day I bought the Robbie Burns book— Yes, yes, I bought it to impress you," he countered, when he realized what he'd said. "Anyhow, she said something to the effect that she'd known men like me and that she didn't want you hurt. Gave me quite a turn. Then I realized she's a Mountie's wife and, even if she did suspect me for what I was, she wouldn't break the confidence...not even to her best friend."

"Mandy is one of the good ones, absolutely trustworthy." Emma smiled. "She went out on limb letting you know what she suspected."

"And putting me right about how I should behave around you...if my intentions weren't strictly honorable, if I weren't ready to at least try to be your hero."

"I'll tell her you succeeded."

"Thanks." He drew a deep breath, then continued, "I never seriously expected to find an Eastern Panther, but then..." He pulled himself to his feet and went to stand close in front of Emma. He put his hands on her arms and smiled into her eyes. "I never expected to meet an Emma Prescott and fall in love. That really threw my investigation for a loop."

"Are you sorry?" She looked up at him, emerald eyes expectantly wide.

"Definitely not." He drew her into his arms and kissed her as he'd been longing to kiss her for weeks.

"Frasier," she breathed when he finally let her come up for air. "My toes are curled so tight I don't think I can walk."

"That's okay." He swept her up into his arms and headed toward the bedroom. "What I have in mind doesn't require you to take a single step." He paused as he was about to push the door open. "By the way, why did you suddenly decide to give me directions to Midnight Jim's camp?"

"At first I honestly had no more than a vague idea about where it was." She grinned up at him. "Just the two-big-pine-trees thing. Then I decided I'd never get anywhere with you until you did actually find an Eastern Panther. So, on the off chance one might be lurking at that abandoned logging camp, I thought and thought...and then I asked my mother. She was the one who always led the way with Dad when we visited it years ago. Seems she has an excellent memory. She's also as good as any Mountie at giving instructions on how to get your man."

****

"The Pug's had attack dog training?" Frasier stared at her as she poured them each a cup of coffee in her cabin the next morning. "Why didn't you tell me?"

She sat down opposite him and grinned. "Would you have believed me?"

"Probably not," he exhaled, picking up his mug.

"Aren't you glad he was able to dig his way out of your dog run and follow me? Seems that hole you made such a fuss about came in handy after all."

"Yeah, well." He leaned back in his chair.

"And he has a name. I think it's high time you started using it."

"Okay, okay, he's Bruiser, the Bruise." He looked down at the little dog, and Bruiser wriggled all over with pleasure. "I wasn't surprised to discover you'd taken self-defense lessons," he continued, looking back at Emma. "I figured you had too much common sense not to have it, considering some of the kids you deal with, then daring to live alone up here. But tripping and head-butting a guy in the gut couldn't have been part of it."

"Fortuitous accident...like both of us coming to live at this great place at the same time," she said, getting up to close a window. "A little cool these days, but what with fieldstone hearths and cozy log fires, a perfect spot to officially begin our relationship."

She turned back to him, green eyes full of suggestive teasing.

"Are we...about to...begin a relationship?" He met her gaze full-on.

"Oh, y-e-a-h." She crossed the room, gripped his shirt front, pulled him to his feet, and into a long, wild kiss.

"Okay," he breathed, when she finally let him come up for air. "Only, you need to know what you're getting into, lady. I'm thinkin' Mandy might have to host a bachelorette party, come spring."

"Suits me. I'll tell her to reserve Nigel."

Over her shoulder he saw Bruiser grinning contentedly up at him. The Pug blinked one eye and Frasier winked back.

A word about the author...

The award-winning author of twenty published books, Gail MacMillan is a graduate of Queen's University.

Two of her nonfiction books, *Biography of a Beagle* and *Ceilidh's Quest*, have garnered Maxwell Medals. Her short stories and articles have appeared in magazines in Canada, the USA, and Europe.

She lives in New Brunswick, Canada with her husband and three dogs.

You can visit Gail at her website:
www.gailmacmillan.ca

Thank you for purchasing this publication of
The Wild Rose Press, Inc.
For other wonderful stories of romance,
please visit our on-line bookstore at
www.thewildrosepress.com.

For questions or more information
contact us at
info@thewildrosepress.com.

The Wild Rose Press, Inc.
www.thewildrosepress.com

To visit with authors of
The Wild Rose Press, Inc.
join our yahoo loop at
http://groups.yahoo.com/group/thewildrosepress/

www.ingramcontent.com/pod-product-compliance
Lightning Source LLC
Chambersburg PA
CBHW070913180626
46817CB00003B/1033